HAVE YOU SEEN THIS GIRL?

Alice didn't want to go into the shop.

She looked at the posters in the window and then at the small ads. A huge headline stood out from one of them. HAVE YOU SEEN THIS GIRL? it said. Underneath was just a photo but Alice couldn't make it out from where she was standing. Inside the shop she saw Rosie moving backward away from the counter, the newsagent still talking, looking like he was counting something off on his fingers.

HAVE YOU SEEN THIS GIRL? The words gave her a mild shock. All those years ago. In Berwick. The day after it happened. The streets of Berwick were covered in photographs. It had been taken from some album, photocopied and enlarged. Someone had put the pictures in plastic sheet protectors, the kind that usually fitted into ring binders. They'd been stuck to trees and lampposts and the inside of people's windows. She'd been at home at the time, so she couldn't have seen them herself; she must have seen it on the television. A reporter standing by a poster. HAVE YOU SEEN THIS GIRL? it said. Everyone was looking for her.

Only JJ had known where she was.

LOOKING FOR JJ

ANNE CASSIDY

Houghton Mifflin Harcourt
Boston   New York

www.GraphiaBooks.com

First published in the UK by Scholastic Ltd, 2004
First U.S. edition 2007

Library of Congress Cataloging-in-Publication Data
Cassidy, Anne, 1952–
Looking for JJ/Anne Cassidy.
p. cm.
Summary: Seventeen-year-old Alice, released from prison with a new
identity after serving six years for murdering a child, tries to keep her anonymity
from the British tabloids, while haunted by memories of her past trauma.
[1. Murder—Fiction. 2. Emotional problems—Fiction. 3. Child abuse—Fiction.
4. Identity—Fiction. 5. England—Fiction.] I. Title.
PZ7.C26857Lo 2007
[Fic]—dc22   2006038269
HC ISBN 978-0-15-206190-6
PA ISBN 978-0-15-206638-3

Text set in Adobe Garamond
Designed by Cathy Riggs

Printed in the United States of America
QUM   10   9   8   7   6   5   4   3   2   1

For my lovely dad, Frank Cassidy

LOOKING FOR JJ

part one

ALICE TULLY

ONE

EVERYONE was looking for Jennifer Jones. She was dangerous, the newspapers said. She posed a threat to children and should be kept behind bars. The public had a right to know where she was. Some of the weekend papers even resurrected the old headline: A LIFE FOR A LIFE!

Alice Tully read every article she could find. Her boyfriend, Frankie, was bemused. He couldn't understand why she was so fascinated. He put his arm around her shoulder and dipped his mouth into her neck while she was reading. Alice tried to push him away, but he wouldn't take no for an answer and in the end the newspaper crumpled and slipped onto the ground.

Alice couldn't resist Frankie. He was bigger and taller than she, but that wasn't difficult. Most people were. Alice was small and thin and often bought her clothes cheaply in the children's section of clothes shops. Frankie was a giant beside her, and he liked to pick her up and carry her around, especially if they were having an argument. It was his way of making up.

She was lucky to have him.

She much preferred to read the articles about Jennifer Jones when she was on her own. It meant waiting until Rosie, the woman she lived with, was out at work. It gave her plenty of time. Rosie worked long hours. She was a social worker and had a lot of clients to see. In any case, the stories about Jennifer Jones weren't around all the time. They came in waves. Sometimes they roared from the front page, the headlines bold and demanding. Sometimes they were tiny, a column on an inside page, a nugget of gossip floating on the edge of the news, hardly causing a ripple of interest.

When the killing first happened, the news was in every paper for months. The trial had thrown up dozens of articles from all angles. The events on that terrible day at Berwick Waters. The background. The home lives of the children. The school reports. The effects on the town. The law regarding children and murder. Some of the tabloids focused on the seedier side: the attempts to cover up the crime; the details of the body; the lies told by the children. Alice Tully hadn't seen any of these at the time. She had been too young. In the past six months, though, she had read as much as she could get her hands on, and the question that lay under every word that had ever been printed was the same: How could a ten-year-old girl kill another child?

In the weeks leading up to the ninth of June, Alice

Tully's seventeenth birthday, the stories started again. Jennifer Jones had finally been released. She had served six years for murder (the judge had called it *manslaughter* but that was just a nice word). She had been let out on license, which meant that she could be called back to prison at any time. She had been relocated somewhere far from where she was brought up. She had a new identity and no one would know who she was and what she had done.

Alice fell hungrily on these reports, just as she sat coiled up and tense in front of Rosie's telly, using her thumb to race past the satellite channels, catching every bit of footage of the Jennifer Jones case. The news programs still used the only photograph that there had ever been of the ten-year-old. A small girl with long hair and bangs, a frowning expression on her face. *JJ* was the little girl's nickname. The journalists loved it. It made Alice feel weak just to look at it.

On the morning of her birthday, Rosie woke her up with a birthday card and present.

"Here, sleepyhead."

Alice opened her eyes and looked upward at Rosie. She had her dark suit on and the white striped blouse she always wore with it. Her hair was tied back off her face, making her look serious and stern. Instead of her usual hanging earrings she was wearing gold studs. It was not the way Rosie liked to dress.

"Don't tell me, you're in court today!" Alice said, sitting up, stretching her arms out, ruffling her fingers through her own short hair.

"You guessed it!" Rosie said. "Here, take this, birthday girl!"

Alice took the present while Rosie walked to the window and pushed it open. A light breeze wafted in, lifting the net curtains. Alice pulled the duvet tight, up to her neck.

"Do you want to freeze me to death?" she said, jokingly.

Rosie took no notice. She loved fresh air. She spent a lot of her time opening windows, and Alice spent a lot of time closing them.

Inside the wrapping paper was a small box, the kind that held jewelry. For a moment Alice was worried. Rosie's taste in jewelry was a bit too artsy for her. She lifted the lid off gingerly and saw a pair of tiny gold earrings.

"These are lovely," Alice said, and felt a strange lump in her throat.

"More your taste than mine," Rosie said, looking in Alice's wall mirror and pulling at her jacket, using the flats of her hands to smooth out her skirt. She looked uncomfortable.

Alice got out of bed and stood beside her. She held an earring up to one ear and nodded approvingly. Then she squeezed Rosie's arm.

"You're on lates this week?" Rosie said.

Alice nodded. She didn't have to be at work until ten.

"I'll be home early. So I'm going to cook a special meal," Rosie said. "And it's not only your birthday we're celebrating. Next Saturday, you'll have been here for six months!"

That was true. Six months of waking up every morning in that bedroom, of eating in Rosie's kitchen, of seeing her name on letters: ALICE TULLY, 52 PHILLIP STREET, CROYDON.

"My mum's coming. What about Frankie?"

Rosie had been making a special cake that had been hidden from Alice. Her mother, Kathy, a funny Irish woman, was helping her.

"He can't come."

She didn't bother to explain. Frankie said he felt awkward around Rosie, as though she were watching him, waiting to tell him off every time he touched Alice. He preferred it when they were alone.

"Oh well. It'll be just the three of us then."

After Rosie left, Alice sat on her bed holding the earrings and looking at her card. There would be nothing from her mother, she knew that. She sat very still for a moment, aware of her own body, trying to read her own sensations. Was she upset? She had other presents and cards. She had Frankie and her friends from the Coffee Pot. Then there was Rosie herself. Rosie with her powerful hug and no-nonsense manner; Rosie who smelled of lemons and garlic and basil and who was always trying to fatten her up. Dear, sweet Rosie. Alice hadn't known that such people existed.

The sound of the letter box distracted her. She got up and took her card over to the mantelpiece and stood it up. Then she walked downstairs to the front door where the morning paper was sticking through the letter box. She pulled it out, taking care not to graze it or tear the pages, and took it back up to the kitchen. Without looking she laid it down on the kitchen table and got on with making her breakfast. She tipped out some cereal and poured milk into her bowl. One teaspoon of sugar was all she wanted. Then she got out the orange juice and poured herself exactly half a glass. Where eating was concerned she had a routine. She wasn't fussed about her weight or her shape. She just ate what she wanted and no amount of persuasion from anyone was going to change that.

She sat down and flattened the newspaper. There it was again, the headline she had expected.

JENNIFER JONES FREE AFTER SIX YEARS
Is this justice?

Her wrist trembled as she lowered her spoon into the bowl and scooped up some cereal. The story was the same as every other one that she had read over the last weeks. *Should Jennifer have been released? Should she stay in*

Britain? Is she a danger to children? Then there was the revenge angle: *Would the dead girl's parents try to find Jennifer?*

As ever, the newspaper gave a brief outline of the story of that day at Berwick Waters. Alice read it. It was just like all the others. She had read them all. If anyone had asked she could have probably recited it by heart.

A bright blue day in May, six years before. The sun was staring down from the sky, but a sharp breeze bothered the bushes and flowers, bending them this way and that. When it died down, the sun's glare was heavy, and for a fleeting moment it might have seemed like a midsummer day.

The town of Berwick. A few kilometers off the main Norwich road. It had a high street with shops and a pub and road after road of neatly laid-out houses and gardens. Beyond the small school and the park the road led out of the town past the disused railway station to Water Lane. A row of cottages, eight of them. Formerly owned by the government, they stood in a small orderly line along the road.

They weren't all run-down. Some were cared for, with conservatories and extensions built on. Others had peeling paint and broken fences. Some of the gardens were colorful and neat, their blooms in geometric beds, their terra-cotta pots standing upright, early blossoms tumbling over the edges. Others were wild with weeds and strewn with broken toys. Above them all were washing lines hoisted up into the sky, children's shirts and dresses struggling in the breeze one minute and hanging limply in the sun the next.

Three children emerged from a gate at the back of one of the gardens and started on the path to Berwick Waters. It was only a kilometer and a half away and they were walking smartly, as though they had some purpose. The lake at Berwick Waters was man-made, filled up some ten years before by the water company. It was over three kilometers long and was surrounded by woodland and some landscaped picnic areas. The water in the lake was deep and children were not encouraged to go there alone. Some people said that families of feral cats had lived in the area and had been drowned when it was filled. At times, during the day, when there was absolute silence, some people said their cries could be heard. Most people dismissed this, but many children were in awe of the story.

On that day in May the children were cold at first, that's why they were hugging themselves, pulling the sleeves of their sweaters down, trying to keep the niggling breeze from forcing its way inside their clothes. Five minutes later it was too hot and the sweaters came off and ended up tied round their waists, each garment holding tightly on to its owner. Three children walked away from the cottages on the edge of the town toward Berwick Waters. Later that day, only two of them came back.

Alice Tully knew the story. She could have written a book about it.

She looked at her cereal bowl and saw that she'd eaten only half of it. She picked up her spoon and continued, chewing vigorously, swallowing carefully, hardly tasting a mouthful. At the bottom of the editorial there was a final quote from an official at the Home Office:

"Like any other offender, Jennifer Jones has been carefully vetted. It was the considered opinion of all those concerned that she poses no threat to children and accordingly she was released under license and is currently living in a safe environment. Any talk of revenge or vigilante action is wholly inappropriate and will be dealt with in the most rigorous manner."

Where was Jennifer Jones? That's what everyone was saying. There were only a handful of people in the country who knew. Alice Tully was one of them.

TWO

IT TOOK a few days for Alice to actually notice the man in the leather jacket. She might have served him each time he came in, but she couldn't be sure. She was on an early shift that week, getting to the Coffee Pot at around seven. Between them, she, Pip, and Jules served hundreds of customers every morning. It was especially busy in the half hour before eight o'clock. There was a constant stream of business men and women in smart clothes, rushing in for a coffee or cappuccino, a Danish or croissant, all served in a handy carryout bag that could be taken onto a train and consumed on the way to work. By eight-fifteen, when the rush trailed off, Alice was usually exhausted and the other two were sneaking upstairs for a cigarette break. That was when there was time to rest, to look around the coffee shop, to get her bearings, and maybe have a drink herself.

The man sat at a table by the window in the smoking section. He had a large cappuccino and a muffin. It took him a while to drink it, and when he'd finished he came up for a refill. In all he sat in the same seat for about ninety minutes each morning. This didn't bother Alice.

There were about ten tables in the coffee bar and, apart from lunchtime, they were usually half empty. If someone wanted to linger, read the newspaper, work on a laptop, or just flick through a magazine, that was no problem. They were about two hundred meters from the station. People were often waiting to meet someone, or maybe just passing the time of day.

When the man in the leather jacket sat down for the third morning running, Alice had a good look at him. He was middle-aged and quite large, his body too big for the tiny tables and chairs that dotted the front of the coffee shop. His head was balding on top and the rest of his hair had grown long and was held back in a straggly ponytail at the base of his neck. The table in front of him was covered in things that he'd unpacked from a battered knapsack that sat on the floor: a camera, a notepad, a map book, some document folders. There was barely room for his cardboard cup of coffee and his pastry. He spent most of his time looking out of the window and making notes. She wondered whether he was a writer of some sort.

She was preoccupied that morning. The night before she and Frankie had had an argument. She had been due to go round to his flat after work but had been a little late because she'd popped into the hairdresser's for a trim. It hadn't taken more than fifteen minutes, but when she'd arrived he'd taken one look at her tightly cropped hair and got into a mood.

"I thought you were going to grow it!" he said, padding up the hall in front of her.

"I never said I was," Alice said, letting her hand slide down the back of her short hair.

The flat was empty, Frankie's flatmates probably still out at college.

"You look like a boy!" Frankie said.

"I like it short."

Frankie sat down on the sofa. He'd left her standing, and the way his legs were spread across the seat it didn't look as though he wanted her to sit down beside him. She tried to keep cheerful. He had his exams and was under pressure.

"Shall we get some takeout? I've got some cash?"

He didn't answer. He glared at the blank screen of the television. She felt tired suddenly and couldn't be bothered with the row.

"I'll go. I'll ring you later," she said and turned.

She hadn't got far when she heard him coming behind her. She kept on walking. Just as she was a couple of meters from the door, he darted ahead of her, blocking her way. In a moment his arms were around her and he was giving her a tight squeeze, squashing her small chest against his.

"Don't let's argue," he whispered, and slid his hands under her T-shirt.

Later, after eating the takeout, they sat watching television.

"I thought you had some work to do," Alice said, looking at a pile of books and folders on the sideboard.

"Tomorrow," Frankie said, stretching back, lifting his arms up in the air, taking up more space on the sofa.

She'd wanted to go home soon after, but he'd held her there on the sofa in a kind of play fight. She made a half-hearted attempt to wrestle him off, but it wasn't going to happen and in the end she lay limp and captive, laughing at him. He began to kiss her gently at first, holding himself up above her as though he were doing push-ups, but then the kisses got longer and he half lay on top of her, rifling her clothes and stroking and touching her until she was dizzy. "I've got condoms," he'd whispered hoarsely, but she had shaken her head and pushed him off. He'd been good-natured about it but underneath she sensed a growing impatience.

Would there be a day when he got fed up with her? Alice thought about this as she cleared the tables in the smokers' area. Some of the daily newspapers provided by the coffee shop had been opened up and left on various tables. She tidied them up, catching the eye of the man in the leather jacket as she did it. He held his cigarette between his thumb and forefinger and nodded pleasantly at her. When he finally left, Jules cleared his table and came walking back to the counter with a piece of paper flapping in her hand.

"That fat bloke with the ponytail? He must have left

this behind. Keep it behind the counter. He might come back."

Alice took it. It was covered in scraps of writing and some doodles.

"It was on the opposite chair. Most probably it slid off the table. Look, there are a couple of phone numbers on it. He might miss them."

But Alice wasn't looking at the phone numbers. At the top there were three names written out and several lines drawn under each of them.

Jennifer Jones

Michelle Livingstone

Lucy Bussell

Alice folded the paper in half and half again. From behind she could hear Pip and Jules talking, but she had no idea what their conversation was about. She folded the sheet over and over until it was a tiny fat rectangle, the size of a biscuit. Then she shoved it in her pocket and took her apron off.

"I'll have my break now," she said.

Jules and Pip were unloading the trays of lunchtime baguettes and packed sandwiches and hardly gave her a look. She walked out of the coffee shop, along the high street, and turned off onto the road that led to Rosie's flat.

It was only five minutes away but she quickened her step, wanting to get there, to be on her own before something inside her exploded.

In the street there was a small white van parked in front of the house. The back doors of the van were wide open and so was the front door of the downstairs flat. Alice stopped for a second. A couple of bags and a suitcase were in the hallway and she could hear the inside doors opening and closing. Someone new was moving in downstairs. She got her key out and quickly opened Rosie's door, walked inside, and shut it tightly behind her. She did not want to meet the new neighbor. She had no time for small talk now. She leaned back onto the door. She was small and she didn't weigh a lot, but for a few moments she pushed against the heavy wood with all the power she could muster. As if that were good enough to keep someone out.

Then she ran up the stairs into the kitchen. With trembling fingers, she got out the piece of paper and flattened it onto the table. The three names stared back at her. *Jennifer Jones, Michelle Livingstone, Lucy Bussell.* Three children who had gone up to Berwick Waters on a spring day six years before. Names that had been plastered over the newspapers for many months. Only one name had remained famous. *JJ. Jennifer Jones.*

Why had the man in the leather jacket written them out? What were they to him?

She rang Rosie. Her fingers rigid, she jabbed at the telephone and asked to speak to Rose Sutherland, and said it was urgent. Rosie's voice, when it came, was slow and steady. She listened to Alice's stuttering explanation and didn't rush to speak. When she did speak, her words were considered. She tried to calm Alice down. It was nothing, just somebody's scribbles. Possibly he was a writer or a journalist. So what? There was nothing for him to find out. This was something she had to be prepared for, would always have to be prepared for. Now that the media knew that JJ had been released there would always be people willing to try and find her. Alice nodded. She had had this conversation many times with Rosie. She knew that Rosie was right.

Replacing the telephone receiver, she seemed to pull herself together. She returned to work and slipped the piece of paper into a gap between the till and the wall.

When the man in the leather jacket came in the next day, she waited until the rush was over and walked across to him, carrying the scrap with her.

"You dropped this yesterday. I thought it might be important."

She held it out. It was crisscrossed with lines from where she had folded it. He looked surprised, pleased.

"Thanks, darling. I wondered where that had got to."

"Are you a journalist?" she said casually.

"No."

"Only, I thought, what with the names, that you were investigating that girl. The one who's just been released."

"Good spot," he said. "Only I'm a freelance detective. I am looking for Jennifer Jones. Only not for a newspaper story."

He tapped his finger on the end of his nose and went back to his papers. Alice gave a rictus smile. Her lips were drawn across her teeth and she nodded her head as though he'd just said something pleasant. Inside, though, she had turned to dust. Going back behind the counter she found herself staring at him, a sudden, intense dislike stirring up inside her. She noticed his hair was greasy and his skin was pockmarked. His shoes were scuffed and the hem of his leather jacket had come down on one side. From where she was standing, she could see him pushing the last crumbs of his Danish into his mouth with one hand while using the other to punch a number into his mobile.

He was despicable and he *was* looking for JJ.

If only he knew that he had found her.

THREE

A WEEK later, when Rosie came home from work one day, she found Alice sitting in a corner in her bedroom wrapped in her duvet. Beside her was a fan heater. It was three o'clock in the afternoon and the curtains were closed and the room was in twilight. The air was heavy and hot. Rosie sighed, squatted down, and pulled out the plug of the fan heater. Alice pulled the duvet around her more tightly and watched as Rosie stepped across and drew the curtains back, letting the daylight crash-land into the room. For a moment she looked as though she were going to open a window. The very thought of it made Alice feel cold, and she pushed herself back into the corner, the duvet up to her nose.

"We need to have a chat," Rosie said, in a no-nonsense voice.

Alice had been waiting for it. It wasn't the first time in the last seven days that Rosie had found her cocooned in her room. Up to then Rosie had made a joke of it, treated it lightly, just one more of Alice's little ways.

But this was different. Alice had walked out of her job.

She'd arrived at the Coffee Pot on time, in good spirits. She'd climbed into her smock and took up her position behind the counter looking out into the street beyond. She'd watched as a line of determined-looking people made their way toward the station, their heads down, their bags and briefcases in hand, some glancing at watches, fishing out travel cards in readiness for the machines.

They'd looked so ordinary.

She'd even served a few: a frothy coffee to go; a croissant in a greaseproof bag; a large latte and chamomile tea for the couple in the corner perched on the seats, grabbing a few minutes before their train.

At eight minutes past eight she'd suddenly felt light-headed. She'd looked down at her body. Thin. She was too thin, too lightweight. Like a piece of paper that the wind might blow away. Somebody was standing on the other side of the counter asking for something, but she couldn't answer.

If they knew. If the woman with the flapping ten-pound note knew who she was talking to. If she had any inkling that she was centimeters away from Jennifer Jones, JJ, the girl from Berwick who had spent six years in prison for murder. What would she say? Would she be so bright and pleasant, commenting on the good weather as she asked for her black coffee and pecan cookie?

Alice had mumbled some words, but honestly she'd had no idea what she was saying. *I am not who you think*

I am, she had wanted to say. Instead she unbuttoned her smock and let it slide off her, stepping out of it, leaving it on the tiled floor like a skin that she had just shed. She was going home because she couldn't go on pretending.

The manager looked at her with concern. It wasn't as though she'd been acting completely normal that week, after all. There had been other things: crying in the toilets, dropping plates, spilling hot coffee on her wrist.

When she'd walked out of the shop she felt a moment's relief. The door closed behind her and she didn't even look around. But it wasn't as easy as that. She found herself walking against the crowds, sidestepping people on their way to work, stepping half on the pavement, half on the road, glancing around from time to time to make sure the trams weren't anywhere near. Then, turning the corner, she was in Rosie's street and she was hit by the quiet. No people, only a car or two seesawing across the speed bumps.

Alice knew the manager would ring Rosie. She could almost hear the bleeps on his mobile as he tapped Rosie's number in and rang her to report Alice's departure. Rosie was an old friend of his. He'd given Alice a job as a favor. Not that he knew the truth. No, Rosie had had other girls staying with her; girls whose families had given up on them and who needed time and space. A safe house where they could make some sort of life for themselves.

Rosie had never had a murderer stay with her before.

"I'll make some coffee, and I want you to come into the kitchen and chat with me," Rosie said, walking out of Alice's room and leaving the door wide open so that a gale could come through it.

Alice heard the water running and the sound of crockery clinking gently, the fridge door opening and shutting, the tinkling of the teaspoons. Then she could smell the coffee, strong and warming. She let her duvet fall away and got up, her legs feeling like twigs. She made her way into the kitchen and sat down quietly on a chair that had Rosie's jacket hanging over the back of it. Rosie placed two mugs on the table, and then pulled a chair along the floor so that she could sit down directly in front of Alice.

"We knew that things might be difficult," she said, grabbing Alice's hand and searching out her eyes. "We knew that someone might come looking for you. That was one of the first things we talked about. You remember? On that day in Patricia Coffey's flat?"

Alice nodded. Of course she remembered that day.

"We are not going to let this get us down. They can look all they like. As far as these reporters, or detectives, are concerned, you've only just been released."

Alice nodded, although Rosie made it sound as though there were a whole group of them searching for her. A posse.

"I rang Patricia this morning just to check on how things were. She says that no one has approached her for any information. I also rang Jill. She's not been contacted, either."

Jill Newton was Alice's probation officer, a thin lady with white-blond hair and tinted glasses.

"The media are looking for a girl who has just arrived in the community. You've been around for over six months. No one is going to put you and Jennifer Jones together."

Rosie half turned and lifted a plastic container from the side. She opened it and took out a shortcake cookie and put it in Alice's hand.

"Eat up," she said, her voice insistent.

Alice didn't usually eat snacks but she knew that it would make Rosie happy. Rosie *needed* her to eat the cookie. She nibbled at its buttery edges and saw a smile break out on Rosie's face. Rosie pushed her chair back and stood up, her baggy trousers showing line after line of creases.

"So what if this detective, this Sherlock Holmes, comes into the café. What's he going to say? He doesn't know your new name! He has no photographs of you! He thinks Jennifer Jones has just arrived. He can ask anyone he likes, but no one will be able to point at you."

The sound of the front door intercom made Rosie stop. She gave a little tut and trotted off in the direction of the hallway. Alice heard her pick up the receiver and then her voice let out a friendly *Hi!* She talked for a moment, and Alice wondered if it was her mum, Kathy, come to visit. She took a tiny bite from the shortcake cookie and then looked at it. Its edges were uneven, like all of the cookies that Rosie made. From the hallway she heard the receiver being replaced and saw Rosie's face at the door.

"The new woman downstairs, Sara? She's got a leak in one of her taps. She doesn't know where to turn the water off from the mains. Okay if I go down there for a sec? I won't be long."

"I'm fine," Alice said, holding the cookie up and nibbling at the edge.

Rosie had brought a box of her homemade cookies with her on their first ever meeting at Monksgrove. Patricia Coffey, the director, had told her about the proposed visit three weeks before it happened. She'd looked forward to it, counted the days, picked three or four different outfits to wear. It had been like preparing for a date with a boy. Not that she had ever experienced such a thing.

"May I introduce Rose Sutherland," Patricia Coffey had said in a typically formal way.

Alice had been walking behind her into the living room of her apartment. She hadn't been called *Alice* then. The new name had been just some dream of the future; a different person, Alice Tully. JJ would step into her shoes soon. But first she had to meet the woman who would take care of her, who would give her a new life.

"This is Alice Tully," Patricia said, introducing her.

Rosie stood up immediately. She was a big woman, wearing layered clothes, a long skirt, a loose blouse, a sleeveless vest; all made from clashing cotton prints that hung like fussy curtains. Her hair was jaw length and neat and her face ruddy. Alice immediately noticed her odd earrings. On one ear was a long beaded concoction, on the other a series of small hoops. Rosie hardly gave Alice a second to take all these details in because she stepped toward her and gave Alice a hug. She'd felt winded by the woman's grip and slightly embarrassed by the show of affection. She'd smiled a little and allowed Rosie to lead her back to the settee.

"I've heard such a lot about you, Alice," Rosie said, using her name.

"Pat's told me a bit about you, too," Alice had said, looking Rosie up and down.

"About my good looks and perfect figure," she said, breaking into a laugh and looking across to Patricia Coffey.

"No," Alice said, sheepishly, "she said you're a social worker and that you like cooking . . ."

They talked on for a while, Patricia Coffey hovering in the background. Rosie told her all about her flat and her life in Croydon. She told her about her mum, who was Irish and who was never happier than when she was doing someone's hair. She described her kitchen and double oven and her recipes and the book she planned to write called *Rosie's Kitchen*. Then she produced a small plastic box that was full of crumbly, sweet cookies.

Alice took one and broke it into four while Rosie talked. When Alice had taken a mouthful, Rosie suddenly slapped the flat of her hand over her mouth.

"I'm just going on and on," she whispered, looking as though she'd done something naughty. "You're not getting a chance to speak!"

Alice told Rosie about the A levels that she had taken a year early; about her results, three Bs; about the university place she had for the following year. She told her which television programs she liked and which books she was reading.

"But do you cook?" Rosie snapped the question at her.

Alice shook her head. Some of the residents cooked, but it had never been something she was interested in.

"Then I'll teach you!" Rosie said.

Later, before she left, Rosie became serious.

"When you move into my flat things won't be easy for you. There'll be a lot of adjustments to make. After living in . . . such a closed community."

Rosie had a sprinkling of crumbs down her front and Alice wanted to brush them away, but she was too shy to do so. What Rosie had really meant to say was that Alice was living in a prison. It wasn't called that, but that's what it was. Even when Pat had told her about the arrangements for her release, she called it a *placement*. Like a job she was starting. Not a life. Not freedom.

She was to leave Monksgrove in January to go and live with Rosie. Only three people would know this: Patricia Coffey, Jill Newton, and Rosie. Everyone else, the staff, the workers, the other residents, would think that she had gone to a further secure unit until her official release six months later. That way the media, the dead girl's parents, her own mother, would all think that she had only just been released, when in fact she'd been living a normal life for over six months. It would give her a better chance to fit in, Patricia Coffey had said. It was their secret, just the three of them. None of them would divulge Alice's new identity or her whereabouts to anyone.

Alice heard Rosie's footsteps on the stairs and then she came dashing back into the kitchen.

"You okay, love? That Sara! She's hopeless and she's a teacher as well! Doesn't even know how to turn the water off at the mains. Still, it doesn't hurt to be neighborly, does it?"

"No, course it doesn't," Alice said.

"So, where were we?" Rosie sat down on the chair again, a little flustered and gasping for breath.

"That no one will ever find out about me living here. About my new life."

"That's right. That detective? He just hit lucky when

he came to Croydon. He has no idea whether you live here or in Newcastle or Brighton or . . ."

Rosie hesitated for a moment.

"What?" Alice said, thrown by this momentary loss of certainty.

"Nothing. Nothing at all."

But it was a lie. Alice knew it because Rosie always fidgeted with her right earring if she was agitated. She got up and started to clear the cups away even though her own coffee hadn't been touched. Alice knew what was going on. In Rosie's mind was the big question. Why should the detective choose *Croydon?*

Alice knew the answer. It had nothing to do with luck.

A birthday card. That's all. Her mum's name and address neatly written on the envelope. She'd taken ages to decide whether or not to send it. *Happy Birthday!* There were no other words, no corny verse. The pen had trembled in her fingers as she wrote the word *Jenny* at the bottom of the page. No *kisses,* no *love from* . . .

She'd left it in her locker at work for two days before posting it. Then it had only taken a second to slip it into the box. Too late to change her mind. When it left her hand she'd felt light-headed for a moment and stood, one hand leaning on the red mailbox, her eyes scanning the street. *It's for my mum!* she'd wanted to whisper.

That had been weeks before. There would have been

a postmark on the stamp. The word *Croydon* in smudged black ink. She knew that. She expected that. What she hadn't expected was for her mother to tell anyone. To expose her.

Why not, though? She'd done it before.

FOUR

THE shopping center was just so big. Alice felt exhausted simply being there. The place was full of people moving back and forth looking purposeful, their hands clutching shopping bags. In places there were lone shoppers walking smartly through the crowds. Often, though, they were steering strollers, or holding the hands of small grumpy children, stopping abruptly to wipe a nose or pick up a fallen toy. They were all looking in the polished windows at the goods for sale, at the signs that said BLUE CROSS DAY, at the mannequins that stood lifelessly parading the fashions.

After a while Alice sat on a bench and looked up at the floors above; the food hall with its neon signs, the giant palms, the roof above with its glass spires that seemed to pierce the fast-moving clouds beyond. It made her feel dizzy.

It was the Saturday before she was due to return to work and she and Rosie were shopping. It wasn't really Rosie's kind of place, but she knew Alice liked it so they occasionally spent time there. Rosie preferred markets, and spent hours at stalls where the owners had designed and made the clothes themselves. "It's more individual, real designer clothes," she'd say, holding heavy velvet skirts up against her, trying on linen blouses that fell into wrinkles as soon as they were touched. She also liked thrift shops where she often picked up expensive shoes and jackets for a fraction of their price. "But someone's already worn them," Alice would say, shivering slightly at the idea. Rosie didn't care. She washed, ironed, or polished the items and took pleasure in showing them off. Alice preferred the mass-produced stuff in the chain stores. She didn't want to look *original.* She liked to look the same as everybody else.

She was carrying two shopping bags. In one was a light suede jacket, something she had jumped on when she saw it on the rack. She'd run her fingers across it, feeling its softness. She'd tried on the smallest size they had and loved the way it sat around her shoulders, lightweight and comfortable, like a loose embrace. In the other bag was some underwear, plain white and black pants, and bras. Rosie had tried to interest her in colored sets, with lace and netting; pretty things that looked like tiny works of art. She didn't want them, though. They were too frivolous, too gaudy.

For once Rosie had bought something. A floaty top from a department store. It had gathered sleeves and a drawstring neck and looked extremely impractical. Rosie had liked it though, slipping it on over her T-shirt in the middle of the store, twirling around in front of a mirror and nodding contentedly to herself. Alice had crept off to look at other things while Rosie paid for it, striking up a conversation with the woman on the cash register as though she knew her.

Alice sat at the café table and waited for her lunch.

Rosie was such a warm person, easy to get on with. That's why she bonded with the girls who came to stay. Sometimes it made Alice feel good. At other times she resented those easygoing ways because it meant that Rosie clicked with everyone she met. Like Sara, the new woman from downstairs. Alice could never do that.

"Here we are!" Rosie said, placing a tray on the table.

Alice picked up the plate with her sandwich. Rosie moved the other things onto the table and then slid the tray between the legs of the chair.

"Are you seeing Frankie tonight?" Rosie said, biting into her sandwich.

Alice nodded.

"You won't be too late, though?"

"No. We're just going for a drink at the college bar."

"Soft drinks, though?" Rosie said.

Alice nodded. It was a ritual they both went through every time Alice talked about going to a pub. Rosie knew that Alice drank beer and wine. Alice knew that Rosie knew. But each time she went they both had to say the same words. Like a mantra.

"What about you?" Alice said.

"I'm going out for an Indian meal with Sara. I'm looking forward to it."

"Sara? You didn't say."

"It's a sort of last-minute thing. I saw her yesterday struggling with her shopping. I helped her in, we got chatting. She's really quite nice."

"She talks a lot," Alice said, remembering the couple of times she had been going out and had met Sara coming in.

"She's a teacher. You know what they're like!"

Rosie was beaming. Apart from work things and going out with her mum she hardly ever went anywhere. And that was why she'd bought herself the new top. Alice felt a stirring of jealousy. Rosie had a new friend. She shouldn't mind but she did. Sara from downstairs, who never stopped talking.

"What does she teach?" Alice said, remembering the pile of exercise books she'd been carrying the last time she saw her.

"Primary kids. Seven- or eight-year-olds."

"Hasn't she got a partner?" Alice said, wishing she had.

"Nope. Like me. Footloose and fancy-free."

Rosie looked embarrassed for a moment.

"Listen to me. I'm sounding like a teenager."

Alice felt a rush of affection. She reached over and

squeezed Rosie's hand. Why shouldn't she have a life of her own?

"Make sure you don't stay out too late!" she said.

"All right, Mum!" Rosie said, smiling, picking up the second half of her sandwich and inserting the pointed end of it into her mouth.

On the way home Alice felt weary. Her shopping bags hung low and her shoulders drooped. She looked into the Coffee Pot as they passed and saw Pip and the manager behind the counter.

"You okay about going back to work on Monday?" Rosie said, softly.

They were leaving the big shopping center behind and approaching the quieter end of the high street. There were fewer people around, although the traffic was still slow, queued up behind buses that hadn't bothered to pull into the stop. They passed the pet shop and the bookshop and a hardware store that had had the sign CLOSING DOWN SALE outside for months.

"I'm looking forward to it."

She'd had just over a week at home. Rosie had insisted that she hadn't been well, that she was off-color, stressed, and needed to rest. Alice had gone along with it although she'd known, deep down, that she was hiding away. She hadn't told Rosie about the birthday card. It was her se- cret. She was allowed that much, now that she was out in the real world. It had unsettled her, though, that her mother had passed on information to someone about where she might be. It sat in her head like a banging door that she couldn't close.

"I'm just going to pay the papers," Rosie said when they got to the newsagent's on the corner of their street. "I'll wait here."

Alice didn't want to go into the shop. The newsagent's son, a short, muscular lad, was always looking at her and trying to draw her into conversation. She walked a few paces on and leaned against a lamppost. An old dog shuffled past, pausing to sniff at her legs and then carrying on. The shop window was full of posters and small ads, and through it she could only just see parts of Rosie's back and the profile of the newsagent talking and laughing. He was probably adding up her bill, tearing the slips off from his folder. Rosie was probably asking after his wife, who had recently had an operation. Alice let out a light sigh.

Frankie was coming for her about eight. They were going to the college where there was a DJ whom Frankie liked. The drinks were cheap and Frankie knew a lot of people. They'd have a good evening, she knew. She found herself smiling thinking of this, and then from somewhere deep down she felt this tickle of excitement, thinking of Frankie's rough, unshaven face against her neck and her shoulder, and the feel of his hands on her skin pulling her so close that she could feel his ribs and his hip bones. It didn't take much for him to scoop her up in his arms and carry her across to the bed. Even if they weren't going to do anything, he liked her there, in the muddle of his sheets, her head, her short boyish hair, on his pillow.

She tutted to herself. She'd let herself get carried away thinking about him. How silly she must have looked standing on a corner in a kind of reverie. She tried to focus on Rosie. How long did it take to pay the papers? She looked at the posters in the window and then at the small ads. A huge headline stood out from one of them. HAVE YOU SEEN THIS GIRL? it said. Underneath was just a photo but Alice couldn't make it out from where she was standing. Inside the shop she saw Rosie moving backward away from the counter, the newsagent still talking, looking like he was counting something off on his fingers.

HAVE YOU SEEN THIS GIRL? The words gave her a mild shock. All those years ago. In Berwick. The day after it happened. The streets of Berwick were covered in photographs. It had been taken from some album, photocopied and enlarged. Someone had put the pictures in plastic sheet protectors, the kind that usually fitted into ring binders. They'd been stuck to trees and lampposts and the inside of people's windows. She'd been at home at the time, so she couldn't have seen them herself; she must have seen it on the television. A reporter standing by a poster. HAVE YOU SEEN THIS GIRL? it said. Everyone was looking for her.

Only JJ had known where she was.

Alice took a few steps along the pavement and then turned to walk back. Like a sentry marching up and down, she tried to pull herself together. These memories from the past had to be fought off, subdued. She went briskly back to the shop to see what Rosie was doing. Was she ever coming out? She steered her eye away from the offending small ad and tried to focus on a poster that advertised a circus and fun fair. There was a picture of a woman in a sparkling skintight catsuit, balancing on a tightrope and holding a long thin pole. She couldn't concentrate though. The headline was there, at the corner of her eye. HAVE YOU SEEN THIS GIRL? The ad with the photograph, and finally, just as Rosie turned and walked toward the door of the shop, she let herself look closely at it.

The picture made her freeze. It was cut from a larger photograph and photocopied. It was stuck to the middle of the postcard, and was just a face. The face of a teenage girl, about sixteen years old.

Her face.

Her hair was longer then, flicking round her jaw. The image was slightly blurred at the edges. Probably it had been taken a year or so before, by one of the workers at Monksgrove, or a visitor taking a shot of a group of residents. She hadn't posed for it, she wasn't that stupid, but somehow she had ended up in someone's photo. And now it was being used to try and find her.

"That man never stops talking!"

She could hear Rosie's voice, feel her closeness, but her concentration was on the small ad. Underneath the familiar face were some words. *Her family longs to hear from her. Last seen in the Croydon area. Reward of £100 for any information on her whereabouts.* Then a phone number.

"What's this?" Rosie said, drawn to whatever was holding Alice's attention. "Oh my goodness. Oh no."

Her voice dropped and Alice knew that she had recognized her. Rosie could see the likeness. Alice couldn't move. Her legs felt like sticks. If she bent her knees they would snap. She was staying there, on the street, next to her picture.

"Let's go home," Rosie said, gripping her arm and pulling her away. "We'll contact Jill. She'll put a stop to this."

FIVE

JILL Newton arranged for them to meet in a bookshop in London a week later. It seemed like a cloak-and-dagger affair, and Alice couldn't help looking carefully around as she walked along the busy street. As though people might be there, in the slipstream behind her, keeping her in their sights.

As soon as she'd seen the photograph in the newsagent's shop window she'd known that there would be others. Rosie herself admitted to seeing at least three (probably more, Rosie keeping it to herself, trying not to worry her). They were dotted about the town center of Croydon like tiny land mines. Someone, the detective in the greasy leather jacket perhaps, was hanging round the corners of her life, waiting to walk up behind her one day and lay an accusing hand on her shoulder.

Before turning into the bookshop, she took a last look around.

It was just after five. The shop had four floors and she stood on the escalator and let it carry her upstairs toward the café. She had never seen so many books before. Jill

Newton was already at a table when she got there. She was sitting with her back to the window, her shoulders straight, her head high. Her blond hair was stiff and she was wearing different black-rimmed glasses that made her look like a secretary who was about to take shorthand for a boss. As Alice got closer she wanted to wave, but Jill was absorbed in some magazine that she was reading and Alice had to tap her on the wrist before she actually looked up.

"Alice, great to see you. Have a seat. I'll get you something. A coffee?"

Alice shook her head. She'd had enough of coffees and lattes and hot chocolates to last her a lifetime.

"How's the job?" Jill said, closing the magazine and slipping it into a bag down by the side of her chair.

"It's okay. I had a bad couple of weeks, but I think I'm okay now."

Jill's coffee was sitting in front of her and she had her hands loosely clasped around it. She seemed very calm, her fingers only moving to pick her cup up and then replace it. Alice, even though she tried to sit still, was fidgety, crossing and recrossing her legs and picking at the sleeves of her new suede jacket.

"Alice." Jill began to speak after a few moments' quiet. "I've had a message from Pat Coffey. She says your mother has been in touch with her. Your mother says you sent her a birthday card. Is that true?"

Alice took a deep breath. Even now, now that she was free, there were no secrets. She nodded.

"Your mother has taken this as a sign that you want to reestablish contact with her. Is that the case? Do you want to see her?"

Alice shook her head. She didn't know exactly why she'd sent the card but she knew that she didn't want to see her mother. Jill Newton seemed pleased with her response.

"That's what I thought. That's what I told Pat. Sending a card to her wasn't exactly the best thing to do. It went to an old address and had to be passed on through friends."

Jill drank the rest of her coffee. Then she pushed the cup and saucer away and turned directly to Alice. She put one of her hands over Alice's.

"Alice, love. We had this plan. That you would live in total secrecy for a number of years, maybe even longer. This would give you a chance to have a normal sort of life. To live in the community. To go to university. To get a job. Find a partner, maybe, have a family of your own. This means total anonymity. There are only three people who know . . ."

"You, Pat, and Rosie," Alice said, feeling her throat tighten up.

It sounded good. A new life. A new start. Like being born again. Except that Alice was carrying a heavy load into that new life. A lot of baggage from the past, weighing her down.

"People who care about you. People you can trust."

Alice nodded. She knew that this was true. She also knew that there were people whom she couldn't trust and that her mother was one of them.

"It means that people from your past have to be left behind. Maybe not for always. Maybe ten years down the line, when you're established, when you've made a life for yourself. Maybe then you could consider some contact with your mother."

In ten years she would be twenty-seven.

"Now, with this business in Croydon we have two options. First we could contact a judge and set up an exclusion order. Stop the detective from coming anywhere within a certain distance of you. If we do this, it will, no doubt, lead back to the dead girl's parents."

Alice swallowed back. The words *dead girl* just tumbled out of Jill's mouth. How easy it was for her to speak of things that she had no involvement in. Those words, *the dead girl*, would have sat heavy on Alice's tongue, like having a mouth full of cement.

"But if we do contact a judge, the press will certainly get hold of the story. It will show them that they've stumbled on your whereabouts. It might mean that you have to move on from Croydon. We might have to find another placement for you."

Alice shook her head. She couldn't leave Rosie. Not ever.

"The second possibility is that we could simply ignore it. A lack of reaction from you, and this detective will think he's looking in the wrong place. After a while he'll move on. He'll suspect that the card you posted to your mother was posted by someone else, somewhere far away from where you live."

"I'm so sorry," Alice said, looking at Jill Newton.

She was causing trouble for everyone, being a nuisance. Jill had had to come away from her office to see her. Pat Coffey was getting phone calls from her mother. Rosie was having sleepless nights. She had seen her, boiling the kettle at ten past four in the morning, sitting at the kitchen table while the sky paled into daylight. It gave her a mild feeling of panic. How long before they got fed up, tired of her? Maybe one day they would let her go. Tell her to look after herself. Then she would have to face the newspapers and television on her own. Possibly, one day, she would be forced to come face to face with the parents. She shook her head. She couldn't stand that. She'd rather fold up and die than be in that position.

What on earth had made her send that birthday card?

Later, after they'd left the bookshop and got to the station, Jill told her about the mobile phone.

"I'm organizing some funds to pay for it. That way you can contact me if anything else occurs. Personally, I don't think it will. This detective won't get a response. Then he'll get tired of looking. He'll give up when his pay stops coming in. Then you can get back to normal."

Jill gave her a little hug before she peeled off to go to a different platform. Alice waited for her train, feeling the warmth of the woman's embrace for ages afterward. When the carriage doors opened, she stepped quickly in and got herself a window seat. The train filled up and she turned to look out of the window, her face leaning on the glass. The next track was empty but there were people standing on the platform waiting. As her train moved off she tried to recall all the things that Jill Newton had said: the two options, the birthday card, the mobile phone. It was hard to concentrate, though. The rhythm of the train and the tightly packed bodies made it easy to just drift off into her own thoughts. All she was aware of was the train rocking gently underneath her, people close by, the window, and the outside world chugging past. She might have even closed her eyes for a moment.

A raw day in January six years before. There was dirty snow on the ground as they carried their stuff in suitcases and black plastic bags down the stairs from the flat in Norwich. Jennifer and her mother, Carol Jones, half walking, half running to the old cream van that was idling by the pavement. Jennifer dumped her bags in the back, next to the dismantled beds and old armchairs that had been carried down in the lift. She kept her tiny knapsack and climbed into the passenger seat while Carol went back up to the flat for the last few things. Danny, a huge man, a pal, her mum had said, was slumped on the steering wheel, holding a tiny cigarette butt in between his thumb and forefinger. When Carol reappeared she was carrying a black bag and the small portable telly that usually sat in her and Perry's bedroom. This made Jennifer feel uncomfortable and she wriggled about on her seat, smoothing down her trousers. She put her hand into her knapsack and felt Macy, her old doll, there and used her fingers to rub at her silky hair. She wished the van were going, driving along the streets instead of sitting by the side of the flats. When the doors closed, Danny sat up suddenly and cleared his throat, flicking the cigarette butt out of the window. Jennifer watched as it landed on a drift of snow, gasping out a last ribbon of smoke before it died completely.

"Quick," Carol said, getting into the front of the van, squashing Jennifer in the middle. "Let's get going."

Danny turned the ignition key and the van spluttered but didn't start. He tried it again a few times and Jennifer felt her mum's leg and arm stiffen on the seat beside her. Danny turned and looked at Carol and she gave him a glowing smile, her perfectly lipsticked mouth opening to show a row of straight white teeth.

They hadn't taken much from the flat. Just their beds, a couple of chairs, small kitchen things, towels, and clothes.

Perry was out at work and unaware of the move that was taking place. Jennifer was sorry about this. She liked Perry. He was only twenty-four, but he'd been nice to her. He'd chatted to her a lot and opened tins of Heinz tomato soup for her when she got in from school on cold afternoons. He was a Star Wars fan and had a cupboard full of his childhood toys. Her mum was always trying to get him to sell them. "They'll make some cash," she said, running her long fingers over Darth Vader, but Perry wouldn't part with any of them.

That's why her mum decided that they had to go.

"He's a complete waste of space," she'd said, when the letter came about the new house. "We don't want the likes of him weighing us down."

So Danny drove them to Berwick.

"I didn't realize it was this far," he grumbled, pulling the van up half on a grassy verge and half off.

There was a road sign attached to the garden wall of the end cottage. WATER LANE, it said. Carol got out and walked toward the middle house. In her hand was a pair of keys with a cardboard label attached to them. She turned and looked back at Danny, who was still sitting in the driver's seat.

"Come on! There's a lot of stuff to shift!" she said with mock righteousness.

Jennifer heard Danny sigh and then turn off the ignition.

47

The three of them stood by the front door, exhaling small clouds of hot air. Around their feet, on the icy grass were suitcases, boxes, and black plastic bags full of stuff that had been hastily packed that morning. Jennifer saw Danny zip his jacket right up to the neck and glance at his watch as her mum fiddled with the keys. When the door opened into a dark hallway, she picked up a couple of bags and followed her mum in.

The cottage was tiny, smaller than she thought from outside. Her mum seemed to take up all the space in the hallway in front of her. Jennifer felt the bags that she was carrying scraping along the walls, and when she looked around Danny was ducking to avoid hitting the light-bulb.

"Is the power on?" Danny said.

"Midday. That's my official moving-in time," her mum said.

A door opened and the three found themselves in a dark living room. Her mum walked over to the window and pulled back a pair of dusty curtains. A faint wash of light made the room seem bigger and colder at the same time.

"Not too small," her mum said. "It's big enough for us, right, Jen?"

Jennifer nodded. Just the two of them again.

"Freezing in here!" Danny said, looking a bit put out. "I'll need some warming up, Carol."

He threw his arm round her mum's shoulder and her mum wriggled out of the hold. She kept her smile but her voice was dripping with cold.

"Everything in good time, Danny. Let's be patient. There's furniture to put up and then we'll see what we can do to warm the place up a bit."

Later, when the beds had been reassembled, the bags and cases unpacked, and the two armchairs sat side by side in the living room, the power came on. The bulb in the living room gave off a blur of light that did nothing to brighten the room. After a while, though, Jennifer could feel the gentle thrum of the central heating. She took her coat off and sat on the edge of one of the armchairs. On her lap was Macy, her favorite doll that she had owned for years. Macy wasn't a *toy*. She didn't *play* with her. She just liked to have her near and touch her hair. From upstairs she could hear the murmur of her mum and Danny's voices and the sound of things moving around, scraping against the floor. The tiny television sat on the floor in front of her armchair and she wondered if Perry would be angry that they had taken it, and what he would say when he realized that they were gone. She'd heard him call her mum a *thief* before, but they'd made up afterward, spending all afternoon in the bedroom while she watched her video of *The Jungle Book.*

After a few minutes, when the voices from upstairs had died down, Jennifer got up and walked into the small kitchen and looked out of the window over the sink into the back garden.

It was long and uneven. The grass was overgrown and there were clumps of bushes here and there that sat hunched against the gray sky. A shed sat halfway along, its door hanging off, and by the side of it a couple of up-ended buckets sat like tiny seats on the ground. A few flakes of snow floated past. She smiled. It was their first ever garden. She looked over the fence to the adjacent garden, which was very different. It looked longer and wider, as if someone had got a bulldozer and rolled it up and down and flattened it out. There was a small play area, with swings and a climbing frame. A girl appeared and ran out toward the swings. She was about her own age, ten. She wore jeans and a zip-up jacket with a hood that was lined with fur. She ran to the very end of the garden and touched the fence, turning to run back as though she were in a race with some invisible person. Looking back toward the houses, the girl suddenly stopped and looked in her direction. She'd noticed the lights, perhaps, and then Jennifer's face at the window. The girl threw her hood off and shook her head, and her thick ginger hair sprang out. Jennifer wasn't sure what to do, so she lifted her hand from Macy's head and raised it for a wave, but the girl shot off and disappeared back into her own house.

Afterward, when she'd been alone in the new living

room for a long time, she put Macy back into her knapsack and went quietly upstairs. The door of her mum's room was closed but not shut. She could hear sounds from inside, a little laugh and then the low voice of Danny, a couple of words, then him clearing his throat loudly. Her mum shushed him and there was a small creak, the bed moving. Jennifer knew the sound of that bed creaking. She knew what it meant. She had had to share her mum and Perry's bedroom and had lain listening to it many times. Sometimes she'd turned round and watched the figures moving under the covers. Once there had been no covers and Jennifer had narrowed her eyes so that she could only see little bits of what was going on. It had made her feel horrible for days afterward.

Jennifer stood by the door, looking in through the gap. She couldn't see much, just the wallpaper. She could hear Danny, though, his breath coming in great mouthfuls, the bed groaning under his weight. She should go away, she knew that, but her hand reached up and gently pushed the door so that it moved back a few centimeters.

They were lying sideways across the bed, her mum's jeans on the ground, Danny's trousers in pools around his ankles. Danny's huge backside seemed to tremble and then slump, his shoulders sinking into the bed. Somewhere, underneath him, was her mum. Jennifer hoped that she wasn't getting squashed.

"What the hell?" Danny's voice made her jump.

The man was half sitting up, his arms pulling at the waistband of his trousers, his money making clinking noises in the pockets.

"What's she doing in here!"

Her mum got up off the bed, kicking her jeans to one side. She reached over and took Jennifer's arm and marched her out of the room.

"I told you to stay downstairs!" she said lightly, pulling the room door closed behind her.

Jennifer looked at her mother's thin body, her tiny breasts inside an old black bra, the rose tattoo on her shoulder, her flat stomach and skinny legs. She was tall, especially in her high heels, but her body was light as a feather.

"I'll tell you what," her mother said. "You go downstairs and I'll get rid of him. We'll get takeout for lunch. How about that?"

Her mother disappeared back into the room and Jennifer walked down the stairs. At the bottom was the black bag that her mum had been carrying out of the flat just before they left. She picked it up and took it into the living room. Heavy footsteps sounded on the stairs, and then Danny shouted, "Bye." She didn't answer. She waited until the front door slammed and then she unzipped the bag. Inside was a single plastic figure. Luke Skywalker.

Her mum had stolen it.

Alice opened her eyes suddenly and remembered where she was. On the train, pulling out of the station before her stop. Had she fallen asleep? Or just been daydreaming? Lost in her own thoughts? She saw that the train compartment had emptied a little. No one was standing and people were looking easier, nestling back in their seats, their faces serene, looking forward to going home.

A feeling of loss took hold of her. Just for a second. She saw her mother's face breaking into a laugh when she asked her about Luke Skywalker. "That bloody toy!" she'd said dismissively.

How long had it been since she'd seen her? Four years? Five?

It seemed like a lifetime.

SIX

THE detective's name was Derek Corker.

Alice found this out a week later, when she met Frankie at his college bar for an end-of-term celebration. The exams had finished and the students were getting ready to go home. Frankie was moving back to Brighton, where his parents lived.

Alice saw the man's name printed on a small card that was pinned to the Student Union notice board. DEREK CORKER, PRIVATE INVESTIGATOR. Beside it was a copy of the photograph that had been in the newsagents. MISS-ING GIRL it said. *Parents are distraught. Please contact with any information. Cash reward.*

It didn't upset her. She felt strangely detached when she looked at it, as if it weren't a photograph of her at all, but of some other person she used to know.

"What's this?" Frankie said, slipping his arm round her waist and hooking her toward him.

She shrugged.

"Oh, that guy. He's been hanging around college for a couple of days. Looking for some missing girl. He's got wads of cash. Keeps buying drinks and flashing his money."

He pulled her toward the bar and she felt light-headed with relief. The photograph meant nothing to him. The face of the girl in the picture was not that of his girlfriend. She squeezed his arm with pleasure and went on tiptoes to kiss his cheek. He turned toward her and, ignoring the surrounding students, he bent down and gave her a fierce kiss on the mouth, sending a wave of desire through her.

Was this love?

The day before he'd bought her a present, a thin gold chain with a flat heart hanging from it. On the back of the heart was the word *Alice,* engraved in italics. She had never owned anything like it.

"Thanks," she'd said, bewildered by her feelings. She was on the brink of tears.

"You've got a lovely neck," he murmured, lying back on her bed. "You should wear things that show it off more."

They'd been in Rosie's flat for a couple of hours in the afternoon. Frankie had spent the day packing up his stuff, ready to transport it all home to Brighton the following weekend. He had turned up unexpectedly at Rosie's door, dusty and fed up. The others in his flat had used up all the hot water and he needed a shower. Plus he'd decided he wanted to give her the gift. Just like that. She sorted out some towels for him and turned away in embarrassment when he stripped his clothes off in front of her and marched off toward the bathroom laughing, the towel dragging on the floor as he walked.

She put the gold chain on and gazed at herself in the mirror. Her cropped hair made her face look small and her neck was long and thin. How pale and serious she looked. What did Frankie find attractive about her? When he came out of the bathroom, he had the towel tied loosely around his waist and she had a shiver of desire for him. He sat beside her on the bed, making no move to get dressed.

"This is brilliant," she said, holding the chain out.

He slipped his hand up the back of her T-shirt and stroked her skin. Then, taking hold of her bra strap, he pulled her gently back onto the bed so that she was lying beside him.

"I'm talking about the chain," she said, breathing in the smell of soap and shampoo from him.

"Mmm," he mumbled, his mouth on her shoulder.

She laid her head back and allowed herself to be kissed and touched, her back arching with pleasure. When Frankie moved across to lie over her, she raised her head and started to back off.

"Not here! Rosie might come back."

Frankie let out a long exasperated sigh. He sat up, his shoulders hunched.

"Not here because of Rosie. Not at my place because of my flatmates! Where then? Are you trying to tell me something? Don't you love me anymore?"

She sat up at this. The word love had been dropped casually in. He often called her *love* and she had signed notes and e-mails to him *with love*. But love in the big sense, with a capital letter? That kind of Love hadn't been mentioned.

"Hey, you're my number one," she said, trying to lighten the tone. "It's not you. It's me. Truth is . . . ," she said, deciding to be honest for once. "The absolute truth is I've not done anything like that before."

His forehead wrinkled up and he gave a jokey look. "You're a *virgin*?" he said.

She nodded.

"But you've had other boyfriends."

She nodded. Now she needed to lie again.

"And you've never . . . ?"

"No."

"Well," he said. "You're right. We should wait for the right moment. It's got to be really special."

He stood up and pulled the towel tightly round himself.

"But right now," he said, "I need another shower. A *cold* shower."

She heard him mumbling to himself as he went toward the bathroom and she straightened the bed, picking

57

up his dusty clothes and laying them flat. The intercom buzzed and it startled her. Her first thought was of Rosie returning and Frankie in the shower. But Rosie had her own key. She picked up the receiver.

"Alice? It's Sara here. From downstairs? I got this package that was delivered earlier today. I took it in because Rosie was at work. I only just noticed that you were back. Could you take it? I'm going out soon."

"I'm coming down," Alice said.

She looked round to see that the bathroom door was shut and the shower was running again. She went quickly down the stairs and opened the front door. Sara was holding an oblong cardboard box that had Rosie's name and address on it.

"Thanks," Alice said. "No school today?"

"I'm having a stress day. I've had enough of badly behaved kids to last me a lifetime," Sara said, giving an exaggerated sigh.

Instead of turning to go, she stood still, with a pleasant smile on her face. She had a pair of dark glasses propped on top of her head and a large canvas bag on one shoulder. She looked lopsided. Alice wanted to close the door but felt awkward about it. She was Rosie's new friend. She looked at Sara's cutoff trousers and flowing top. She had an air of the beach about her, as if she were on holiday.

"Right," Alice said, edging the door shut.

"How are you feeling?" Sara said, moving closer, her

foot over the doorstep. "Rosie said you were a bit out of sorts the other week."

"I'm better now," Alice said.

"You're so thin! I was saying to Rosie how unfair it is that some people are so skinny. Me? I'm always a stone or so overweight. You'd think I'd be thin with all the running round I do. In the classroom, I mean."

"Well," Alice said, making a determined turn toward the stairs, "I ought to go."

"Right. Tell Rosie I'll give her a call."

Sara gave a bright smile and turned away toward her car that was parked a way up the road. Alice backed into the hallway and closed the door. She took the stairs two at a time and once in the flat she put the cardboard box on the kitchen table.

Frankie appeared at the bedroom door dressed. His hair was still wet and it was making the back of his T-shirt damp.

"Got to go!" he said.

He leaned down, put his hands on her shoulders, and kissed her lightly on the mouth, his tongue flicking past her teeth.

"See you tomorrow," he whispered.

The Union bar was packed with small groups of students making their last farewells. Frankie held her hand and they threaded through the crowds and found a couple of his mates at a table over in a corner. The table in front of them was full of empty pint glasses.

"Hiya, Ali!" Frankie's flatmate said.

She nodded and smiled at the other couple of lads sitting, looking bleary-eyed from too much beer. Frankie went off to get a round and she sat looking around the bar, repulsed by the sticky floor and the smell of drinks and cigarettes, and yet oddly pleased to be there.

"Are you a student?" one of the strange faces said.

"No. I'm starting at university in September," she said.

The lad nodded, but he wasn't really paying attention. Frankie was at the bar, and she sat back, thinking about her own university course.

In September she would be moving into halls of residence in Sussex. A new student, one among many thousands to start a course, to meet new people, to get her qualifications. She would pack all her things in the back of Rosie's car and they would drive there. Rosie would help her carry her things up and down until they had everything in her room. For a lot of students it would be their first time in a small room of their own, away from their families. A tiny single bed with desk and bulletin board. A chair, a telly, a wardrobe, some drawers. A sink and, if they were lucky, a toilet and shower room attached. She had done it before, though. A small room of her own, in Monksgrove. In the prison.

She tried not to let this bother her. It would be a totally different situation. She would be free to come and go as she pleased. She would be among normal people. Young men and women whose worst crime was to smoke dope or pinch a CD from WHSmith's.

Frankie placed the beers on the table, a number of the lads signaling their thanks. She pulled her glass toward her and took a drink of the ice-cold lager.

"My mum wants you to come over and stay with us for a week," Frankie suddenly said.

"What?"

"In Brighton. In August. I could show you around, maybe we could take a visit to the Sussex campus. It's not that far."

"That's really nice of her . . ."

"Hey. I want you to come. We can spend a lot of time together. You can meet my kid sister, Sophie, and my mum and dad. I've got my own room up in the loft. A double bed, the lot. It's like a tiny apartment. I think they had it extended in order to get rid of me."

A double bed. Alice felt a tingle of embarrassment. It was only a piece of furniture, but it meant so much more.

"Hey, there's the bloke with the money," one of the other lads said, reaching across Alice to nudge Frankie.

At the bar, a couple of meters away, Alice could see the man with the ponytail. He was still wearing his battered leather jacket, even though it was a warm day and stifling inside the bar.

"That's the guy," Frankie said to her. "The detective."

She watched as the man leaned his elbows on the bar. In one hand was a rolled-up bill, like a cigarette between his fingers. The girl behind the bar gave him a big smile and took his drink order. Alice couldn't hear but she thought the girl mouthed her thanks, so perhaps the detective had said, "Have one yourself."

"Who's he looking for?" one of the lads said.

"Some missing kid. Used to go out with a student so the parents think she might be lodging around here."

"That's her business. I wouldn't tell him nothing. Even if I knew where she was."

"Even if he offered you money?"

"Nah, not me," one of them said.

"How much, though? I only see him offering tenners," another said.

"It's an interesting point," Frankie said, sitting upright, getting into the argument. "How much would it take for you to rat on someone."

"And there's the other issue," someone else said. "Surely the parents have got a right to know?"

"If you knew where she was and there was a reward of a hundred quid, would you tell?"

The argument went on but Alice had stopped listening. She drank more of her beer, holding the glass in front of her face. The detective was holding his hand out as the girl counted his change. He said something to her and then in his other hand, as if by magic, there was a piece of paper that he gave her to look at. The photograph of JJ, Alice was sure.

The girl looked at it for a few moments and then shook her head. He took it back, putting it into one of the giant pockets of his jacket. He turned away from the bar in her direction. He was holding three pints of beer in a kind of triangle between his two hands. He caught her eye for a second and she looked away, back to Frankie, who was leaning forward, cutting the air with his hand, arguing a point with the others.

Out of the corner of her eye she could see him place the drinks on a nearby table. She put her glass back and let herself glance in his direction.

He was still looking at her. His face a little confused. His eyebrows tensed.

She looked away, holding her breath for a moment. Then she picked her glass up again. She held it steadily, although she didn't drink any. She looked from Frankie to the others, all looking relaxed and arguing about how much money it would take to betray someone. Thirty pieces of silver, perhaps.

Had he recognized her? Had he been looking at her photograph for so long that she had become like a real flesh person? Never mind that she had had her hair cropped and lost weight since then. She had the same eyes, the same lips, the same pale skin. She was JJ.

Suddenly she couldn't sit there for another minute. She stood up, knocking the table slightly, the glasses clinking together, some of the beer spilling over the edge. The lads all looked at her.

"Whoa!" Frankie said. "Careful."

"I'm just going to the toilet," she said.

The noise in the bar seemed louder, the smell stronger, the floor more sticky. She didn't feel well, she needed to be outside, in the fresh air. But as she moved away from the table, the detective stepped across and blocked her way. She had no choice but to stop and look up at him.

"Excuse me," he said. "I know you, don't I?"

She stood very still, not answering him, focusing on his puffy cheeks, his hair, slicked down and pulled back into a ponytail.

"I do, I'm sure. I know you from somewhere!"

She opened her mouth to speak. Could it be this simple? To be found out here, in this bar, in front of everyone? To have her new life end in seconds, her feet stuck to the floor of a tatty bar in front of dozens of drunken students?

"I . . . I . . ."

He smiled suddenly and clicked his fingers in a dramatic way.

"You work in the coffee place by the station. You found some of my papers one day."

"Yes," she said, the tension draining out of her so that she felt light-headed. As though she might float up and away.

"I must pop in again," he said. "Next time I'm around there."

Then he turned and went back to his table and she stumbled on out to the toilet. Once inside she splashed her face with water and stood bent over the sink, letting the droplets fall off, ignoring the sound of people coming in and out behind. Let them think she was drunk, she didn't care.

The argument at the table had finished when she got back and the lads were sitting quietly, their beers in front of them. One of them was passing a joint around, each person inhaling and passing it on.

"I've got to go," she whispered to Frankie.

She had no intention of sitting there while dope was being smoked. That was something serious that could get her in trouble with her probation officer. Just a little thing like that could send her back.

Frankie walked her to the bus stop.

"Will you come, in August? To Brighton?"

"Absolutely! If Rosie lets me."

"Oh . . ."

"She will. You might not be her favorite person but she knows how I feel about you."

"She's like the mother from hell!" he said, and then, as

though the thought had just popped into his head, "What about your own mum? What was she like?"

She was taken aback. He'd hardly ever mentioned her background or her family. It was as if he'd *understood* that it wasn't something she wanted to talk about.

"She was a model," Alice said, seeing a bus turn the corner. "Really glamorous. Still is, I suppose. But I don't see her anymore."

An honest answer. Another thing Alice didn't have to lie about.

SEVEN

AT HOME, in her room, Alice took a picture of her mother out of her bottom drawer. It was one of five that she owned. A professional shot, taken by a photographer, her mother sitting on a wrought-iron chair in an over-grown garden. She was hugging one of her knees, her chin leaning on the back of her hand, her eyes fastened to the camera, her lips parted in a toothy smile.

Carol Jones was beautiful. There was no argument about that.

Alice remembered loving her mother's looks from a very young age. Just as she loved the smell of her and the feel of her clothes. Looking closely, she focused on the pale skin and the dazzling smile. The straw-colored hair was pulled back in some kind of clasp and there were wispy bits hanging forward. Her even white teeth con-trasted with the perfectly lipsticked mouth. How could anyone not have been affected by such a face?

Alice looked up. From the other room she could hear the sound of Rosie's voice. She was having a drink with Sara. The two women had been there when she'd got back from seeing Frankie. Sara had started chatting to her immediately, but she didn't feel like talking so she'd left them alone.

There were other photographs, but Alice didn't want to get them out and start poring over them. She swallowed a couple of times. There in her throat was the old ache. "Don't dwell on your relationship with your mother," the counselor had said. But how could she not think of her? When she had been so proud of her, so glad to have her for a mum. No matter what she did.

Carol Jones didn't have to make an effort to look good. She stepped out of bed in the morning and her blond hair seemed to flop into position, her eyes bright, her skin creamy. All she had to do was throw on a pair of jeans, a T-shirt, some big earrings, and red lipstick and she was ready. Her high heels she always left until last. They were usually lined up by the front door, ready for her to choose which pair to wear. Thin heels and strappy base in summer; in winter it was ankle boots with fiercely pointed toes.

When Jennifer started nursery school, Carol did a modeling course. She had a portfolio of photographs and for a year or so she worked for a couple of photographers; modeling for a clothes catalog, promotional work at exhibitions, some fashion displays for chain stores.

She had photographs of herself on the wall of the living room. Big glossy pictures: on a beach wearing swimwear, in a garden wearing an evening dress, in a city center in a smart suit and fake glasses. Carol pointed to them when she had visitors. "I'm a model," she said, proudly. Jennifer used to sit and look at them. Face after smiling face; different hair, different clothes, but underneath it all was her mum's smile.

There was money for a while. It paid the rent of a flat in a tree-lined street. It paid for new furniture, clothes for her mum, and lots of toys (her favorite was a special model doll called Macy). It even paid for a holiday in Spain, where her mum had a different bikini for every day of the week. Modeling was busy work, though, and Jennifer couldn't be part of it. She spent a lot of time with other people. A woman called Simone looked after her sometimes, taking her to school and picking her up. She was a big lady who walked very slowly along the road, pausing at each corner to get her breath. She hardly spoke, and Jennifer had to carry on a conversation with herself most of the time. She usually pulled Macy, her model doll, out of her knapsack and chatted to her.

And what have you been doing today, Macy?
I had a top model job in the palace today.
Did you see the queen?
I did.

Sometimes her gran looked after her. This was worse than being at Simone's. Her gran lived in a flat that was two bus rides away. She had a small dog called Nelson who would sit on her knee growling at Jennifer. She had to be very quiet there because Gran had sewing to do and liked to watch television while she was working.

Occasionally Jennifer stayed in the classroom with the teacher. She sat at her desk while Miss marked lots of books. She drew some pictures and kept one eye on the playground. Eventually she'd see her mum dashing through the school gate, half running, half walking toward the classroom, coming through the door out of breath and apologizing.

Now and then, when her mum wasn't working, she would pick her up from school on time. It delighted Jennifer to see her waiting, standing head and shoulders above the rest of the mums. Her fair hair was streaked with blond, and sometimes she wore it hanging loosely round her face. She'd be in the middle of all the gray-faced women, talking animatedly, her mouth opening and closing. In the summer she wore as little as possible: a strappy top that showed her tattoo, shorts that exposed her long brown legs, and round her ankle a tiny chain. When she saw Jennifer coming across the playground her face beamed. She might have been standing in front of an important photographer.

Everyone who saw them together was impressed. When Carol Jones squatted down to hug her daughter, the other mums seemed to watch with envy. Jennifer reached up to hold her mum's hand as they walked home from school and knew that people were looking. Men stared at her. Women gave her sideways glances. She knew that she must be with someone who was important. All the while her mum pulled her by the hand and walked on, her head in the air, her body swaying slightly as though she were practicing for the catwalk, her spindly heels scraping along the ground.

There were bad days as well. Sometimes there were headaches and her mum had to lie in the dark. Sometimes she felt sick or had a pain and had to be left alone. Often her mum was in a mood; a minicab hadn't arrived on time or her photographs weren't right.

Jennifer picked Macy up at these times and went into her room.

What job are you on today, Macy?

I'm doing a fashion show. On a catwalk.

Wonderful.

Macy had a whole box of clothes, different outfits for the seasons, for casual or evening, for work or play. One of Jennifer's favorites was her ski suit. It was all in one, a shocking-pink color, and she had matching skis and tiny dark glasses.

After what seemed like hours and hours of playing on her own, she would tiptoe into her mum's room, get on the bed, and lie beside her. If her mum was feeling better she turned and gave Jennifer a sleepy hug. If she wasn't she just lay still, hardly breathing. So Jennifer left her alone all through the rest of the day and sometimes even the night-time. She'd reappear the next morning while Jennifer and Macy were having breakfast together.

"What's the time?" she'd say, yawning, bending over to give Jennifer a kiss. "I must have slept for hours! Thanks for not waking Mummy up, love. It's too late for school now, you'll have to stay home."

Jennifer was happy. On those days she had her mum all to herself. She'd help her to sort out her clothes and tidy up her makeup. She'd flick through the picture port-folio, sorting out the glossy prints. She played in the bath-room while her mum lay soaking in bubbles. Sometimes her mum let Jennifer put Macy in the water and wash her hair. Later, they'd watch television together, her mum smelling of shampoo and cream, her hair still wet, hang-ing in thin strips around her face.

After a while the work dried up. There were other girls who were more unusual looking or had better hair or looked more mysterious. It was nothing personal. Just business. The photographers stopped calling and the agen-cies just asked her to leave a message. "We'll get back to you," they said, but they never did. Her mum searched everywhere for jobs, showing her photographs to agen-cies. She left Jennifer with Simone or her gran; a couple of times she left her with neighbors. It was a bad time.

Early one morning, when it was still dark outside, she took Jennifer to Simone's. Simone was in a giant pink dressing gown and her hair was sticking up. Her mum stood in the hallway getting ready to leave. She was full of sparkle beside Simone, in skintight jeans and fitted leather jacket, her hair parted at the side and pulled back into a severe bunch at the back of her head, her lips looking pink and wet. She had a glittery scarf wrapped round and round her neck and Simone, in between a couple of yawns, remarked on it.

"I bought it in Bond Street," her mum said. "Must go . . ."

But as she turned to go, Simone put her arm out and held her there for a moment. Simone's arm, plump and red, her fingers short and stumpy, holding on to the leather jacket.

"Go inside, Jen," her mum said.

Jennifer backed around the door but she could still hear them talking.

"I will pay you." Her mum's voice was whispery. "I'm getting some back pay this week! All right?"

Later that week Jennifer was surprised to see Simone at the school gate, waiting with the other mums, wearing the glittery scarf that had come from Bond Street. It sat awkwardly round her chubby neck and didn't go with her grubby jacket. It probably still had her mum's perfume on it.

There were a lot of headaches then. Her mum spent a lot of time in her bedroom with the curtains drawn.

Alice heard the sound of the flat door closing. Then a moment later she heard Rosie's footsteps padding along the hallway to her room. She placed the photograph under her pillow. Rosie gave a light knock and then walked in. It had always been like that. Rosie, knowing she could come into Alice's room whenever she wanted. Alice didn't mind. She had had enough locked doors in her life.

"You all right, Alice? You looked a bit peaky when you came in." Rosie sat on the edge of the bed and Alice felt the mattress sink down.

"No, I'm fine. It's just . . . Well, I'm not that keen on . . ."

Alice pointed downward, meaning Sara.

"She's all right. Her school is having a theater trip and she wondered if I wanted to go. I said fine. It's free, after all. Do you want anything? Tea? Coffee?"

Alice shook her head, "I just thought I'd have a lie down."

Rosie nodded and backed out of the room, making exaggerated tiptoe movements, giving Alice a little wave at the door, as if she were going out for a long time, not just moving into another room.

Alice pulled the photograph out from under the pillow. She realized then that she'd never shown any of her mum's pictures to Rosie. *What would she think?* she wondered. Would she think that Alice looked like her mum? Alice shook her head. Apart from the fact that they were both thin there was almost no resemblance. She was small and plain. Her mum was tall and glamorous.

She was gripped by a sudden feeling of sadness. Where was her mum now? At that very moment? Was she lying on a bed thinking of Jennifer, the daughter that she hadn't seen for years? They'd been joined together once, she and her mum. How could they be so far apart?

No one really understood. *Did your mum abuse you?* the counselors asked. *Did she hit you? Hurt you? What about all the men she knew? Did any of them touch you?*

Just after her sixth birthday Simone refused to look after her anymore. Instead of seeing her moon face at the school gates, she would now see her mum, her blond hair blown here and there by the wind. She wasn't always cheerful, and sometimes she forgot to put her red lipstick on, but Jennifer was thrilled to see her all the same.

One day a photographer rang. He had some work for her mum. The receiver made a ding noise as her mum replaced it and she danced up and down the tiny hallway. Jennifer and Macy watched.

"All I need is to get my foot back in the door," her mum said, peeling off her clothes, standing stark naked at the bathroom door.

Her foot in the door. It was an odd image and Jennifer thought about it for a few minutes. Then she took Macy into her mum's bedroom and sat on the bed while she got ready. Her mum sprayed herself with perfume, rubbed cream into her skin, her arms, legs, her stomach and back, her tiny breasts. She was humming and posing in the big mirror like she'd done before, when she'd had lots of model jobs. She held her clothes up, outfit after outfit, almost as many as Macy had.

"The studio's only ten minutes away. I won't be more than a couple of hours."

Jennifer thought of Simone then and felt a rumble of worry.

"Will I have to go to Simone's?" she said.

Her mum stopped and looked at her for a moment.

"No, love. Not today."

Jennifer pursed her lips. Did that she mean she had to go to Gran's?

"I want you to be a really big girl today and stay on your own. That's all right, isn't it?"

Jennifer was surprised.

"On my own?" she said. "By myself?"

"Like a really big girl. I'm going to leave you in the front room with a video on. I've got something to drink and cookies and when I go out the front door I'll start the film and I bet you that I'll be back even before it's over."

"I'm allowed to watch a video on my own?"

"Just for today. Just this once because it's very important."

Her mum tidied up the living room, pulling the big armchair in front of the television. She put a glass of orange soda and a bowl of chips on the coffee table. Beside it were a couple of tiny chocolate bars.

"You're not to answer the front door to anybody. Nobody at all. Do you understand?"

Jennifer nodded, feeling very serious.

"Nor the telephone. Just let it ring. The answering machine will pick it up. And . . ." Her mum looked around, hesitating. "Don't touch anything. Things that you shouldn't . . ."

Her sentence hung in midair, and then she looked at her watch.

"I'll have to run. You'll be all right, won't you? Look, it's two o'clock. I'll be a couple of hours, probably. Back at five at the latest . . . You can watch the video. Then the telly. You'll be fine."

And then she left. She didn't return until eight o'clock. Jennifer was on her own for six hours. The flat got dark, but she and Macy sat tightly together on the settee, the light from the television making the room look blue.

After that it was easy. Her mum left her on her own for a few hours, a whole morning or afternoon, a day that seemed to stretch out forever. Just now and then at first. Then once every week, a couple of times every week, then every afternoon after school.

Jennifer got used to being alone. What choice did she have?

Alice was lying back on the pillow, the photograph

loosely in her fingers. From somewhere else in the flat she could smell meat cooking and hear the sizzle of the frying pan. Rosie was making something. There was the clink of cutlery and the sound of cupboard doors opening and closing. She even thought she could hear some low music playing, and Rosie's voice humming along.

She sat up. She wanted to be there, in the kitchen, with Rosie. She left the photograph on the duvet and walked out of her room, along the hallway, her throat dry, her eyelids heavy. The kitchen was warm and the air full of the smell of onions. Alice let herself sink into it. When the music stopped Rosie must have sensed Alice there, because she turned round and looked at her with some concern. Alice took the two steps she needed and sank into Rosie's arms, her head pushing into her soft breasts, her arms clinging tightly.

The counselors had never really understood. In those early days her mum hadn't actually *abused* her. She'd simply deserted her, cast her off. *Abandoned* her.

EIGHT

THE good news came in a phone call from Jill Newton.

Alice was helping Frankie to pack the last of his books and clothes into cardboard boxes. They were lined up in the hallway of the flat, waiting for his dad to turn up for the journey back to Brighton.

The other students had already left for home so the place was almost empty. Alice could hear the echoes of her footsteps as she walked in and out of various rooms, picking up bits and pieces of Frankie's stuff. All that was left were the basic pieces of furniture: beds and wardrobes, a settee and coffee table, kitchen table and chairs. Several things in the kitchen had to be counted in order to make sure that the students got their deposits back. Alice stood at the cupboards and checked the kitchenware. There was eight of everything, cutlery and crockery. She counted the saucepans and the oven dishes and ticked them off the list.

Frankie was in the bedroom putting some papers into a bag.

"All done?" she said.

"Um," he murmured.

Frankie's mood was not good. She had arrived later than she'd said and he had immediately wanted to know where she'd been, what she'd been doing. When she told him she'd been helping to count stock at work, he'd looked at her with disbelief. Because he had hated any job he had ever had, he expected her to hate hers. She didn't, though. She liked working in the café. It was all so ordinary. Serving people, making drinks, cutting slices of cake, or using the silver tongs to pick up the syrupy Danish buns. It didn't bother her if the manager asked her to stay on for a short while, to help out with other things. But Frankie had been waiting, and he demanded to know where she had been. His questions had an undertone, as though he thought she hadn't been at work at all.

"How long till your dad gets here?" she said, trying to ignore his mood.

She walked up behind him and put her arms around his broad back. She could feel the tension in his muscles, so she hugged tightly, rubbing her face on the back of his T-shirt. He was so warm, so solid. She loved the feel of him, the fact that he was big and could shake her off in a second if he wanted.

"About an hour," he said, his voice softening as he turned toward her, his arms folding across her back, half lifting her off the ground. She tilted her face up to look at him and felt her eyes blur as he leaned down to kiss her.

Her eyes closed and her lips opened as she waited for his mouth to touch hers.

The ring tone of her mobile sounded. She pulled back, the sound startling her. She still wasn't used to having a mobile, let alone receiving calls. Frankie let her go, his face on the edge of a pout.

"Who's that?" she said needlessly.

She walked back out into the hallway where she'd left her bag and rummaged through it until she produced the mobile. On the screen was the name JILL. From back in the bedroom she could hear the plastic sacks being dragged across the floor and dumped by the door.

"Hello?" she said uncertainly.

"Alice," Jill said. "How are you?"

"Fine. Is anything wrong?"

That was her first thought. She stood in the hallway, the mobile clamped to her ear, and imagined the worst. She had been found. Her secret was out. It gave her a cold, clammy feeling, even though it was a hot day and stuffy in the flat. Frankie came out of the bedroom and gave her a long-suffering look. He made his hand into the shape of a mobile and held it at his ear. *Who is it?* he mouthed at her.

But she was listening to Jill and couldn't focus on what he was asking.

"Good news, Alice," Jill was saying.

Good news. This was a phrase that Alice hadn't heard much.

"We've managed a clever decoy trick with the press. I don't suppose you remember Michael Forrester, a support worker at Monksgrove? Probably not, as you hardly had anything to do with him. Anyway, Patricia Coffey had information that he'd been meeting with a reporter. Obviously her first thought was to dismiss him, but after a chat with me we decided to try something. We produced some fake documents that indicated that Jennifer Jones had been placed abroad, in Holland, with an English family."

Holland?

Frankie had come up behind her. He was standing close enough to listen. She turned and put her hand up to fend him off. *I won't be a minute,* she mouthed, trying to catch what Jill was saying.

"Sorry, Jill, I missed that," she said.

Frankie gave a dramatic sigh and turned his back, walking out of the room. The door closed slowly, as if in slow motion, behind him.

"The idea is that Jennifer has been placed with an English family in Holland for three years. She will go to university there and live a quiet and private life. Afterward she may stay in Holland or choose to come back to live in Britain. Patricia Coffey has phrased the whole thing to look as though it were part of an international agreement.

The European Resettlement of Offenders Strategy. It's very convincing."

She walked to the room door, holding the mobile at her ear. Frankie had gone back in the bedroom. She could hear drawers being opened and closed. *Holland, for three years*. It certainly had a ring of truth to it.

"So these papers were left around when Forrester was in the office. Patricia engineered some kind of emergency and left him on his own."

Jill Newton's voice was buoyant.

"Guess who rang a couple of days later? A national newspaper! They wanted confirmation that Jennifer Jones was living in Holland with an English family. Patricia denied it, of course, but we expect them to publish in the next couple of days."

"Publish?" Alice said, her heart sinking. "It's all going to be in the papers again?"

Her voice had dropped to a whisper and she walked to the corner of the room, as far away from Frankie as she could get.

"This is good news, Alice. This is the end. Once the papers accept that you're out of the country they will stop hounding you. This detective will go away. You'll be able to relax and live a normal life. When you start university in September no one on earth will know that you're anyone other than Alice Tully. Believe me, this is the best possible news."

After several more optimistic statements Jill rang off. Alice was perplexed. It was all going to be in the newspapers. Every detail would be dragged up again. She could just imagine the headlines: Berwick Waters Murder. Jennifer Jones Escapes Justice! Jill Newton was sure it would be the end. Once the press thought that JJ was out of the country they'd stop looking. They'd forget about it.

Alice plonked down on the arm of a chair. *Forget.* It was such a simple word; as if part of the brain could just wipe itself clean, delete information so that it was no longer there. The silly small things of life forgotten: a birthday card, a book to take back to the library, a tube of toothpaste from the supermarket. But the big things of life. They were ingrained. They lived in the fibers of the brain, in the tissue and the blood. They would always be there, curled up, sleeping in the subconscious, until something prodded at them. Memories that flickered into life and filled her head with pictures. A trip out for three children that would live with Alice for the rest of her life. A hole dug in the ground, the skeletal face of the feral cat, the splashing of water, the sight of blood, like a shocking red rose blooming from a child's head. How could she expect the press to forget when she never ever would? She sat there for a few moments gripping her mobile phone. Beneath her feet the carpet was threadbare. In places it was thin enough to see through.

She found Frankie lying across the bare mattress on

the bed that he used to use. Alice could see the tension in his face. He hadn't always been like this. At the beginning he had made her laugh all the time.

"What's wrong?" she said, sitting beside him.

He turned away from her, pushing his face into the mattress.

"You're seeing someone else," he said, his words muffled by the mattress.

"What? Of course I'm not!" she said wearily.

They'd had conversations like this before. Frankie quizzing her about who she was with and where she'd been on the evenings and days when she wasn't with him. He didn't understand that she liked time on her own, or was happy to just stay in with Rosie. Sometimes she had to lie, like when she was meeting Jill Newton. He didn't trust her and she didn't know what she could do about it.

She lay down beside him and put her arm around his waist and began to kiss his shoulders.

"I'm not seeing anyone else," she said, between kisses. "It's just you and me."

She felt him turning and waited until he was face to face with her.

"I've never met anyone like you before," she said, her voice husky.

He was staring hard at her, his eyes dark, shifting slightly from side to side, as if he was scanning her for any sign of lies.

"I'm sorry," he said, after a minute, his big arms pulling her closely to him. "I just want you all for myself. I can't help it."

She felt his mouth on her neck, his lips pushing hard into her skin, as though he might bruise it. She put her hands up, cupping his face, pulling him toward her and then lifted her head so that he would kiss her.

Poor Frankie. It wasn't possible to have people, to own them, as though they were possessions. Alice knew that. It was something that JJ had learned the hard way. A long time before.

When the modeling work finished and her mum locked herself in her bedroom for days and weeks, Jennifer had to live with her gran. She slept in the sewing room, on a small camp bed in the corner. There wasn't much room with her gran's giant sewing machine and the various plastic stacking boxes that were full of her equipment: materials, patterns, and threads.

"Don't you touch any of those, Jenny," her gran said. "That's my job, see, it's what I get paid for."

Jennifer knew this already. Her gran made clothes for children's shops. She'd seen the piles of trousers and tops, the skirts and tiny pairs of jeans that her gran sewed up. She'd even been given some of them to wear from time to time.

During the day, she had to move out of the tiny room

so that her gran could work. That meant she had to sit on the sofa in the living room, changing Macy's clothes, watching the television set that seemed to be on all day long whether her gran was in the room or not. Nelson had an armchair to himself and from time to time she caught him looking at her in a bad-tempered way. She tried to ignore him and spent her time chatting to Macy.

After a week her gran told her that she'd have to stay for a while. They'd have to try and find her a new school because the old one was too far away.

"When's Mummy coming?" she said.

"I don't know, Jenny. I wish I knew," her gran said, taking a cigarette out of a pack and lighting it up.

There were lots of phone calls, mostly late at night. Jennifer heard her gran talking, her voice low and urgent, her words sharp and ugly. Once, she got out of bed and walked into the hallway. Her gran's back was facing her, her shoulders hunched. Even though Jennifer couldn't see her face she could tell that she was angry. The top of one of her arms wobbled as if she were pointing her finger at someone and her legs were stiff, like a sentry on guard duty. Jennifer imagined her face all screwed up, her lips pursed up into a little bunch.

"She is not my responsibility. She's been here too long already. You can't just dump her when it's not convenient . . . I don't bloody well care what sort of a job . . . I'll have to contact social services . . . I can't have a kid living with me. I'm warning you. You keep this up much longer and she won't be here when you come back . . ."

A growling sound startled Jennifer. Her gran turned round to see what it was and saw Jennifer there. Nelson was standing at the door of the living room, baring his teeth.

"I've got to go," her gran snapped and replaced the handset. "Jenny, you should be in bed," she said, walking along the hallway, lifting her foot to shoo the dog back into the living room.

"Was that my mum?" Jennifer said.

"Yes. She sends her love and says she's going to come and get you soon. Come on, now. Back into bed." Her gran took her hand and led her back to the tiny bed, tucking the covers around her. She stood up to go and then hesitated, bending over to give Jennifer a peck on the cheek, leaving behind her the aroma of cigarettes. The room door clicked shut and from the living room she could hear the sound of the television and her gran's voice, lighter, cheerful even, talking to Nelson.

The schools were all full up, her gran said, when she asked. There wasn't really much point in her going anyway because her mum would come one day and take her off to live somewhere else. Then she'd have to start all over again looking for another new school. So she spent her days in the living room watching television. In the background there was the rumble of the sewing machine and by her side, in the armchair, she could see the disapproving face of Nelson, his tiny paws crossed in resignation.

One Tuesday, after she'd been at her gran's for weeks, her mum came unexpectedly. The doorbell rang, and when her gran went to answer it Jennifer heard the familiar voice. In seconds, as though she'd flown straight past her gran, her mum was there, in the living room beside her.

"Jennifer, love," she said squatting down in front of her. "Mummy's missed you!"

Jennifer couldn't speak. She just looked in astonishment. After many days of the dreary flat, the grumpy dog, and Gran's fog of cigarette smoke, her mum bending down in front of her was like an apparition.

"Haven't you got a kiss for me?"

Jennifer threw her arms round her mum and hugged her tightly, weaving her fingers in and out of each other so that she could keep hold of her. Her face buried in her mum's neck, she inhaled the scent of her perfume, felt the tickle of her hair and the cold metal of her earring.

"Look," her mum whispered, trying to disengage herself. "I've bought you a present!"

But she wouldn't let go. Over her mum's shoulder she could see her gran standing by the telly giving both of them a sour look.

"And I've got something for you!" her mum said, straining to look around at Gran, whose expression didn't change.

Jennifer felt a pang of resentment. Why was her mum bothering with Gran? Hadn't she been talking to her on the telephone for weeks? Wasn't this Jennifer's turn? She closed her eyes for a moment, blocking out her gran's square head, the little curl of smoke that was twisting its way up to the ceiling. Later, when her mum had gently pulled her hands away from her neck, they sat on the sofa together. Her mum put a wrapped present on her lap. Jennifer, feeling light-headed, let it lie there, feeling over it with her fingers.

"Are we going home?" she said.

"Not right now, love. Gran's probably told you that Mummy's had a few problems. But I've got some more modeling work now and I've got a chance of a flat soon. As soon as that comes through I'll come and get you. You'll have your own bedroom again, and we can paint it any color you like. That'll be good, won't it?"

Jennifer nodded. There were so many things she wanted to ask. Her mum was fidgety, though, sitting on the seat for only a few minutes, then getting up to pace up and down before perching on the arm of Nelson's chair. Although she'd taken her coat off, it was simply draped over the seat, ready, close to hand. She wasn't going to stay long, Jennifer knew. She kept her eye on her all the time, on her face, the back of her hair. If she didn't let her out of her sight, then maybe she wouldn't be able to go. Her gran didn't seem bothered at all and kept bending over to pet Nelson. After a while she brought in a mug of tea, which her mum held and blew across but didn't actually drink. Eventually she stood up and picked up her coat.

Jennifer felt a sense of panic, like a tiny figure jumping up and down inside her chest. On the sofa, lying by Macy's side, was the present, unopened because Jennifer didn't have the time. She had to keep alert, find things to say to her mum to keep her there. But the words wouldn't come, and the tiny figure inside her seemed to be laughing hysterically. *You can't do anything to stop her going!* it seemed to say. So she pushed herself back into the settee and sat there rigidly, as though she were tied there and couldn't move. She looked her mum over. She'd had her blond hair cut short and was wearing a long leather coat over some white trousers. Her shoes were glittery, as though someone had sprinkled gold dust on them. She was like a princess.

"What about the child?" Her gran pointed her cigarette in Jennifer's direction.

Her mum ignored the comment. She carried on sorting through her bag and finally pulled an envelope out and gave it to her gran. Her gran took it with a sneer and then placed it on the mantelpiece behind a potted plant.

"As soon as I hear about this flat, then I'm going to come and get you, so don't get too comfortable here!" Her mum leaned over and combed her fingers through Jennifer's hair.

Jennifer couldn't speak. Her tongue felt thick and heavy, and even though she wanted to walk to the front door and say good-bye she found she couldn't move. Her eyes misted over. Could this be it? Could the visit be over? Was her mum to disappear again?

Don't go, she wanted to say, but it was too late, her mum's coat had swished out of the living room and there was a final "Bye, love!" from out in the hall and the front door clicked shut. She sat on the sofa as still as could be, her eyes blurring with tears. After a few seconds her gran walked back into the room and went straight to the mantelpiece. She opened the envelope and pulled out some money. She flicked through the notes, her lips moving silently as though she were counting. Looking up she caught Jennifer's eye.

"There now," her gran said. "You've seen your mum. Doesn't she look well?"

She nodded, her throat too dry to speak. Her mum shone out, wherever she went. Once she had been with Jennifer all the time. Now it was different. She was just a visitor, and Jennifer had to live in this tiny room and all she had to look at was a mean little dog sitting on its own chair.

"Open your present," her gran said, looking much happier.

With heavy hands she pulled the paper off.

Inside was a doll in a box. A model doll. It was *Macy,*

International Catwalk Model. She looked puzzled. She already had Macy. Turning to the side she saw dear old Macy sitting against the arm of the chair, wearing her evening dress and tiara. Why should she want another Macy? She pulled at the cardboard, tearing it untidily until she had the second Macy out in her hands.

There was an odd sound. It wasn't her gran. She had tucked the money into her trousers and was picking up her mum's leftover tea. Then she went out into the kitchen and Jennifer heard her humming to herself. The sound came from Nelson, staring at her from beneath his overgrown hair. She could see his mouth open and his teeth bared. The noise was a low growl like a drill coming from far away.

Why was he doing that? Didn't he know that she had just lost her mum again? Was he so stupid? In her hand was the doll, like a dumb twin, lying, staring up at her. Just a plastic shape really, not like *her* Macy. It was wearing jeans and a cutoff top; casual stuff that *her* Macy never chose to wear. The gravelly growl of the stupid mean little dog was still going on so she turned and said *shush* in a loud whisper.

He didn't stop, though. He just carried on as though he were a radio that someone had switched on. Even though he didn't move or open his mouth, the noise, the drilling sound, seemed to get louder and louder. She looked round toward the door. Possibly her gran was on the sewing machine. But there was silence coming from there. It was only when she turned her head back that the growling seemed to grow and grow and the strangest thing was that Nelson appeared to get bigger in front of her eyes so that his head took up all the space on the armchair.

Then she saw it. On the floor there was a sprinkling of glitter. It had come off her mum's shoe. Like magic dust it lay there, the only reminder that she had of her mum's visit. Apart from the doll. She looked down and saw its ugly face, nothing like *her* Macy. She picked it up in one hand as though it were a stick, not a doll at all. She looked at the giant dog on the chair who simply would not keep quiet. Then she raised the plastic Macy above her head and brought it crashing down on the dog's back. There was a moment's silence then a terrible cry, a howl. She didn't wait, she brought the doll thumping down again and again until the howling was louder than the drilling noise, until she felt someone's hands on her shoulders, shaking her, picking her up by the skin and flinging her backward so that she bumped against the side of the settee.

The drilling had stopped.

There was just a yodeling whine and the dog was lying on the floor with her gran bent over it.

"You horrible, wicked girl. You wicked, nasty girl, get

out," her gran screamed at her. "Get out. Go into your room. I don't want to see your face for the rest of the day."

Jennifer stood up, reached over and picked up the *real* Macy, and went back into the sewing room. She pulled the duvet off the tiny bed, crept into the corner, and wrapped it around herself.

It wasn't possible to have people all for yourself. It was something Frankie would have to learn.

His dad arrived about four. He was not what Alice had expected. A small man with a shiny bald head. He shook her hand formally, as though she were someone important. Then he spent some time opening the rear of the car and flattening the backseats so that Frankie's stuff could go in. The three of them went back and forth, up and down the stairs, carrying the boxes. Every time Alice came face to face with Frankie's dad he made some funny little comment. *This'll give you muscles! This'll put hair on your chest! What've you got in this, Frank? Gold bars?*

When they were all packed up, Frankie locked the front door and the two of them stood on the pavement while his dad, giving a little wave, got into the driver's seat and waited.

"August the fourteenth. You'll come and stay with me."

Alice nodded. This had all been agreed, but Frankie was just repeating it for safety.

"Rosie says she'll drive me over."

Frankie huffed. "Check up on me, more likely."

"She looks after me. She wants to make sure you're not taking advantage of me!"

"Better not tell her then."

"What?"

He bent down and kissed her neck, whispering in her ear. "That's precisely what I am going to do. Take advantage of you."

She waved as they drove off, standing in the same position until Frankie's dad's car turned out of the street. Then she picked her mobile out of her bag and pressed the button for ROSIE.

NINE

FRANKIE had been gone for almost ten days when the story appeared. Jill Newton rang Alice at eleven o'clock on the evening before and told her that it was about to break, that it would be the lead story in at least two newspapers the following morning.

It was a blow. As each morning had passed bringing no sign of the name *Jennifer Jones* in the newspaper, a tiny bud of hope had grown inside her. The press was no longer interested in where JJ was. They had ignored the story, thought it unimportant. So what if she was in Holland. What did they care?

It had given her a feeling of recklessness. She'd walked out of the flat with a spring in her step. She'd smiled at the postman and didn't even mind having a few minutes' chat with Sara from downstairs. She went into the newsagent's on the corner and bought some mints, scanning the rest of the papers and feeling buoyant that she hadn't been mentioned. The newsagent's son, whose name was Stuart, chatted to her about the buses, the traffic, the weather, her job at the Coffee Pot. She didn't mind. Leaving the shop she felt lighthearted, weightless, as though she weren't walking at all but gliding along.

And then, on the morning after Jill Newton rang, the newspaper slid through the letter box and thudded onto the mat. They both heard it. Rosie gave a sigh and went downstairs to collect it. Alice sat at the kitchen table, spooning up her cereal, chewing and swallowing, her knees and feet close together, the music from the radio drifting over her head. She had kept to her routine, got up early and showered, washing her hair and getting ready for work. Rosie had fussed around her but she'd tried to shake her off. "I'm fine," she'd said several times, even though all her body weight seemed to have dropped down to her feet and she walked around her room heavily. Pushing her bowl away, she heard Rosie at the bottom of the stairs, the paper rustling as she straightened it out to read. Several footsteps sounded and then stopped, the paper crinkling. Rosie had paused, her eyes glued to the story. More footsteps and Rosie appeared puffing slightly, the newspaper opened in front of her.

"It's not so bad," she said.

But that was Rosie's newspaper. They both knew that the others, the tabloids, would be worse, much worse.

JENNIFER JONES REPORTEDLY
ON EUROPEAN OFFENDERS SCHEME

It was a small headline at the bottom of the front page. Rosie laid the big newspaper across the kitchen table and turned the pages. On page six was the full story. It was brief, just the main details with a quote from Patricia Coffey, Director, Monksgrove Secure Facility. *"I cannot confirm or deny the whereabouts of Jennifer Jones. I am not at liberty to comment on any of the residents at Monksgrove, past or present."* Lower down was a quote from the probation authorities in Holland. *"We do not comment on individual cases. We can only say that in Holland ex-offenders are given every opportunity to start a new life and to become responsible members of society."*

"You'd hardly notice it," Rosie said.

Alice didn't answer. She gave Rosie's arm a squeeze, picked up her jacket, and went out to work. Luckily there was no sign of Sara from downstairs so she put her head down and marched up the street, past the newsagent's, and in the direction of the Coffee Pot. There would be no avoiding the newspapers there, she knew that.

Even though it was just after seven, Pippa and Jules were already serving. A small queue of sleepy-looking commuters stood along the counter and one or two were sitting at the tables, blowing on steaming cups. They all looked a bit distracted, a couple with newspapers under their arms. On the rack were the café's own papers, untouched, still lying neatly in their folds. No one seemed bothered.

This pleased Alice. For the first time since the previous

evening she felt her spirits rise. Looking round she saw that the queue had disappeared and Jules and Pippa were talking quietly, Jules using a cloth to rub over the glass surface of the counter, Pippa stacking cups and mugs within easy reach. Behind them the cappuccino maker was hissing like a steam train. Everything was so normal.

It wasn't until eleven-thirty, when she was due her break, that she sat down by the window and unfolded one of the papers with the intention of reading about herself. The headline was everything she thought it would be.

CHILD KILLER GETS NEW LIFE IN HOLLAND

She felt curiously cold about it. As if she weren't sitting reading about it but were watching herself, from a distance, like an actress in a film. It didn't take long to scan the first article. The usual phrases were there: *Berwick Waters, dead girl, prostitution, glamour model, hidden body* . . .

"What you reading?"

It was Pippa's voice. She was standing looking out of the café window, her mobile at her ear.

Just the news, Alice was about to answer, but Pippa started to speak into the mobile, turning slightly away.

Alice flicked through the inside pages. She was looking for other references to the story. Turning to page four she had a momentary shock. Her mother's face was staring back at her. A photograph, taken the previous day, at her home *in the north of England*. Alice sat very still, looking at the picture. Behind her she could hear Pippa's voice talking on her mobile and the clinking of cups and plates. The sound of the traffic from beyond the glass was suddenly amplified by someone coming into the café. She let it all fade into the back of her mind as she searched out the photograph. Her mother, in front of her, for the first time in four years.

Did she feel anything? Was there a tremor of emotion? Or just the rock-hardness of her chest, her feelings trapped inside ribs of stone.

Carol Jones looked older, her face a little chubby. Her hair was still blond but it looked tired, as though it had been combed and teased once too often. Her smile was wide and the painted lips were still there. She was wearing a low-cut top and the mark of her cleavage showed as a dark line. Behind her, on a strategically positioned shelf, was a photograph of Alice as a baby.

She looked away from the picture and back to the story. The headline was suitably dramatic:

NOT ALLOWED TO SEE
HER DAUGHTER

Carol Jones, attractive 34-year-old former model, had tears in her eyes yesterday when she spoke of her long separation from her daughter, Jennifer Jones, the notorious killer of a 10-year-old girl at Berwick Waters six years ago.

"I know that my Jenny did a terrible thing and I know that some people say that she should be in prison for longer. But to me it seems as though she is still in prison because I'm not allowed to have any contact with her. I don't know where she is or what she's doing. I'm not even allowed to have a photograph of her."

Carol Jones, recently remarried, had to stop frequently in order to compose herself. Her husband, a 40-year-old sales consultant, was holding her hand. "Carol thinks of her daughter all the time. She is appalled that the authorities have sent her out of the country. Carol needs her daughter. Jennifer needs her mother. She even sent her a birthday card. There is a permanent home here for her. She doesn't need to go and live in Holland."

Alice stopped reading. She looked around the shop before tearing out the page with her mother's picture. She folded it up and put it in the pocket of her smock. Then she took the remainder of the paper and put it into the garbage bin. The picture crinkled in her pocket and she rubbed it with her fingers. She almost smiled. A *permanent home* for her with Carol and her new man. A home with her mother. It was all she had ever wanted, and it was the one thing she had never had.

During the first few years at Monksgrove she talked a lot to Patricia Coffey.

"Call me Pat," she said, at the first session.

She was a big, tall woman, with hair that reached down past her shoulders and glasses that hung on a string around her neck.

Jennifer couldn't do that, though. She called her Miss instead.

She sat on one end of a settee in an office. There were stuffed animals nearby—a giraffe, a hippo, an elephant, a lion, and a monkey. When she was talking she held them and moved their arms and legs.

Patricia Coffey wanted to *chat* about her life. She poured her some juice in a big glass and then sat in the armchair and started.

"I wasn't at the trial, Jennifer, so I just want to confirm some details with you."

Jennifer nodded, her hand reaching out to touch the lion, her finger running along its back.

"You lived with your mum until you were six and then with your gran for a year, I think?"

"Yes, Miss. A year."

"And you didn't have much schooling at that time?"

"No."

The lion was soft. She pulled it away from the other animals and hugged it like a cushion.

"And then you went back and lived with your mum for about six months, I think?"

She nodded, her fingers combing the lion's mane. It could have been six months, it could have been less.

"You were in care for a short time and spent weekends with your mother. Eventually you went back and lived with your mother. This was when you were eight?"

"Yes, Miss."

"Your mother and you then seemed to live at different addresses, a few months here and there. This was when your mother was with a couple of boyfriends."

She changed her mind about the lion and replaced him. The monkey was much nicer. He had arms that she could move about.

"Then your mother found a more stable relationship in Norwich and you lived with her, until you were offered the house in Berwick?"

She looked up. Patricia Coffey had her glasses on, with the bits of string hanging down the sides. Her hair was heavy, hanging down each side of her face. She looked a bit like a horse.

"So, it's reasonable to say you had a fairly unstable childhood?"

Jennifer nodded.

"But you were never abused? Hurt?"

She shook her head, her front teeth cutting into her lip. No, she was never *actually* abused. She cradled the monkey while Patricia Coffey carried on talking. Its fur was soft and its eyes glittered. It had tiny hands and feet like those of a baby.

"You could have that monkey if you like," Patricia Coffey eventually said. "Take it back to your room."

She half walked, half ran along the bright corridors, feeling the bounce from the carpet underneath her feet. The monkey was casually sandwiched under her arm as she went past a couple of other kids, sitting talking with each other. They looked up as she passed but their faces were closed off from her. She was notorious. She had killed her friend. Everybody knew.

In her room she put the monkey on her pillow and stood back to look.

She still wasn't used to her surroundings. The walls were pink and gray, and so was the duvet. She had a chest of drawers and a desk as well as an armchair. It was plush, not what she had thought it was going to be like. The door was wide open; it had to be like that. At night it was closed but not locked. In the corner, like a bird on a perch, was a tiny closed-circuit camera.

It was all very comfortable, and yet she felt awkward, as if it were some sort of waiting room that she was in. Not a *bedroom*. The monkey had fallen forward so she moved him onto the chest of drawers. She sat him against the wall and watched as he tipped over to the side. He was too soft by far; that was why she couldn't find the right place to put him.

She sat down heavily on the bed with the monkey on her lap, her fingers rubbing at its fur. The words *unstable childhood* went through her head and she pictured Patricia Coffey's funny horse face.

Why was everyone so interested in her now? When it was too late to change anything? What was the point? The monkey's eyes stared up at her and she had a sudden feeling of impatience with it. *Stupid child's toy!* What did she want it for? She took its arm and flung it aside. Then she pulled the duvet around her and sat in the corner of the bed.

Alice ended up in the stockroom. It was quiet in the café and she was using the time to tidy up the wholesaler's packs of coffee, tea, chocolate, and biscotti. The room was tiny, barely enough space for two people to pass each other. She didn't mind. She liked sorting out the stock, putting it in use-by-date order, checking through the boxes of paper cups and lids, plastic spoons, knives, and forks. Counting up, matching stuff against the master list, seeing if anything was running low. It was all about organization. Without well-stocked backup the café might run out, and then where would they be? She stood back feeling satisfied. It was good to know that everything was in order.

Brushing the dust from her smock she felt the crinkle of the paper again. Finding some space she sat down cross-legged on the floor, took the newspaper picture out of her pocket, and spread it out in front of her. Her mum's face smiled again. *A permanent home.* Her mum believed it, she was sure.

How could she explain it to anyone? She hadn't been hit, punched, locked away. She hadn't had anyone screaming at her, ordering her about, insulting her. She'd just been sidelined, forgotten about. She'd been left with friends and family, the social services, complete strangers; finally when there was no one else, she'd just been left on her own. That brilliant smile, that lipsticked mouth, the sparkling eyes, those were for her once, but as she grew up they had turned away and were gazing in a different direction. Jennifer had been an inconvenience, and whenever her mother had a new set of friends, a new boyfriend, a new modeling job, she simply cast her off.

She did it so beautifully, with promises and toys and kisses. And every time Jennifer believed her. This was the last time she would have to stay with Gran or be in care or stay in with Perry. After this time it would all settle and there would just be her and her mum. *Just the two of us.*

But each time there was the choking hurt of it. The days when they'd been together were full of brightness and color. But slowly, with a look, a phone call, an extra hour in the bathroom, Jennifer knew that things were changing. The days turned from color to black and white, and she was alone again; the plastic smiles of another foster placement, or her gran's weariness. Inside she felt each separation like a blast of cold. She couldn't be angry. She just had to wait until one day the door would open and there her mother would be, resplendent in a matching outfit, her hair hanging wispily, her skin glowing, her mouth pouting with the need for forgiveness.

Except in Berwick it had been different. Then her mother hadn't abandoned her. She had done something much worse. She had *used* her, and Jennifer had hated her for it.

Alice folded the picture up again and was about to replace it in her pocket when she suddenly thought, *Why?* Instead she screwed it up and tossed it into the bin, with all the empty packaging and foodstuffs that were past their sell-by date.

Later, just before she was due to go home, she was surprised to see the man in the leather jacket, the detective, Derek Corker, struggling in the door. He was carrying a laptop case as well as a knapsack, and he had a couple of newspapers under his arm. Pippa was about to serve him but Alice edged in.

"I'll get this one," she said. "You have a break."

Derek Corker gave her a smile of recognition.

"We must stop meeting like this," he said. "A large latte and a Danish to go."

"To go?" she said.

"Yep, I'm moving on today. My investigation? That girl I told you about? It's come to nothing."

"Oh," Alice said, a smile settling on her face. The newspapers looked ruffled as if he'd been reading them somewhere.

"I'll still get paid, though. So it's no skin off my nose."

"Have a good trip," she said, handing him his change.

"Sometimes people don't want to be found," he called.

She nodded, watching him as he struggled out of the café door and walked toward the station.

TEN

THE flat smelled of rich spices. Alice inhaled the aroma all the way up the stairs, speeding toward the top, keen to see Rosie and tell her about the detective's departure. When she threw open the kitchen door, she saw Rosie seated at the table. Opposite her was Kathy, her mother. Both women were cradling cups of coffee.

"Hi, Kathy," Alice said, grinning at the older woman, her heart racing.

"Hello, Alice love," Kathy said.

"How are you?" Alice said, lightly, pulling a chair out, easing herself down on it.

"Never been better, sweetheart."

It was her usual kind of answer. Kathy was a relentlessly cheerful woman who didn't seem to have a bad word to say about anybody. Rosie adored her, phoning her almost every day, talking for ages, and then going through the conversation again with Alice, keeping her up to date on her mum's new clothes or hairstyles.

Kathy was very different from Rosie. She was smaller and thinner and dressed up every day as though she were always getting ready to have her photo taken. She wore pantsuits from Marks and Spencer's and her hair, a shocking red color, was always neatly styled. Her skin was perpetually tanned from frequent holidays to an apartment in Majorca that she owned.

"My neighbor is going to the Maldives for her holiday!" Kathy said, looking faintly shocked. "It's a long way to go to lie on a beach."

"But it's beautiful, Mum, I'd love to go there."

"Honestly," Kathy said, turning to Alice, pulling her into the conversation. "I've tried to get her to come to Majorca for the last five years. Will she come?"

"I'll come," Alice said.

She was only joining in the playful banter, but a strange light-headed feeling came over her because she suddenly thought, *I could go! Why not?*

"You come any time you like, sweetheart," Kathy said, picking up her coffee mug and peering into it. "Maybe you can persuade my Rose to come as well. Yuck, I've had enough of this coffee. I'll be running to the loo all the way home."

"I'll drive you," Rosie said, picking up the cups and taking them to the sink. "You'll be okay on your own, won't you, Alice?"

Alice nodded, pushing down a tiny blip of disappointment. She had looked forward to having Rosie to herself. She had envisaged the two of them chatting about the newspaper story, about Derek Corker and his hopeless detective work. She was feeling pumped up with confidence. He'd stood next to her, talked to her on three occasions, and yet he'd never once realized who she was.

And then, floating around the edges of her mind, was this idea that she might go with Kathy to Majorca. It had only been said as a joke, but why not? She so much wanted to talk to Rosie about it, to hear Rosie's soothing words and feel that finally, after many months, things were going to be all right.

But Rosie's car keys were rattling.

"I'm not an invalid," Kathy was saying. "Tell her, Alice, that I'm capable of getting the bus!"

Alice shrugged her shoulders. "She likes taking you home," she said, rolling her eyes as if she also was vexed with Rosie's overprotective attitude toward her mother.

"I suppose so," Kathy said, sighing, as though it was something she had to bear.

Alice leaned across and gave Kathy a kiss on her powdery cheek. She listened for a few moments as the two women disappeared down the stairs. She would have to be patient. She and Rosie had the whole evening to talk.

She walked into her bedroom, pulling her T-shirt off, intending to have a shower. Beside her bed, on the floor, was her carryall bag, partly packed for the trip to Brighton to stay with Frankie. She'd pulled it out the previous weekend and chucked a couple of things into it but hadn't got any further. Now it would be a rush, making sure that the clothes she wanted to take were washed and ironed. It didn't matter. The main thing was that she was going. She sat on the bed and peeled her jeans off. Lying back, stretching her arms and legs, she thought of Frankie. He had rung her every day since he left. He missed her and *loved* her, he'd say, and she'd felt mildly embarrassed at his words.

How lucky she was. She had Rosie, Frankie, a place at university. She had a bag to pack and a trip to Brighton to look forward to. She was even thinking of going to Majorca to stay in Kathy's apartment. How normal was that? Her new life fitted her comfortably, like a favorite chair that she could curl up in.

And yet the past was there. It always would be. *You can't change what happened,* Patricia Coffey had said over and over. *No matter how much you think of it or cry about it, you can't change a single second of it. The only thing you can change is the future.*

I don't deserve a future, she had said. *I can't go on and live my life normally when I took someone else's life away. How can I do that?*

You've got to. Otherwise two lives have been wasted. You have to go on now and make a good life for yourself, to make up for what you've done.

Is this what she meant by a good life? Alice wondered. Is this enough? To go to work every day? To have friends?

To become educated? For what, in the end? To become a wife, a mother? Would it be better if she went abroad and worked among the hungry and the desperate? If she could prevent others from suffering and dying, would that make up for what she did six years before on Berwick Waters? Would it then be a life for a life?

Alice turned on her side, pulling her knees up to her chest. Feeling her insides harden up, she closed her eyes and let the day come back into her head. In May it was, cold but sunny, and she had to keep shielding her eyes with her hand. The other two up ahead, chatting away to each other, their sweaters tied round their waists. Three of them out for a day's adventure. On their way into the reservoir Michelle told Lucy to be careful of the cats. "They hate people," she said, in her know-all voice. "They blame people for flooding the land and drowning them. Don't look straight at them because they might scratch your eyes out."

Alice reached out and pulled the corner of the duvet toward her. She was too warm by far but it didn't matter. She let the feral cat creep into her thoughts. The memory of it uncurled in her head. Its face was bony, its skin stretched across its skull. On that day it had appeared from nowhere and sat on the ground staring heavily at her. She'd backed away, startled by its glare. It had seen everything and hadn't flinched. Just raised its paw and started to clean itself, ignoring everything else, not even glancing over at the girl's body on the ground.

She choked back a sob and pulled the duvet over her face. Three children who went out for an adventure. Only two came back. The knowledge of it would always drag her backward in time. No matter how many years passed it would always be there, attached to her by some invisible thread. She tried to curl herself up into a ball, to cover herself completely with the stifling duvet. At times like this she wanted to disappear, and no amount of hugs from Rosie or text messages from Frankie could change that.

She should have died on that day. Perhaps, in a way, she had.

Later, after a long cool shower, she put up the ironing board in the kitchen and started to sort out her clothes. She heard the front door open and waited for Rosie's footsteps and for her to appear at the kitchen door, her face beaming with some story about her mum and then a hug for Alice. She would be deliberately upbeat, trying to take Alice's mind off the newspapers, and then she'd show Alice the meal she'd cooked, probably something special to make up for the rotten week they'd both had.

As Alice pressed the iron's face onto the board she felt an aching inside her for Rosie's presence. Where was she? Why was she taking so long to come up the stairs? Footsteps sounded then, but not just Rosie's. Someone else was coming as well. Had Kathy come back for some reason? Seconds later she heard voices. It was Sara from downstairs. She was immediately irritated. Why was Sara always hanging round? Waiting to talk to her or Rosie, coming up and sitting in the kitchen as though she owned the place.

"Look who I've brought back with me!" Rosie said, coming in through the kitchen door, her mouth in a sort of wide smile that Sara couldn't see from behind. Alice immediately softened. It wasn't Rosie's fault and Sara would probably be gone in a half hour.

"Hi, Alice. I'm glad I've caught you. I wanted to chat with both of you."

"Cup of tea?" Rosie asked.

"No."

Alice noticed something odd about Sara. She looked different. She was wearing a dark suit and not carrying a bag. In her hand was a set of keys, a big bunch as though she had lots of doors to open.

"I think you both should sit down," Sara said, in an odd bossy way.

"What's the matter?" Rosie said, looking from Sara back to Alice and then back again.

Sara looked taller, that was it. Alice looked down at her feet and noticed her high-heeled shoes and light-colored tights. The suit was fitted at the waist and made her look slimmer altogether. It looked expensive; she hadn't seen her wear anything like that before.

"You look smart," Rosie said, pulling a chair out and sitting down. "Are you going somewhere nice?"

"It might be a good idea to sit down, Alice," Sara said, ignoring Rosie's question. Sara said it in a tone of voice that suggested she was used to being obeyed. Maybe she wasn't such a bad teacher as she made out to be. Alice bent down and switched the iron off at the plug and then pulled out a chair to sit beside Rosie. She glanced over at the kitchen clock. It had just turned six. She hoped Sara wouldn't be long.

"What's this all about?" Rosie said, raising her eyebrows, giving Sara a pleasant smile.

Sara didn't sit down. She had her hands clasped behind her and looked as though she were going to make a speech. Alice had a sudden bad feeling about it.

"I may as well be completely straight with you. My name is Sara Wright and I work for a Sunday newspaper. A couple of months ago we had a tip-off that Jennifer Jones had been released early and was living in South London. Through some other contacts we were able to pinpoint a number of teenage girl placements in this area and it didn't take long to find out which of them was Jennifer—"

"What?" Rosie spluttered. "You're from the newspapers?"

Alice looked from Rosie to Sara and then back again. Rosie's expression was of total disbelief. Her hand shot sideways and grabbed Alice's arm. Sara looked a little un-comfortable but rushed ahead as though she had a lot of words to get out in a short time.

"When we were sure that Jennifer Jones had been placed here, we made plans to investigate the situation. I rented the flat downstairs and have spent the last six weeks or so collecting information."

"You've been spying on us?" Rosie said.

Alice couldn't speak. She looked at Sara without blinking. Her eyes felt like stones, ready to drop out if she wasn't careful.

"The newspaper I work for is a quality journal. When we knew that Jennifer was living here, we decided not to make a splash of it. We decided to wait and go for a more analytical approach. We wanted to see what sort of person Jennifer . . . Alice was. How she fitted into the commu-nity, and so on."

"You told us you were a schoolteacher," Rosie said, her voice dripping with disappointment.

"We made plans to write an article about Jennifer . . . Alice. It was going to be a prelude to my writing a book about the whole case. The . . . incident at Berwick, the trial, the aftermath, Alice's new life. That's why I moved in downstairs. Not to expose you, Alice, I could have done that six weeks ago. No, no. I wanted to get to know you. I wanted to be able to write a serious book about you and your new life. To show the public that it is possible for people to change."

"Why didn't you just ask me?" Alice said.

Sara's face softened and she leaned forward, resting her hands on the back of a chair.

"I knew you would refuse. I thought if I came to you, you would just disappear, go somewhere else."

This was true and Alice knew it. It didn't make her feel any better. She looked at Sara's suit and smart shoes. That was the difference. In the past Sara had dressed like a schoolteacher. Baggy tops, jeans, jewelry, a giant bag that looked as though it held a set of exercise books. She'd been in disguise to fool them. Rosie had liked her, taken her into the flat and made her drinks and homemade cookies. She had trusted her, made plans for theater visits, when all the while Sara was a person in disguise. Just like Alice, really. Poor Rosie, she was surrounded by fakes.

"I want to write a serious piece about you, Alice . . . Jennifer . . ."

That was it. That was the final straw.

"My name is Alice Tully. I am not Jennifer Jones. Not anymore. That's what you people don't understand. I am a new person."

"That's exactly it. That's what I want to write about!"

Rosie let go of Alice's hand and stood up suddenly, the table rattling as she did so.

"Why tell us this now? Why now? When it's all died down."

Sara's composure crumbled for a moment and she began smoothing her skirt down, picking at the jacket buttons.

"I had no intention of doing anything this soon. I have the lease on the flat for another month. The trouble is that my editor wants to go with the story now. With all this stuff about Jennifer being in Holland, it would be a marvelous coup."

"You'd expose Alice now?" Rosie said, her voice cracking.

"No, no. That's why I'm talking to you now. I believe that if we three could come to an agreement, if we could cooperate on the story, then I could put my editor off publishing it for a while. At least until Alice goes to university. That way she could avoid some of the . . . notoriety. Also if she . . . if you were prepared to cooperate, then the article would give you a chance to have your say. To tell your side of the story. Surely that's worth thinking about?"

Alice slumped back in her seat. She had known it was too good to be true. The detective leaving, the newspapers getting it wrong. These were just cruel jokes to make her feel better. They had known where she was all along.

"Even if Alice agreed, her probation officer would never allow it. It could put her in danger, for goodness' sake!"

"From the girl's parents, you mean?" Sara said.

"And others. You know what it was like at the time of the trial. No, no. I certainly won't have it. Alice cannot be put in that position."

"I'm afraid she won't have any choice. What I'm saying is that my editor wants to go with this story with or without Alice's help. I think it would be a better story if she had a say."

A moment's silence lay on the table between them. Rosie sat down heavily. Alice looked round at the ironing board, the iron facing her, the sleeve of one of her shirts hanging down. She felt her eyes misting up. That was it. That was the end. There would be no trip to Brighton, no plane ride to Majorca, no room in halls at the uni. It was all a mirage because they would never leave her alone. Rosie caught her eye. Her eyebrows flickered with misery and then she seemed to pull herself together.

"We don't have to decide this very minute?" she said, softly.

"No," Sara said, even though there was a hint of urgency in her voice. "We'd need to know soon, though. My editor wants to run the story this weekend, but if you agreed to cooperate I think I could persuade him. He trusts me. He knows I'll do a good job."

Rosie nodded. "And meanwhile you won't tell anyone where Alice is?"

"You have my word," Sara said.

Alice wanted to laugh. The word of a liar.

"We'll let you know," said Rosie. "In a couple of days. Now, I'd like you to leave us."

Sara nodded solemnly as though a great contract had been made, as though something momentous had happened. She turned quietly and stole out of the kitchen, her high heels making only the slightest sound on the floor. When Alice heard the downstairs door close, she had a sudden feeling of nausea. She stood up and turned to the sink, but before she could move Rosie enveloped her, her big arms holding her firm, Alice's face pushed into the soft fabric of her blouse.

"It's all over." She choked the words out.

"No, it isn't. It's not all over. We'll deal with this, you'll see," Rosie said, her voice a whisper.

Alice nodded, her head pushing into Rosie's soft flesh. The words had been spoken but they were low and quiet. Insubstantial, liable to be blown away in a puff of air.

part two

JENNIFER JONES

ELEVEN

THE girl with the ginger hair was called Michelle Livingstone. She introduced herself to Jennifer the day after they moved into Water Lane. She knocked at the door of their house just after ten in the morning. Jennifer was up and dressed but her mum was still sleeping.

"I live next door. My name's Michelle. My mum's a secretary and she works at my school. I saw you moving in yesterday. Was that fat bloke your dad?"

Jennifer mumbled, "No," her eyes transfixed with Michelle's orange hair, which sprung out wildly from each side of her head. Someone had parted it down the middle, a completely straight line, and put a couple of barrettes in at the front to hold it in place. It looked like it might uncurl itself and spring free at any moment.

"I've got a den and some dressing-up stuff and it's my birthday in two weeks' time. What have you got?" Michelle demanded, trying to look past Jennifer into the tiny hallway of the house.

"A lot of things," Jennifer said. "But we haven't unpacked everything yet."

"My best friend is called Lucy. She lives at number two. Well, she's not my absolute best friend. Lucy just hangs around a bit. But she's all right. She usually does what I tell her. Who's your best friend?"

Jennifer looked at Michelle with consternation. She didn't have a best friend.

"My mum's a model," she said, ignoring the question. "You could come over later and I'll show you her photographs."

Michelle's expression was a mixture of irritation and interest.

"I've got to go now, my mum's calling me," Jennifer lied, closing the front door.

Later, before her mum got up, she took out the stolen Luke Skywalker figure and thought about Perry alone in the flat, wondering what had happened to them. He'd see all their stuff had been taken, the beds, the armchairs, the bits and pieces from the kitchen. He'd notice immediately that his portable telly was gone. Poor Perry. He would probably go round the neighbors asking about them, maybe he would even call the police. The whole day would have gone by before he noticed that Luke Skywalker was missing. Jennifer held the figure out. Its arms and legs felt stiff, as though no one had ever played with it. She took it into the living room and stood it on the mantelpiece. It looked shiny and new. Not like Macy. She was old and scuffed and her outfits looked tatty and out of date. It didn't matter. Jennifer still kept her. Maybe, in years to come, Macy would be worth money, like Luke Skywalker.

When her mum finally got up, she made her a cup of tea.

"Do you think Perry will come and find us?" she said.

Her mum shook her head.

"I don't think so. Perry will be all right on his own. He was far too young for me."

"What about your job?"

Because her mum was between modeling jobs she had taken some bar work. It meant she was out a lot late at night and Perry hadn't liked it. Neither had Jennifer.

"I'm concentrating on my modeling. All that smoke, anyway. It's bad for the complexion."

Jennifer didn't say anything about money. She didn't mention paying the rent or buying stuff. Maybe her mum was right, and this time she would get her picture on the front of a magazine. She looked idly out of the back window and saw some movement in next door's garden. It was Michelle with someone else. The ginger curls stood out, bobbing busily here and there at the end of the garden. The other girl was less clear. The two of them were doing something and had their backs to Jennifer so she couldn't see very well.

"What you looking at, Jen?"

"There's a girl who lives next door called Michelle," she said.

"Right next door?" her mum said. "The posh lot?"

Jennifer shrugged.

"Why don't you ask her around to play?"

"We don't *play*," said Jennifer, offended. She was almost eleven. In September she would go to secondary school. She didn't *play* anymore.

"Well, tea, then. Or just to chat. That's what girls do, isn't it? I could make something for her to eat. It'd be a way of getting to know the neighbors."

"What about the other girl?"

Jennifer saw Lucy Bussell then. She was carrying a big pile of stones to the far corner of the garden. Michelle was walking behind her, talking and gesticulating with her arms, and Lucy turned round for a moment to answer. She was smaller than Michelle, much smaller. She looked younger as well, maybe only about eight. She was thin and had almost no hair that Jennifer could see. She was wearing a zip-up jacket that looked a couple of sizes too big. She looked cold, her mouth pursed against the air.

"Whatever," her mum said, gulping down her tea. "Want to come shopping with me? See what the town's like?"

Jennifer washed up the cup while her mum got ready. When she came down the stairs she was wearing skintight jeans and boots and a small leather jacket that barely covered her bottom. Around her neck was a bright pink scarf with tassels. She'd put her makeup on and tied her hair up on top in a scraggy ponytail.

"Don't want to look a state, do I? I might be paying rent on this place but that doesn't mean I can't dress well, does it?"

There was still snow on the ground when they shut the front door behind them. Her mum had to step carefully along the icy path and was shivering by the time they got to the end of the road.

"An apartment in Spain, that's what we need," she said, pulling Jennifer's arm through hers.

The main street was only a ten-minute walk away. There was a pub and a garage and half a dozen shops: a tiny Co-op supermarket, a couple of newsagents, a launderette, a Chinese fish-and-chip shop, and a clothes shop.

"Not exactly Bond Street, is it?" her mum said.

A few flakes of snow fluttered by as Jennifer and her mum went into the Co-op. They emerged a short while later carrying four plastic bags of shopping. The walk back to the house was uphill and Jennifer held her head low to avoid the bitter wind hitting her face.

"Maybe Danny'll come and give us a ride up to the superstore," her mum said, the snow dotting her hair. "It's bloody expensive there."

Later, after they'd unpacked the shopping, Michelle

called for her again. This time Lucy Bussell was with her, looking pale and tiny. Close up, her face had the look of a mouse. All she needed were the whiskers. Michelle spoke immediately, businesslike.

"You can come in my house, if you like. Lucy and me have dug a grave in the back garden."

Jennifer's first instinct was to say no. She didn't like the bossy tone of Michelle's voice. She was startled by the mention of a grave, though. *A grave?* she thought. Her mum's footsteps sounded up the hallway behind her.

"It's freezing here. Why don't you bring your friends in?" she said, coming right up to the door and giving her best model-girl smile.

Jennifer grabbed her coat off the banister.

"I'm going next door," she said, pulling the front door closed behind her.

"That's her mum," Michelle said to Lucy. "She's a model."

At her front door Michelle pulled out a single key that was attached to a variety of fobs: a tiny shoe, a pair of dice, a troll, a plastic skateboard. She opened the door and the three of them walked in. The heat on the inside hit Jennifer immediately. She stood for a second and let it soak through her. The house, although the same as Jennifer's, looked very different. The hallway had hidden lighting and looked longer and higher. So did the lounge. The kitchen was the biggest surprise, though. It had been extended and was a giant room with fitted units and a big old-fashioned stove. She paused and looked around at the pots and pans that were hanging from the ceiling and the jars and bowls, plates and jugs that seemed to cover every surface. The room seemed busy.

A woman was standing by a worktop measuring out ingredients from packets. She had an apron on with pictures of rabbits all over it and her hair, ginger and curly like Michelle's, was pulled back behind her head. She looked round and gave a smile.

"Hi, you're from next door?"

"Hello," Jennifer said.

"We're busy, Mum."

Michelle grabbed hold of Jennifer's sleeve and led her out into the garden. The cold air seemed to shoot up her nose and into her ears as the back door clicked shut. The other two walked briskly up the garden, but Jennifer slowed, wishing they could have stayed in the kitchen longer. She rubbed her hands together to keep them warm. Michelle looked back and gestured to her to hurry up. Jennifer quickened her steps reluctantly. When they got to the end, Michelle made a *shush* sign with her finger and then pointed to the ground. In front of her, Jennifer could see a mound of stones. A small hill of pebbles and bits of rock.

"What is it?" she said.

"It's a grave, *obviously*."

"Whose grave?"

"Not *whose* grave. It's not a person's grave, silly. It's a bird."

"Mine."

The word came from Lucy. Jennifer was taken aback because the girl hadn't spoken before.

"She found it in her garden," Michelle said, hooking her thumb at Lucy.

"It lived on my tree. Now it's dead."

Lucy's voice was squeaky, as though it needed a spot of oil.

"You can see if you like," Michelle said, and squatted down, flinging the stones to the side. In the middle was a tiny brown bird lying on its side. Its feathers looked soft and velvety, and it just seemed as though it were sleeping.

"Are you sure it's dead?" Jennifer said.

"Course it's dead, most probably killed by one of the wild cats," Michelle said, looking affronted.

"We said a prayer for it," Lucy said, quietly.

"Wild cats?" Jennifer said, imagining tigers and lions.

"Up at the reservoir. They live there, tons of them. They come around here for food. They eat anything. They're cruel."

"I've got to go," she said.

She was feeling gloomy and wished she hadn't come. Before she had walked a couple of paces, Michelle ran up to her and was whispering in her ear.

"Come back, after lunch, when Lucy's gone. I'll show you my room and my things. You can show me your mum's model pictures."

She looked round. Lucy was staring at the ground where the dead bird was. It didn't seem right, her coming back when Lucy wasn't there. On the other hand she had said she'd show Michelle her mum's model shots.

"Okay," she whispered and ran off up the garden.

School was easy. She'd been to six different ones over the years. A week after moving into Water Lane she was led into the classroom by the head teacher and introduced to the pupils. She'd been through this before. In the past she'd been nervous, looking along the rows of strange faces. This time it was different. In the corner, by the class library, was Michelle, and beside her an empty space that had been saved. The head teacher left and the lesson went on. Michelle was smiling at the other kids. She laid her hand on Jennifer's arm in a proprietary way. She had already met the new girl. She also knew the new girl's mum who was a model and had had her photograph in clothes catalogs.

At lunchtime Michelle took Jennifer to the office to pick up her lunch.

"How's your first morning?" Mrs. Livingstone said, looking up from her computer.

"Very nice," Jennifer said, smiling.

Lucy was in a younger class, so Jennifer looked around for her in the dining room.

"Most days she goes home for dinner. Sometimes she's in Reading Club. I usually don't hang around with her at school," Michelle said, with a hint of annoyance. "Anyway, she's too young to be my best friend."

Jennifer relaxed. This made her feel a bit better. The younger girl had been giving her and Michelle doleful looks for the last few days.

"She's very timid," Jennifer said.

"Her dad left home . . . She just lives with her mum and two brothers."

Jennifer already knew this from her own mum, who had made it her business to find out stuff from the neighbors. She'd seen Lucy's mum herself a number of times. She was a small thin woman who was always wearing athletic clothes, as if she were about to go and play a game or run cross-country. Jennifer had only ever seen her standing around, though, talking to people outside the shops or to the other neighbors in Water Lane. She had a loud voice that seemed to carry, so that Jennifer often heard her before she saw her.

"Stevie and Joe boss her a bit," Michelle continued. "My mum says that they get away with murder. Stevie's never had a job and Joe should really be at a special school."

Lucy's brothers did look odd. Stevie, the older one, was nineteen but small, like Lucy, with thin hair and sunken cheeks. Joe was only fourteen but was as big as a man, heavier and broader than his older brother. They were always together and wore army trousers and jackets as if they belonged to the military. Only they weren't members of any group, her mum had told her, they just dressed up to please themselves. Her mum had been inside Lucy's house chatting to Mrs. Bussell and she had shown her their room, which was full of military knick-knacks. "They've even got replica guns," her mum said, "hanging on the walls, and helmets and boots and tents."

Jennifer didn't like them at all. When she walked past them they used their fingers like pretend binoculars and followed her steps as if she were some kind of enemy. Jennifer felt sorry for Lucy having to live with them.

"Lucy's so tiny. She reminds me of a sad little mouse."

Michelle opened her mouth to speak but appeared to be struck dumb by this image.

"She's all right," she said finally. "No one'll ever bully her with brothers like that!"

After school they walked arm in arm through the village, sheltering for a while under the shop awnings when it started raining. Sidestepping the dark glassy puddles, they walked up to Water Lane.

A man was coming out of Jennifer's gate. He had a sports jacket on and the hood was up. He was carrying a big bag over his shoulder.

"Oh look," said Michelle, "I wonder if that's a photographer."

The man opened a car door and struggled to put the bag in, then he stood back and pushed his hood off his head. It was Perry. Jennifer's hand immediately rose to wave, but he didn't seem to register her presence and quickly got into the car and slammed the door.

"Maybe he's just taken some pictures of your mum," Michelle said.

"I'll have to go in," Jennifer said.

"Can I come?"

"Later, when I've done my homework. I'll come and call for you."

The house was quiet and dark. She switched the hall light on even though it was only three-thirty in the afternoon. Her mum wasn't in the kitchen or the lounge. Jennifer ran upstairs. She was in her bedroom, and the door was tightly shut.

"Mum," she called. "Did Perry come?"

"I've got a migraine, Jen."

"Can I come in?" she said, turning the handle.

"I'm better on my own," her mum said, her voice scratchy. As if she'd been crying.

She went back downstairs. The place was so quiet. As if no one had spoken in it for weeks. She went into the living room and sat down. The small television was still there. Perry hadn't taken it back. The mantelpiece was empty, though. Perry had rescued Luke Skywalker and taken him back to all the other Star Wars toys.

Jennifer felt glad. That's where he belonged.

TWELVE

BERWICK Waters. Jennifer had expected it to be mysterious. In her mind she imagined a thick, dark forest edging onto a flat glassy lake; a place of intrigue and possible danger.

A school trip was planned. Miss Potts and a couple of the other teachers were taking their classes up to the reservoir for the day. The children would do a six-kilometer hike around the lake. They had to bring a picnic lunch and wear sensible shoes. Even though Michelle didn't seem particularly excited by the prospect, Jennifer was looking forward to it.

She woke up early. Unusually, her mum was already up. The bathroom door was closed and she could hear the sound of the shower running. She went downstairs to have breakfast and then make up her packed lunch. After a while her mum came into the kitchen. She was all dressed up.

"You going out?"

"Yep. That photographer who rang yesterday? I'm going to his studio."

"Is it for a magazine?" Jennifer said.

"Could be."

Jennifer hoped so. Her mum had been moody over the last week or so, keeping to her room, getting up late, lying on the carpet in the living room watching the tiny television. She hadn't felt like cooking, nor going to the launderette, nor doing any shopping. A couple of times she'd even suggested that Jennifer take the day off school so that they could get the bus into Norwich and do some window shopping. In the past, Jennifer would have jumped at the chance. A day out for her and her mum; there would have been nothing better. But this time it was different. She liked school. She had her place next to Michelle and they often did their work together. At lunchtime they sat in the soft chairs in the hall or, if it wasn't too cold, on the bench by the playing field. They swapped books and magazines and shared their lunches. They were best friends. Michelle had even given Jennifer a spare key fob that she had with a tiny skateboard and fluffy heart attached to it. Just so that they could be the same. Sometimes, when the head teacher was out, Mrs. Livingstone let the girls go into the stationery cupboard and tidy up the packs of exercise books and boxes of pens and felt-tips. On the way home they usually let Lucy walk with them. The younger girl listened with awe to all their gossip and chatter, and it was as if they were reliving their day by telling it all to her.

Jennifer didn't want to take the day off school.

The day before the trip to Berwick Waters her mum asked her again.

"Just this once. Just to keep me company?" she'd said with an exaggerated pout.

Luckily, Michelle called for Jennifer just at that moment.

"We could go on Saturday," she'd said, rushing to answer the front door. "Or Sunday?"

But her mum had forgotten about the offer and shuffled off into the kitchen. That afternoon she'd come home from school and found her lying across her bed still in her dressing gown.

How different she looked a day later in her long tan coat and black trousers. Her hair had been curled and looked lighter than usual. She had pale lipstick on for a change and hardly any eye makeup.

"Fingers crossed. Maybe this will be my lucky day," her mum said.

They'd lived in the house for more than six weeks and there had been no modeling work. They didn't seem to be short of money, but Jennifer knew, from past experience, that if her mum wasn't working at *something* the money would dry up.

"I might be a touch late," she said. "You'll be all right, though, won't you?"

It wasn't really a question so Jennifer didn't bother to answer. She stretched the cling wrap out so that it covered her sandwich and put it into a tiny plastic box. She knew how to look after herself.

Arriving at the reservoir, Jennifer felt a twinge of disappointment. It was just a woodland park set around a giant man-made lake. There were paths everywhere and signs with arrows pointing the way. There was nothing wild about it at all.

Miss Potts had told the three classes, the other teachers, and an assortment of mums to assemble in the main picnic area. Standing on one of the tables above them all, she gave a short talk. Fifteen years before, the Water Board had dug out the lake and filled it in order to service the nearby towns with water. Because of what happened in Berwick, she said, people for miles around had ample drinking water. She stopped and looked round expectantly, but no hands shot up with questions. That was it. It had no dramatic history. Once it had been a farmer's fields. Now it had a sculpted lake and woodland.

Jennifer's mood dipped. The teachers stood with their arms crossed and the mums were huddled together looking up at the sky.

It was a dull day, the sky crammed full with clouds. A strong wind splattered them with raindrops from time to time. The daffodils that fringed the paths were almost bent double and the trees waved their branches agitatedly. The surface of the lake was rippled and looked like the color of dishwater.

It was too early in the year for the snack bar to be open, but several of the kids used the toilets and the rest sat on the wooden benches and waited. After a few minutes, Miss Potts handed out armbands: red, blue, yellow, and green. Different teams had to make their way round the lake collecting information about the wildlife, which they would fill into a small booklet that had been prepared by the water company.

"Keep your adult leaders in sight," she said. "And no one should go off the main paths, especially not by themselves. And the most important thing of all is that no one is allowed to go anywhere near the lake."

Just as their groups were about to leave, Jennifer looked over to Lucy's class and saw that she was wearing a red armband.

"Lucy's on the same team as us," she said, nudging Michelle. "Maybe we should ask her to walk round with us? In a threesome?"

"Nope. Mouse can find her own friends!" Michelle said, striding off, following the leaders of their team.

Jennifer frowned and quickened her step to keep up. Michelle had taken to calling Lucy *Mouse* behind her back. It made her feel uncomfortable and she wished she'd never said it in the first place. She'd wanted to tell Michelle to stop it a number of times but hadn't quite managed to say the words. She opened her mouth to call after her, but Michelle had sprinted ahead and was talking to one of the teachers, her ginger hair bobbing animatedly. Looking round she saw some of the younger kids with their red armbands, one or two holding clipboards, the others with their booklets in plastic covers. Following behind them, walking by herself, was Lucy. Jennifer felt a niggle of guilt. Before she had moved to Water Lane, Lucy had been friends with Michelle. Nowadays the girl seemed to be on her own a lot, or hanging round with one of her mad-looking brothers. She seemed tired and the booklet was flapping in her hand. It didn't even look as though she had a pen or a bag. Michelle seemed quite happy up front so Jennifer hung back and waited until Lucy caught up with her.

"You all right?" she said.

Lucy nodded. She was wearing her giant jacket again and her hair had a zigzag part and was hanging limply down each side of her face.

"Where's your packed lunch?"

Lucy put her hand into one of her pockets and pulled out a tinfoil square.

"My mum made a sandwich," she said.

"Here, do you want a pen? To fill that in?" Jennifer said, pointing to the booklet.

"Got one!" Lucy said, and produced a pen from her other pocket.

They walked on, a distance behind the others. To the rear, the next team was starting their walk. Jennifer had an odd feeling. As though she were in a kind of no-man's-land. Lucy didn't seem to notice and was chatty, her squeaky voice rising and falling.

"My mum's got to have an operation. She's got a sore heart. Stevie says she has to wait for months and months. That's not fair, is it?"

Jennifer shook her head. Her mum had told her that Mrs. Bussell was waiting for heart surgery. She felt sorry for her, the woman had a lot on her mind. Her husband had left her and there was some talk of Mrs. Bussell not being able to cope. Michelle's mum had no sympathy. It was Mrs. Bussell's own fault, she said. The woman smoked thirty cigarettes a day.

"Look, a cat," Lucy suddenly said, pointing into the bushes.

Jennifer swung around to look but couldn't see anything. One of the teachers from the group behind was catching up with them. She linked Lucy's arm and pulled her on.

"Did you see it?" Lucy said.

"No, come on. We'll get left behind."

"My mum said that years ago, before I was born, they all got drowned. There used to be just fields here and they filled it up with water without telling anyone." Lucy's voice was picking up speed. "The cats didn't know. Nobody knew. One day it was a field and the next day it was a lake. My mum said she saw cat bodies floating about on the top of the water. She fished one out. It was stiff, she said, and its fur was all mangy."

Jennifer didn't answer. She pictured Mrs. Bussell, in her athletic clothes, tiptoeing through the mud and reeds, pulling a dead cat out of the lake.

"They don't like people. They avoid us, Stevie said, and if I was to go near one it would attack me."

"No . . ."

"It's a secret. Only people in the army know what they're really like. Stevie told me."

Jennifer hadn't heard this bit of the story. She thought of Joe, the younger brother. He was only fourteen, Mrs. Livingstone had said, but he looked big enough to do a man's job.

"Have you ever seen a cat attack someone?" Jennifer demanded.

"No, but Stevie has. Him and Joe come up here at night to hunt them, but I'm not supposed to tell. They bring their guns. They've got a den."

"Guns?" Jennifer said, exasperated.

"Stevie says they have to try and get rid of the cats."

"Cats what?" Miss Potts said, a few meters behind them, her voice booming out.

"About the drowned cats, Miss," Lucy said.

Miss Potts tutted. Her head moved from side to side

as though she were trying to see something. She picked up a whistle that was hanging on a string around her neck and put it up to her lips as if she were going to blow it. Some boys who were running rather close to the lake saw her movement and scooted away. She let the whistle drop.

"They lived here, when there was no lake. Then, when the water came they all drowned."

"Lucy, dear, that story's just a myth."

"So there are no wild cats?" Jennifer said.

"There are *feral* cats. Not domesticated. They mostly live round the picnic areas."

"And no cats were drowned?"

"Possibly. I'm sure there was some wildlife that suffered when the reservoir first filled up . . . Honestly, look at that stupid boy!"

Miss Potts went striding off in the direction of a boy who was halfway up a tree. Several others were standing round the trunk holding branches and trying to knock him off. The sound of a whistle pierced the air, and from a dozen spots around the lake small groups of children appeared and looked in the direction of the sound. Further up, with a finger of the murky water of the lake in between them, was Michelle. She made an impatient signal for Jennifer to come and join her.

"We'd better hurry up, or we'll get left behind," Jennifer said, hooking Lucy's arm and quickening her step.

"We've got to get to the top end of the lake for our lunch. And we've got to fill in this book."

As they walked on Jennifer looked around to see if there were any cats. None. She did a drawing of a wildflower and helped Lucy to do hers. She described the weather and ticked some boxes on a wildlife quiz. She pulled Lucy by the hand up a steep incline, all the time trying to hurry her steps so that they could catch up with Michelle. She huffed and puffed as she got to the top, feeling Lucy's weight like a sack of potatoes. Standing at a height, she looked around and saw some of the other kids walking in little groups. Catching her breath, she stood for a moment and peered into the trees and scanned the edge of the lake below. There were no cats that she could see. *None.*

The red armbands were all sitting at the picnic area at the top of the lake. Michelle was with a girl called Sonia, whom they weren't usually friends with. Jennifer frowned and walked over, Lucy following her. The girls had unpacked their lunches on the wooden table and filled up the remaining benches with their bags. There was hardly enough room for Jennifer to sit, let alone Lucy.

"Sorry we're late," Jennifer said, looking directly at Michelle, who was averting her eyes, glancing at her food or across the lake.

"Can we sit down?" she tried again, her voice cheerful,

though her shoulders were rounded, her knapsack getting heavier by the minute.

"Suit yourself," Michelle said. "There's room enough."

Sonia, the other girl, looked round at Lucy.

"There's enough room for a *mouse,* anyway."

Jennifer caught Michelle's eye for a second. She could hardly believe it. Michelle had told her! She had gossiped to Sonia about something Jennifer had said. How could she?

"Mouse?" Lucy said, looking round.

The two girls burst out laughing.

"Squeak, squeak," Sonia said, looking straight at Lucy.

Jennifer gave a look of fury and turned away, pulling Lucy by the hand and going across to another table. They sat with their backs to the two girls and unpacked their lunch. They ate in silence, Lucy playing with the tinfoil in which her sandwich was wrapped, folding it into shapes. Jennifer gave a weak smile, but she was squaring her shoulders, making her back like an iron door, shutting out the others, closing herself against them. When they'd finished and the teacher blew the whistle to start, Jennifer took Lucy's arm and surged ahead, her irritation propelling her so that the two of them covered the remaining few kilometers in less than an hour.

"We've won!" Lucy said when they arrived back at the original picnic area.

Although it hadn't been a race, they were the first

back. A couple of the mums took their booklets, and then Jennifer went to the toilet. Lucy followed her and Jennifer sighed. Was the girl going to cling to her all day? Emerging from the block, she stood for a minute looking into the distance. There were groups of kids coming toward them, and she could see Michelle among them.

Then, in the corner of her eye, she saw a sudden movement. Looking round she came face to face with one of the feral cats.

It was on a mound behind the bins. It was straggly and thin, its haunches sticking out, its fur flat and dull. Its ears were stiff and upright, as though it were listening for the smallest sound. It seemed to be tiptoeing around the grass, its big black eyes looking here and there, its shoulders hunched with anxiety. She moved toward it and stopped abruptly because the cat had turned to look directly at her, its dark eyes pinning her to the spot.

"Do you see it?"

Lucy was behind her, her voice no more than a scratchy whisper. Jennifer looked at her with irritation. She wished Lucy would just go away. When she looked back, the skinny cat had disappeared.

"I've got to go," she said, and strode across the grass toward the other kids who were coming up to the end part of the walk. She didn't look back and hoped that Lucy wasn't following. After a few minutes she reached the first group, among them Michelle and Sonia.

"Hi," she said, forcing a smile.

She was going to pretend that nothing had happened. To try and get things back to normal. She and Michelle. Best friends.

"Do you want to come round my house afterwards? My mum's had some new photos done today. We could have a look."

"Nah," Michelle said, threading her hand through the other girl's arm. "I'm going round to Sonia's. Why don't you ask Mouse?"

Sonia smirked and Jennifer stood still and let them move ahead. There was a great lump of hurt in her throat and she tried to swallow it back. In the distance she could see Lucy leaning against a tree. She felt an overwhelming dislike for the tatty girl. She didn't want to see her again that afternoon; she didn't want to be anywhere near her scruffy jacket or her uncombed hair. She turned and walked off toward the public footpath in the direction of the road. It wasn't allowed, she knew that. She was supposed to wait for the teachers, but she'd had enough of Berwick Waters. It was only a crappy park, anyway.

She didn't cry until she got back to Water Lane and pulled her key fob out of her pocket. The tiny skateboard and pink fluffy heart blurred in front of her as she opened the door.

"I'm back!" she shouted, her voice cracking.

Her mum's long tan coat was hanging on the banister and her shoes were laying at angles at the bottom of the stairs.

"Mum?" she called up the stairwell.

There was no answer, and when she went into the kitchen there were fragments of paper all over the table and floor. She picked them up, crouching down to pull a couple from under the cupboard where they had drifted. She fitted the pages back together. GLAMOUR GIRLS AGENCY. BEAUTIFUL MODELS FROM ACROSS THE GLOBE.

Her mum hadn't got the job. Should she go up and see her? Bring her a cup of tea? Probably not. It was better to leave her on her own.

THIRTEEN

JENNIFER had only spoken to Mrs. Nettles, the head teacher, once, on the day that she started at the school. She was a small, plump lady with curly gray hair that flicked around the sides of her ears. She wore dresses made of flimsy fabrics that floated around her, with jackets that didn't fasten and usually billowed out like capes as she walked up and down the main corridor of the small school. She had a big voice that seemed to fill up the assembly hall, and her face was jolly, as if she were always remembering something funny.

She wasn't smiling on the morning after the trip to Berwick Waters.

"What on earth were you thinking of? To walk off on your own, in the middle of the reservoir? To leave the school trip without permission? How could you? How dare you!"

Jennifer was standing in the middle of the room. She'd been called there as soon as school began. It hadn't been a surprise. Miss Potts had arrived on her doorstep the previous afternoon, just after four, demanding to see her mum. Jennifer had lied and said she was out at work. The teacher had been furious when Jennifer shrugged, unable to say why she had left the reservoir on her own. Miss Potts had had to leave someone else in charge. She no longer had the whistle round her neck. No doubt she'd had to give that over to some other teacher who could blow it to keep order among the children.

When Mrs. Nettles finished speaking, she stood up and wafted across to a filing cabinet for a brown cardboard file. She opened it as Jennifer stood awkwardly. Her feet were tightly together and she didn't move a muscle, as though she were balancing on the top of a high pole. Mrs. Nettles was rustling sheets of paper, making little *tsk* sounds, and Jennifer looked away, out of the window. She saw the rest of her class being led across the playground toward the playing field. Michelle was there in the middle, walking next to Sonia. It gave her a bad feeling, a tightness in her chest. The sound of Mrs. Nettles's voice made her look back.

"Jennifer, your records have finally arrived, and I see here your education has been a little erratic."

She nodded, even though she had no idea what *erratic* meant.

"You've missed an awful lot of school over the years. And lived with your grandmother for a while. Foster placements as well . . . But you're back with Mum now, I see. And is Mum all right? The new house and everything? Are you settling in?"

She nodded again, eager to please the head teacher, keen to get out of her office and back into class.

"This walking off, this going off on your own, seems quite out of character. Did someone tell you off?"

"No, Miss," she said.

"I don't know what's happened. Honestly, Jennifer, when you're on a school outing you must stay with the teachers. Never, never, never go off on your own. Anything could happen to you, and it would be our responsibility. Do you understand?"

"Yes."

She had to sit in the far corner of the school office at a tiny desk and fill a whole page with writing. *Ways to Behave on a School Trip*. From time to time she looked across at Mrs. Livingstone, who was typing on a computer and putting letters into envelopes. When she was standing up, making a cup of tea for Mrs. Nettles, she gave Jennifer a tiny smile.

After the writing was finished, Jennifer looked out of the window and saw her class walking back across the playground. They looked flushed and smiley, having run round the school field, no doubt playing rounders or mixed football. At the end, linked arm in arm, were Michelle and Sonia. Jennifer felt her mouth go dry.

Her mum hadn't been up when she left that morning. This worried her. She remembered days like this from times before when things started to go wrong. Then there were no pound coins for dinner money, no five- or ten-pound notes for shopping, no loose change for the sweet shop. Small things, really, but they suddenly mounted up, and then there were social workers at the door, her mum in floods of tears. Or maybe her mum wasn't there any-more, and Jennifer had to sit in an office and smile at a secretary (not unlike Mrs. Livingstone) who was typing at a computer and putting letters in envelopes.

Watching Mrs. Nettles flutter in and out of the office, she put her elbow on the table and leaned her chin on her hand. She didn't want it to be like that again. They had a house and she had a school. And Michelle. For the first time she had a real friend. Except that, since yesterday, for some reason that she couldn't quite work out, everything had changed. She put her hand in her pocket and pulled out her key ring. She rubbed her finger across the skate-board and then felt the furry heart. It was like a tiny hand-bag. Macy had had one like it once, but Macy was old now, lying in a cardboard box with all her outfits around her. She had shown her off to Michelle, who said she looked funny, like she was in a coffin; as though Macy had died and was waiting to be buried. Thinking of this sud-denly made Jennifer feel sad, as if Macy really had died. Her eyes blurred and she swallowed back a few times and turned her head away from Mrs. Livingstone, who was nearby, flicking through a pile of papers, whispering to herself. What had she done wrong? Just because she'd felt sorry for Lucy? She lifted the key fob to her face and rubbed the fluffy heart on her cheek.

After break, she was allowed to go. She picked up her bag, closed the office door carefully, and walked along the edge of the corridor toward her class. Everyone else was in lessons and she quickened her steps, not wanting to be too late. The smell of lunch was in the air and she could hear the sound of trays clattering against each other as the kitchen staff got everything ready. She gave a tiny knock on the classroom door. When no one called out, she opened it a few centimeters and slipped through the gap. A music lesson was under way. She was relieved. No one seemed to notice her as she came into the room. Half the desks were covered in keyboards. Kids in headphones were looking at music sheets and tentatively pressing keys. In the corner there were some drums, and a group of boys seemed to be squabbling over them. The teacher was sitting with a couple of girls with Spanish guitars and didn't seem to notice her. An adult helper was wandering round. Through the glass, in the back corridor, were half a dozen kids with recorders. Michelle was among them. Jennifer was struck with indecision for a moment, but then she put her bag down on a chair and picked up a recorder from the instrument store and went out. There were six girls in a row, reading off sheet music that had been tacked to the wall.

"Hi," she said, walking up and standing beside her friend.

"Um," Michelle murmured, the recorder still in her mouth. Sonia said nothing, but her eyes settled on Jennifer and stayed there.

"I've been in Mrs. Nettles's office."

Michelle kept her gaze on the music sheet that was on the wall. Sonia took her recorder out of her mouth.

"Do you want to go to the convenience store at lunchtime? I've got some money?" Jennifer said.

Michelle didn't answer, didn't even acknowledge that she had spoken to her. She started to play the recorder, the notes rising and falling, her fingers moving up and down. Jennifer stood glued to the spot, her chest welling up with anxiety. She put her recorder in her mouth and turned to the music sheet. What could she say? She didn't know what else to say. She blew into the instrument, her fingers finding the holes, her head feeling heavy.

"Maybe she should go to the convenience store with Mouse?"

She heard Sonia's voice underneath the notes. She didn't turn to look, but felt Michelle nodding in agreement with her new friend. She blew harder, her recorder making a discordant sound. It startled her and she stopped abruptly. She knew the two of them were sniggering; she could almost *feel* Michelle's body shaking with laughter. She didn't look at either of them. She stared through the glass of the classroom door and saw other kids chatting, smiling, enjoying themselves. She shouldn't have come out here. She should have stayed in the classroom, avoided Michelle, given her time to forget the day at the reservoir.

"Poor little Mouse. Living with her nutty mum!"

"Don't let her say that!" Jennifer said.

"What's it to you?" Sonia said, moving forward in front of Michelle and squaring up to Jennifer.

"It's not nice . . . ," she said, gripping the recorder tightly, her shoulders pushing forward toward Sonia.

"Don't wet your knickers about it!" Sonia said in a baby voice.

Jennifer hated Sonia. She couldn't stand to look at her silly face for a minute longer. She raised the recorder and banged it on her forehead. A single second was all it took. It was only plastic, but it still made a *thwack* sound. Her hand seemed to vibrate for a few seconds afterward, but the rest of her was still, like a statue. She watched as Sonia's face reddened and crumpled, and then a long wail came from her ugly mouth. Jennifer stepped back, her arm dropping down by her side, the weapon hanging silently.

Sonia's hands rose and covered the spot where she'd been hit. She looked like she might topple backward for a moment, but Michelle was there stopping her from falling. Jennifer caught her eye and held it for a second. Michelle had a look of shock on her face, but there was a glint in her eye that Jennifer couldn't quite read, couldn't quite understand.

Then there were adults around, pushing past her, pulling her back, marching her into a corner, shouting words at her. She didn't register much of it, she closed her eyes, feeling tired. Someone snatched the recorder from her hand, and once it was gone she felt a trembling sensation in her shoulders and upper arms. She looked toward Sonia and Michelle. They were being ushered into the classroom, Sonia being held up by Miss Potts, followed by the other adult and a gaggle of excited children. On the wall, the tacked sheets of music flapped where they had been dislodged by the commotion. On the ground were a couple of recorders that had been dropped; probably one of them belonged to Sonia.

She was alone in the corridor.

The sound of footsteps made her turn. Mrs. Nettles was striding toward her, her clothes flapping out, her face grim. Jennifer turned away and looked through the glass into the classroom. Michelle was looking out at her, her expression one of awe.

That look in Michelle's eye. That strange glint. It had been *excitement*.

Her mum had to see Mrs. Nettles. Jennifer had to wait in Mrs. Livingstone's office while the head teacher spoke to her. She sat at the same tiny desk that she'd written at just an hour or so before. Mrs. Livingstone was still there, but she didn't look or smile at her. After a while her mum came out of the head teacher's office, her face in a pout.

"Come on," she said quietly, glancing over at Jennifer.

She hadn't dressed up. She was wearing some old jogging trousers that Jennifer had seen lying across the banister that morning. Her hair was loose with some strands hanging over her eyes. She was round-shouldered and looked fed up. Jennifer wondered whether she would tell her off, shout at her, send her to her room. She knew she wouldn't, though. Her mum hardly ever told her off about anything.

At home she sat in the living room watching daytime television. At a little after four there was a knock on the front door. When she opened it she found Michelle, on her own, carrying the school bag she had left behind. For a second she looked awkward and then, as though nothing had happened, she walked into Jennifer's house and started to speak.

"Sonia's fine, just a bruise on her head. You should have seen her! Mrs. Nettles put her in the backseat of her car to take her to the surgery! She was looking all around as though she were the queen being driven by a chauffeur! She had it coming really, she's got such a mouth on her. I never meant to say a word to her about Lucy. She just sort of wheedles things out of you, before you even know you've said it. I don't like her. Specially now. Now every-one's feeling sorry for her!"

"Hello, Michelle," her mum said, passing through the hallway.

"Hi, Mrs. Jones," Michelle said, and then without so much as a breath she carried on, "What about you! What did Mrs. Nettles do? Has she expelled you?"

Jennifer shook her head.

"I'm suspended for five days, and then there has to be a meeting between me and Sonia and I've got to write a letter . . . You know."

"Look on the bright side! Five days off school!"

Jennifer nodded. There was a bright side. They were friends again.

FOURTEEN

MR. COTTIS, the new photographer, first came to the house at the end of the Easter holidays. He drove up in a black van. It looked brand-new, as if it had just been driven out of a showroom. He got out and stood looking at the houses. He was tall and thin and was wearing tight jeans and a black sweater with no coat. He had a completely bald head and glasses that seemed to go darker as he stood there.

Jennifer and Michelle were hanging around, bored with their holiday pastimes. Michelle walked straight up to him.

"Are you looking for Carol Jones, the model?" she said.

He nodded, his face breaking into a smile.

"She lives there," Michelle said, pointing. "This is her daughter. She's my best friend."

"Thank you very much, young lady," he said and did an old-fashioned bow.

"Come on," Jennifer said, embarrassed at having been pointed out to a complete stranger.

The small park near the shops was empty except for Lucy Bussell's brothers. They were in the play area. The older one, Stevie, was leaning back against the climbing frame; the younger one, Joe, was messing around with a football. They were both wearing the bottle-green trousers and camouflage jackets that they had on most of the time. Stevie had a distant expression on his face, and Jennifer was immediately reminded of his sister, Lucy.

They'd not seen much of her in the previous weeks. She'd been unwell, off school. During the holidays she'd been indoors a lot. Michelle had even knocked for her a couple of times, but she'd not come out, saying that she was looking after her mum. Jennifer had been relieved. It meant that she and Michelle could be on their own.

Joe was zigzagging around the play area. His body was taut, trying to keep the ball up in the air, bouncing it off one foot. His limbs were moving like clockwork and his face was heavy with concentration. Stevie was completely still, only his hand moving back and forth with a cigarette.

They could have walked away, ignored them, headed off to the other end of the park and sat on one of the benches. Michelle had different ideas, though.

"You're not supposed to be here. It's for under twelves. See the notice," she said, pointing at a faded notice board behind the swings.

Stevie didn't respond. He didn't even acknowledge

that she'd spoken. He stayed in exactly the same position, his legs splayed, blowing little rings of smoke into the air. Joe gave his ball a fierce kick and it hit the fence with a thud.

"You're not supposed to be smoking here!" Michelle continued, her voice louder.

Stevie's eyes flicked in their direction. They settled on Jennifer.

"You tell him," Michelle said, drawing Jennifer in. "You tell him he's breaking the law!"

Jennifer frowned. Couldn't Michelle just leave her out of it? Stevie's gaze had stayed on her, and it was making her feel uncomfortable.

"Let's go," she said in a half whisper.

"Why should we? This park's for us, not them!"

A smile broke out on Stevie's face, and he flicked the rest of his cigarette in their direction. Michelle stood with her arms crossed as the butt flew past her and dropped a few centimeters from Jennifer.

"That's it, start a fire!"

"Get lost, you brats," Joe said, walking toward them, bouncing the football off his knees, first one then the other.

"I'm going!" Jennifer said, fed up with the row.

"How's your mum?" Stevie suddenly said.

Joe dropped the ball and it rolled toward her. She picked it up, looking quizzically at Stevie.

"What?" she said.

Joe snatched the ball from her hands and turned away.

"How's your mum?" Stevie repeated, his mouth open.

She stared at him, waiting for some sort of insult, when he put his tongue out and started to lick his lips.

"Gross," Michelle said. "I'm telling my mum about this. The police could prosecute you. You wait."

The football whizzed past her head and hit the notice board. Jennifer took Michelle's arm and pulled her away, out of the park.

"They're not worth it," she said.

Walking toward her house she saw the photographer, Mr. Cottis, coming out of her gate. He looked momentarily surprised to see them and edged past with a big shoulder bag and a small case on wheels. He looked like someone going on holiday. The girls stood back until he got his stuff out onto the path.

"Are you finished?" Michelle asked unnecessarily.

He hardly answered, just nodded his head and cleared his throat and got into his van. They watched as the shiny black van did an awkward three-point turn and then stuttered a bit before it drove off up the road.

"I wonder what the photos will be like!" Michelle said, her voice full of wonder, the upset of moments before gone.

"Let's go and see," Jennifer said, the tension draining out of her.

Finding the living room empty, looking unused, she led Michelle into the kitchen.

"Mum's probably getting changed," she said. "You stay here and I'll go and see."

She ran up the stairs and without thinking pushed open her mum's bedroom door. The room was in darkness so she clicked on the light. She expected to find the room empty and had half turned to go to the bathroom. But her mum was there, lying on the bed on her side, her knees drawn up. Her eyes were closed but she wasn't asleep, Jennifer could tell because she was holding her hand up to shield herself from the sudden light. Jennifer clicked the light off and went across to the curtains, pulling them back.

"I didn't know you were in here!" she said. "I thought you'd gone for a bath!"

Her mum was wearing a short skirt and a white blouse and tie. Like a schoolgirl. She had short white socks on as well, the kind that Jennifer wore herself.

"Has the photographer finished?" she asked.

The room was a mess. A chest of drawers had been moved and on top of it there was a globe, just like the one they had in school. There were books and papers strewn across the bed, as if someone had been doing homework. There was a chair in the middle of the floor that had been brought up from the kitchen and it was making everything look untidy. She took hold of it and pulled it to the side.

Then she noticed the money. Three pink notes. Fifty-pound notes.

"You got paid!" she said uncertainly.

Her mum nodded.

"When will you get the photographs?" she said, sensing something not right.

Her mum sat up, stretching her long legs out.

"Why are you dressed like that?" Jennifer said, edging the door shut behind her, afraid that somehow, without warning, Michelle might appear at her shoulder.

"That's what you do in modeling," her mum said. "You dress up in other people's clothes."

"Will it be in a magazine?"

"Not this time, love. Now, I think I will have a bath," she said, and walked past Jennifer into the hallway.

Jennifer came slowly downstairs, each foot pausing a second before continuing. She was not sure what she was going to say to Michelle about the photographer, not sure why she felt so gloomy.

"You'll have to go," she said, walking into the kitchen. "My mum's got a headache. It's the bright lights they use. It gives her a migraine."

Michelle looked miffed. She took her key fobs out and rattled them indignantly.

"I'll call for you later," Jennifer said.

Michelle didn't answer and the front door closed loudly behind her. Jennifer stood uncertainly at the bottom of the stairs. She expected to hear the water running from the bathroom, but there was no sound.

The house was silent. As though no one were home.

FIFTEEN

THE ambulance came in the middle of the night.

Jennifer was woken up by the sound of voices from out in the lane and lights shining through the window. She got up and looked out, craning to see what was going on. The ambulance was untidily parked and its back doors were wide open, throwing a shaft of light onto the lane. Two paramedics were wheeling a chair carefully down the garden path of Lucy's house. They were going slowly, one of them tucking a cover round someone. Mrs. Livingstone was there in a dressing gown, but there was no sign of Michelle or Lucy or even the two boys. When the chair turned out of the gate, she saw that it was Mrs. Bussell who was tucked up, only her small head visible above the blankets.

Jennifer moved away from her window and into the hallway, standing at the door of her mum's room. She opened it slightly and could hear soft snores coming from her mum's bed. Her mum had been at work all day on a photo shoot, so she decided not to wake her. She put her slippers and dressing gown on and went downstairs.

Opening the front door she felt the air, crisp and cold, making her skin tingle. The ambulance doors banged shut and it moved slowly away. Then she saw her neighbor pulling Lucy by the hand toward her own house, talking slowly, her voice soft and soothing.

"What's happened?" Jennifer asked.

Mrs. Livingstone guided Lucy into her path and sounded mildly cross.

"You should be in bed, Jennifer."

"Is Mrs. Bussell ill?"

"Yes, but she'll be all right. Is your mum up?" Mrs. Livingstone said, getting a bunch of keys out of her dressing gown pocket.

"Yes," Jennifer said, lying. "She's in the bathroom."

Jennifer looked at Lucy's worried face as Mrs. Livingstone led her into the door. She turned toward Jennifer and spoke in a whisper.

"Tell her that poor Mrs. Bussell has had a heart attack. The boys have gone with her to hospital. I'm looking after Lucy. Now, go back to bed. No point in everyone losing sleep."

The front door shut quietly and Jennifer backed into her own house. Going up the stairs she could hear her mum turning over on her bed, coughing lightly. It was better for Mrs. Livingstone not to know that her mum had slept through the ambulance. It made it seem as though she didn't care, when really she was just too tired to wake up.

Once in her room she found herself over by the window again, looking out. The lane was empty. It was four o'clock and it was ages till she had to get up for school. She lay down for a moment but couldn't rest, couldn't even shut her eyes. In spite of the seriousness of it all, she felt strangely invigorated by the situation. She put her bedside light on and sat cross-legged on top of her quilt, not even feeling the cold.

Mrs. Bussell was ill. What was going to happen to Lucy?

Michelle told her the following morning.

"She has to stay with us! In my bedroom. Mum's already got the camp bed out and cleared away a load of my things so that she can fit it in!"

"Will her mum be okay?" Jennifer said.

"Yes. I mean she's ill and all, but she'll get better. Trouble is she'll have to go into a nursing home for a couple of weeks so that means I'll have Mouse in my bedroom."

"Don't call her that," Jennifer said.

"You don't have to put up with her. She's got my pink duvet cover and Mum says she can borrow some of my clothes if she wants. Mum thinks it's fine, she says it's only for a couple of weeks, and that we have to be kind to her now that both her parents are out of the way. Otherwise she'd have to stay with her brothers."

"That'd be awful," Jennifer said.

"Maybe. But I don't see why she has to stay with *us*! Her brothers are going to stay in the house. Mum says *they* can look after themselves. I don't see why they can't look after Lucy. She's their sister, after all, she's not mine!"

"It's not so bad," Jennifer said. "It'll only be for a couple of weeks."

"That's easy for you to say. She's not hanging round your bedroom the whole time."

For the next week Michelle was in a constant bad mood and it was all Jennifer could do not to fall out with her. She moaned all the time about Lucy's clothes all over her bedroom, Lucy using her hairbrush, Lucy talking in her sleep.

"Even worse, my mum wants us to have a picnic for Lucy's birthday!"

"That might be nice," Jennifer said.

"But why should she? Lucy's not her *daughter*. That's up to her mum and dad!"

"But her mum's ill . . ."

"And her dad's gone. Exactly!"

Michelle gave a single clap of her hands as if she'd just proved something. Jennifer didn't know what to say.

"Can I come to your house? After school?" Michelle said.

"I don't know. My mum might be working. Mr. Cottis might be coming."

"Does he come every day?"

"Not every day."

Mr. Cottis came twice a week, maybe three times.

"I'll call for you later," Jennifer said. "We could go to the park."

"We'll have to take Lucy."

"That's okay." Jennifer shrugged.

Turning into Water Lane she saw his van parked outside her house. Michelle made grumbling sounds but peeled off into her own house and Jennifer opened her front door and went in. Mr. Cottis's bag and suitcase on wheels were lined up in the hallway as usual, making it hard for her to get past. The kitchen door was open and she could hear him and her mum talking.

"Say hello to Mr. Cottis," her mum said, pouring her a cold drink from the fridge.

"Hello," she said, smiling and looking at another man who was seated at the table dipping a cookie into a hot drink.

"This is Mr. Smith," her mum said, gesturing at the other man.

Jennifer smiled at both of them and walked out of the kitchen with her drink in her hand. She headed straight

173

upstairs to get out of the way for a while. She didn't like Mr. Cottis. He was too thin, his shoulders poking through the sweaters he wore. She'd never seen him sitting down, only leaning against something, stiff like a ladder. His glasses were disconcerting. One minute they were dark like sunglasses, and the next they were ordinary and she could see his tiny blue eyes staring at her. She didn't feel relaxed when he was there. She hadn't seen Mr. Smith before and only noticed his thin spiky hair and his pierced ear, a tiny hoop with a cross hanging on it.

It was her mum's job, though, and she had to get used to the visitors. Mr. Cottis, her mum said, was acting as a kind of *agent* to get her work. Some of it was in outside locations and occasionally there had to be some home shoots. Hiring a studio was expensive, she said, and with modern technology really high-quality pictures could be obtained in ordinary surroundings.

There was a good side to it. There was a lot of money in the house. Her mum kept a pile of notes in a box in the wardrobe. There was to be no bank account, she said, because she didn't want the tax people to know how much she earned. It had meant new clothes, a settee, lots of pocket money with which Jennifer had bought teen magazines and a bright pink cassette player that worked with batteries. Her mum was feeling generous. In the future it would pay for a holiday, maybe even a car in the long run. Why not?

There was a bad side. In previous weeks Mr. Cottis had found a lot of work for her mum. Almost every day she'd been up early and out on a shoot of some sort. On the days when she was at home Mr. Cottis came round. It meant that she was rushed and a bit forgetful. The groceries had run low and she had given Jennifer a fifty-pound note to go down to the Co-op and get what they needed. The washing had piled up and she'd had to take it to the launderette. Her mum explained, "You have to take the work when it comes, Jen. You know how long it took me to get back into modeling!"

However fed up she got, she had to admit that it was better than the times when her mum was lying around not doing anything, miserable with one headache after another.

"You could always go to Gran's for the next few weeks. She hasn't seen you for a while. You could just visit, until I get this work over and done with."

"No, no, I don't want to go to Gran's!"

She had no intention of going to Gran's. It wasn't that she didn't like her; over the years she had got used to her gran's way of life, to the new dog that sat on Nelson's chair, to the tobacco smoke and the sound of the sewing machine thundering away in the back room. It was just that visits to Gran's were dangerous. They often started with a day or two and ended up as a couple of weeks, or maybe longer. No, she had a school and friends and her own house, and she and her mum were together. She might not see much of her, but she'd still rather be there, sleeping under the same roof. If it meant waking up in the middle of the night and standing for a moment to hear her moving around in bed, she'd put up with doing everything else—making do, enduring Mr. Cottis and his long thin fingers and bony knuckles, his bag and suitcase on wheels blocking the hallway. It wasn't the kind of life she'd thought they would have when they moved into Water Lane, but it was better than living with her gran.

She heard a soft knock on her door.

"Jen, are you going out to play?"

She opened the door. Her mum was on the landing beside Mr. Cottis and his bags. Behind him, pausing on the top stair, was Mr. Smith, his earring glinting under the light.

"I don't *play*, Mum! I'm too old for that!"

"I know, love. Are you going out with Michelle? Here's some money for fish-and-chips, if you like."

She held out a ten-pound note.

"Okay," Jennifer said.

"We're going to set up a few shots in my room and tea might be a bit late. Anyway, you'd get bored if you hang around here. We'll be about an hour or so."

"All right."

Her mum had asked her to go out before so she didn't mind. She changed out of her school uniform and into some new jeans and a top that had been bought the previous weekend. She tucked the ten-pound note into her back pocket and went out, grabbing her sweatshirt. From inside her mum's room she heard things being moved around. They were probably setting up the camera and the equipment; big lights that flooded the room, making it look like a film set, her mum said. It was the lights that made models look so beautiful. It was the lights that were going to put her on the front cover of a magazine.

Jennifer called for Michelle, who came out immediately, closing her front door quietly as if she were escaping from somewhere.

"My mum's friend's giving Lucy a haircut, so we can be on our own. We could listen to some music, read some mags."

Michelle had taken to calling magazines mags. She had also begun to make fun of all the games they had played in the past, calling them kids' stuff. Since Lucy had moved in, Jennifer had noticed Michelle trying to be more grown up, using swear words more often, and talking about periods and tampons and problem pages and even boyfriends. She had even insisted that they have new nicknames. She was to be Ginger, after a pop star, and Jennifer was to be JJ. Lucy wasn't to have one, Michelle said. She was only a visitor. It meant that Lucy often didn't know what they were talking about and couldn't join in.

"I'll have to go back for the cassette player."

"Be quick. We can get away before Lucy's finished, and then my mum won't tell me off."

Jennifer ran back into her house. The furniture moving had stopped and there was just a low mumble of voices from the room next door. She picked up the cassette player and gathered up the tapes, and was about to go out of her room when she heard a strange sound from next door. A yelp. As if someone were in pain. She listened again, her body tense, and she heard it a second time. It was her mum's voice. She dropped her cassettes and went out on to the landing and knocked loudly on her mum's door.

"Mum, are you all right?" she shouted.

There was a sound of movement, a cough, a mumble, her mum's voice. The door opened a crack.

"What's up, love? I thought you'd gone out."

"Are you all right? I thought I heard you cry out."

"I'm fine," she said, the door relaxing a little, opening back.

She could see her mum's head and neck. She was wearing the school blouse and tie again. A gruff voice came from behind and her mum turned away to say something. The door opened a little more and she could see Mr. Smith sitting on the bed, wearing a shirt and tie just like her mum's. As though they were both schoolkids. Mr. Cottis was standing to the side, leaning against the chest of drawers, his glasses darkened in the brightly lit-up room.

"I'm fine. We're just doing a few situation shots." She lowered her voice. "We won't be long. You run off now, love, or else I'll get into trouble with Mr. Cottis."

Jennifer stood on the landing for a few moments before going back into her room to collect her things. She didn't like Mr. Cottis. Mr. Smith, neither. She didn't like the photographs with the school ties. She'd never seen any of those on the front of a magazine.

She walked down the stairs slowly, listening at every step for a sound from her mum's room. She felt jittery, as though something might jump out at her. She didn't know exactly what was going on, but it was different from any modeling her mum had ever done before. She gripped the cassette player and hesitated. She didn't want to go out and spend time with Michelle. She might want to talk about her mum's career and how she herself wanted to be a model when she grew up.

Outside, she saw Lucy standing next to Michelle. Her hair had been cut and styled and it made her look quite pretty. She was wearing some fashionable clothes; probably things that Mrs. Livingstone had sorted out for her. They were clean and ironed and she looked normal, just like any other kid, relaxed and happy. Michelle was not happy. She seemed exasperated.

"I've told her she can't come with us," she said crossly.

Jennifer looked sternly at the pair of them. She really couldn't be bothered. She glanced back up to her house and felt a great lump of frustration at her throat. She didn't know what was happening in her mum's room. And yet deep down, in a way that she couldn't have explained to anybody, she did know. Mr. Smith in his school uniform, his silly little earring swinging back and forth. Mr. Cottis, stiff as an ironing board, standing behind a camera. Maybe his bony face broke into a smile of some sort, possibly he took his glasses off and looked through the camera lens with his cold blue eye.

"She can't come, can she, Jennifer?" Michelle continued.

Why her mum? Other mums had jobs. Mrs. Livingstone was a secretary. Why couldn't her mum do something like that? Even her gran sewed up clothes for people to wear. Why couldn't her mum be like her?

"You're too young to hang around with us," Michelle said. "Isn't she?"

Lucy looked the best that Jennifer had ever seen her. Without her hopeless mum and her awful brothers, she seemed to be stepping forward. Even with her mother lying in a hospital bed, she seemed happier than ever.

"I can come, can't I?"

"No," Jennifer said, her throat turning to steel.

"Why not?"

"Go away! You can't come! Go and visit your mum or something!"

Lucy looked startled, her mouth hanging open. Jennifer felt a sudden fury. What was the girl upset about? Wasn't she being looked after? Cared for? Wasn't her mum being nursed back to health? What did she have to whine about?

"My mum's coming home next week," Lucy said, uncertainly, a hopeful smile on her face.

"Maybe she will. Maybe she won't," Jennifer said.

"What?" Lucy said, her mouth bunched up.

"Maybe she won't come out of hospital at all. Maybe you'll never see her again!"

Michelle looked astonished.

"That's not true, is it?" Lucy said, looking at Michelle, her eyes becoming glassy. "She's coming home next week. That's right, isn't it?"

"Course she is!" Michelle said.

"You don't know," Jennifer said, unable to stop herself, "her mum might be dead. At this very minute, she might be DEAD."

"No, she's not!" Lucy said, a sob coming out.

"Don't say that to her, I'll get in trouble with my mum!" Michelle said, her words coming through clenched teeth.

But Jennifer couldn't stop. Why should she stop?

"LEAVE US ALONE!" she shouted. "GO AWAY! GO AND FIND YOUR MUM!"

"You're mad, you are. You're MAD!" Michelle said, grabbing Lucy by the arm and taking her off down the lane, her arm protectively around Lucy's shoulder, as if she were her best friend in the world.

Jennifer swallowed back and sat down on the pavement. She turned her cassette player on as loud as she could and sat there until much later, until her front door opened and Mr. Cottis and Mr. Smith came out, both laughing at some joke.

Mr. Cottis raised his hand to wave at her, but she didn't wave back.

SIXTEEN

LUCY forgave her.

It was something Jennifer could hardly understand. How vile she had been. What horrible things she had said. On the way to school the following morning, Jennifer ran up behind and put her arm around her.

"I'm really, really sorry. I was in a bad mood and I never meant that about your mum. Course your mum's coming home. Next week. I heard Mrs. Livingstone say it!"

"Okay," Lucy said.

"You're my friend? Really?" she said, giving Lucy a hug.

"Yes, of course."

Lucy was walking with a spring in her step, Michelle on one side and Jennifer on the other. She didn't seem to hold a grudge. She was like a puppy dog, bouncing along the lane, an invisible tail wagging behind her.

Unlike Michelle, who was grumpy and round-shouldered all the way down to the main road. "You could have got me in a lot of trouble with my mum!" she hissed, and only cheered up when they got to school and Lucy ran off to her classroom. Jennifer slipped her arm through hers and said, "Hey, Ginger, you're still my best friend, aren't you?"

At lunchtime, a few days later, they sat in the corner of the library flicking through magazines.

"Look at this, JJ," Michelle said, in a loud voice.

Michelle liked the other kids to hear them use their nicknames. It wasn't enough to just use them when they were alone. Michelle wanted everyone to know. Even though Jennifer sometimes felt a bit silly calling her friend Ginger, as though she were some kind of pet. Michelle loved it, though, and seemed to fiddle with her hair whenever she heard the name, pulling her long curls out or sweeping a great clump of it back off her face. Jennifer's own name, JJ, was less pleasing, just a couple of initials that didn't really mean anything. She looked at the magazine. Michelle was pointing at a picture of a pop singer that they both liked. She'd seen it a dozen times and had one like it on her bedroom wall.

"And here, look, there's that nail polish that I'm going to get!"

Jennifer didn't answer. She was bored with the magazines and fed up with sitting inside every lunchtime. She looked out at the playground. Some of the kids from her class were playing rounders, and she had a desire to be out there, running round, feeling the fresh air on her face. But she and Michelle didn't do those things now. They were too babyish. She noticed the younger kids and, in the middle of them, Lucy.

"Since Lucy's been staying with you, she doesn't hang around us at school so much."

Michelle nodded, opening a new magazine to the back page and working her way forward.

"It's like she doesn't need to be with us now. She's got her own friends."

"She's not staying with me permanently!"

"I know *that*. I'm just saying."

They were quiet for a minute.

"Is your mum coming to the picnic on Sunday?" Michelle said.

The picnic was to be up at the reservoir. It was Lucy's birthday treat and Mrs. Livingstone had invited Lucy's brothers and Jennifer's mum.

"I think so," she answered.

Jennifer wasn't sure if her mum was going to go to the picnic. She'd asked the previous night.

"I'm really busy this week, and on Sunday morning Mr. Cottis has got me a session."

"On a Sunday?" Jennifer had said flatly.

Mr. Cottis seemed to be everywhere. Either he was visiting her house or telephoning or her mum was talking about him. A horrible thing occurred to her. Was Mr. Cottis her mum's *boyfriend*? Jennifer didn't like to think about it.

"Amateur photographers. It's good money. I don't like to turn it down, love."

"But it's not all day?"

"No, maybe I could make it back. What time is the picnic?"

"About three o'clock. If it's dry."

"I should get back by then. If I don't, you can explain, can't you?"

Jennifer nodded. She could explain if she had to.

"Tell you what, I'll give you some cash to buy Lucy a nice present. How about that?"

There was plenty of cash, Jennifer knew that. It should have made her feel good. They could pay the rent, buy the groceries, have money for clothes and holidays. She just didn't feel relaxed about it. It was all in a box in her mum's wardrobe. Sometimes she went in there and took it out and looked at the notes lying untidily inside. It gave her an uneasy feeling, as though it didn't really belong to them, as if her mum had robbed a bank or something. When she put the box away in her mum's wardrobe, she covered it with sweaters and shoes.

On Sunday the weather was dry, so they joined in the lane at the back of the houses to walk up to the reservoir. There was a train of people, everyone carrying something, Mrs. Livingstone shouting instructions. Lucy was up at the front, saying, "This way, this way!" in her scratchy voice.

Mr. Livingstone, who kept asking everyone to call him Frank, laid the blankets on a flat area of grass that sloped down to the edge of the lake. Mrs. Livingstone unpacked the food, plastic boxes of sandwiches and bags of chips. She had even baked a cake and brought candles. On it were the words HAPPY BIRTHDAY, LUCY.

"Perhaps Carol will get here later," Mrs. Livingstone said.

Jennifer nodded but knew that her mum wouldn't come. Mr. Cottis had picked her up in his van much later than she'd expected. She'd been annoyed when he finally came, whispering loudly to him in the hallway, her words too muffled to hear but her voice forced out, like a hissing kettle. Jennifer had come out of her bedroom to say good-bye but the front door had slammed shut and she'd been left alone in the house, the sound of Mr. Cottis's van driving off up the lane.

She hadn't really expected her to come. She knew her mum wouldn't sit on a blanket and chat to Mr. and Mrs. Livingstone. She couldn't imagine her eating sandwiches and singing "Happy Birthday." It was a picture that just wouldn't form in her head. It was as unlikely as her mum putting an apron on and making a cake with the words HAPPY BIRTHDAY, LUCY on it.

Lucy had a new dress. She looked clean, her skin pink and shiny, her thin hair pulled up into a ponytail. She told them about the card she got from her mum. She was coming home soon, she said. Jennifer was enthusiastic about it, nodding her head and saying, "That's good!" Trying to make up for the awful things she'd said a few days before. Lucy's brothers were wearing their usual: oversized dark-green jackets and heavy boots. Stevie's trousers had a camouflage pattern but Joe's were plain green. Lucy was thrilled with everything and kept getting up to walk around the blanket and sit in a different place. The brothers looked uncomfortable, as though they'd rather not be there. Whenever Stevie was asked if he wanted anything, he grunted, nodding or shaking his head. Joe was more polite, saying, "No thank you, Mrs. Livingstone" or "Yes please, Mrs. Livingstone."

Michelle hadn't dressed up. She was wearing the same clothes as she'd had on the day before, as if she couldn't be bothered. Jennifer knew it was deliberate. Michelle loved dressing up, but she wasn't going to do it for Lucy.

They ate and drank and Mrs. Livingstone lit the candles and they all sang "Happy Birthday" to Lucy. After the rubbish was tidied away, Michelle's dad stood up and started to flex his legs.

"Anyone fancy a walk?" he asked.

"No thank you, Mr. Livingstone," Joe said, buttoning his army jacket up to the neck, as though it were deep winter.

"Do call me Frank," Mr. Livingstone said.

Mrs. Livingstone got up.

"Come on, you three, come for a walk!"

Michelle shook her head, but Lucy stood up and walked toward her. Michelle looked directly at Jennifer and rolled her eyes. Jennifer was thrown. She didn't mind going for a walk, but she didn't want to upset her friend.

"Oh, you lazy pair!" Mrs. Livingstone said, striding off with Lucy at her side, her husband up ahead.

They watched as the three of them walked away. Jennifer wanted to make a joke, but Michelle's face seemed to harden as she kept her eyes on her mum and dad and Lucy, looking every bit a family. The brothers were mumbling together at the other end of the blanket. Stevie lay back suddenly, his head on the ground, his big boots pointing up to the sky. Joe laughed for no reason, as though someone had just told him a joke.

"What are you laughing at?" Michelle demanded.

He didn't answer. He just laughed and nodded his head, as though someone had just said something that he agreed with. Stevie raised himself up on his elbows and looked at the girls. Beside his brother, his head looked small and bony, his eyes narrow, like slits.

"Don't say nothing to him," he said.

"Why? Why shouldn't I?"

Michelle knelt on the blanket, her shoulders squared, ready for an argument. In the distance, her parents had become tiny figures. Jennifer wished she'd gone for a walk with them. She didn't like the Bussell brothers. There was something *dangerous* about them.

"Don't . . . ," she said. "Don't let's argue."

"Don't let's argue," Stevie said, repeating her words. He gave her a childish grin, showing a mouthful of crooked teeth.

"He's not very bright, is he? Your brother?" Michelle said.

Jennifer's shoulders sank. Why couldn't Michelle just leave it?

"You shut your mouth," Stevie said, without moving a muscle. "Or I'll come over and shut it for you!"

"I'll tell my mum!"

"I'll tell my mum," Stevie mimicked Michelle's voice.

"Stop it!" Jennifer said, louder than she meant to.

Stevie's face turned toward her. He was no longer angry. There was a flicker of something behind his eyes, like a light going on in a distant room of a big house.

"How's your mum?" he said, his lips turning up at the corners.

"She's . . . she's all right."

Jennifer hated his expression. Hated the way his body lay in front of her, his legs open, his camouflage trousers making him look like an oversized action figure.

"Her mum's a model!" Michelle said.

Why did she have to say that? Jennifer wished she

would keep quiet. It was her business and her mum's. She didn't go round to everyone saying that Michelle's mum was a secretary.

"A model? Is that what she calls it?"

"A model," Joe repeated his brother's words.

"What do you mean?" Michelle said. "She *is* a model. I've seen her pictures. She's been a model for years, hasn't she, Jennifer? She's even had her face in magazines."

Jennifer nodded halfheartedly. She'd shown Michelle her mum's portfolio. Eight years' worth of photographs. Hundreds in the first few years, but less and less as time went on.

"Yeah, I'll bet she's had more than her face in magazines," Stevie said.

"A lot more," Joe said, giving a horrible laugh.

"What do you mean?" Jennifer said, even though she knew exactly what they meant.

"How come she has all these blokes visiting her every day? If she's just a *model*?"

Jennifer was puzzled. Blokes visiting her? What did he mean?

"You mean Mr. Cottis? He's her agent. He's the photographer, see?"

"Is that what he calls it?"

She looked at Michelle, who seemed as bewildered as she was. Her mum probably did have visitors. Amateur photographers. She had to take the work. It was her way of getting back into modeling. Jennifer knew that. She looked with disdain at the two Bussell brothers. Not half a brain between them. Stevie, lying back, his hand resting lightly on his crotch. Joe looking at her, then back to his brother whose hand had begun to press against his camouflage trousers.

She stood up. She wasn't going to stay. In the distance, she could see Mr. and Mrs. Livingstone with Lucy in between them, a pretty picture, walking among the trees, the lake glittering beside them. She should have joined them. It might have been fun. But she was stuck on the blanket, like being marooned on a boat in the middle of the lake, and Michelle's voice was still droning in her ear. Why couldn't she just shut up?

"She's beautiful and she'll end up on the cover of a magazine. And she'll make a lot of money. Isn't that right, Jen?"

Jennifer couldn't speak. There was a sick feeling inside her. The cake and the sandwiches and the fizzy drink were gurgling in her stomach.

"Yeah. Some prostitutes do make good money."

Joe laughed again, a great bellow. Stevie just lay there, looking at her, his hand rubbing at his trousers. Jennifer turned and walked away. After a few steps she began to run. Behind her she heard Michelle's voice.

"Jen, don't go. I'll tell my mum and dad, I'll tell on them. Don't go. I'll get in trouble. Don't go off, my mum'll be worried!"

She didn't stop. She didn't turn back. She ran till her breath was ragged, leaving the lake and the woods behind her, out of the gates and into the lane and on toward the houses.

SEVENTEEN

SHE ran into the house through the back door and the first thing she saw was Mr. Cottis's suitcase on wheels parked in her hallway. It startled her for a second, sitting upright, its handle stiffly against the wall. She hadn't expected it to be there. She went to the bottom of the stairs and looked up. The stairwell was dark, as though it were night. All the doors on the upstairs landing were shut. There was only the faintest of sounds; mumbling voices, the scrape of a chair leg, the creak of the bed. Her mum was in and she'd brought him with her.

She felt exhausted. She had no strength to walk up the stairs, to push her mum's room door open and check that the camera was there as well as the big lights and Mr. Cottis with his roll of film.

Because her mum was not a prostitute. She was not. She was a model.

She turned away from the stairs and went into the living room. In the cupboard she pulled out her mum's portfolio: a big leather folder full of pictures. She lay it in the middle of the floor and opened it. The first few pictures dated from before she was born. Her mum (just *Carol* then, *16-year-old from Ipswich*), in shorts and T-shirt on a beach, the sea crashing into the shore behind her, her hair blowing wildly, the white teeth against her perfectly lip-sticked mouth. How beautiful she was.

After she was born it was all professional shots. Carol Jones in an evening dress, a feathery boa around her neck; in a city suit, a pair of black-rimmed glasses making her look serious, every bit the businesswoman; in jeans and a checked blouse, like a cowgirl, her hair in bunches at the side of her face. Dozens of catalog photos: her mum mod-eling dresses, casual clothes, nightwear, sportswear. She stopped abruptly at a picture of her mum in a pink ski suit. The background was a view of a snow-covered mountain and a ski lift. It wasn't real, she knew that; her mum had never been skiing. She closed her eyes for a moment and sat there, still as a statue, a memory coming back to her, like a bird in the distance, coming closer and closer. And then she saw what it was. Macy in her ski outfit. Her lovely Macy, *International Catwalk Model.* Now she was in a cardboard box upstairs. Michelle said it looked like a coffin. The thought of it gave her a feeling of great heavi-ness, as if it were her fault that Macy was dead, when it wasn't her fault at all.

She looked back to the portfolio. Even though there

were no recent pictures of Carol Jones, she knew with absolute certainty that her mum was a model. Not a prostitute. A model.

Out in the hallway was the suitcase, neat, its edges square. Would Mr. Cottis have photos of her mum? Recent ones? He was her agent. He must have photos of her to show to people, so that she could get work. That was how it happened, she knew.

She left the portfolio open on the floor and went out to the suitcase. It had a zip all the way round. She squatted down and flicked the zipper back and forth for a second before pulling it along so that in moments the suitcase was open, its front hanging down, a flap of plastic drooling onto the hall floor.

Inside were brown paper envelopes. Lots of them. They had handwriting on them, single words: FIFTIES, SAILOR, SCHOOL, NAUGHTY. She picked up the one with SCHOOL on it and opened the envelope. Some photographs spilled out onto the hall floor, but it was too dark to see them so she scooped them up and took them into the living room, placing them down beside the portfolio.

She winced when she looked at them. Picture after picture. Her mum, lying on the bed, a school tie around her neck, books and paper strewn around her. The rest of her clothes gone, not there. She looked away with embarrassment. Then back again. She'd seen her mum with no clothes on. Skinny, with tiny breasts, the rose tattoo on her shoulder. She'd watched her getting out of the bath, running across the landing, looking at herself in the mirror. She'd seen her mum naked. But never like this. Never like this.

A knocking sound made her jump. Someone was at the front door.

She stood up quickly, stuffing the photographs back into the brown envelope, her throat gripped by a feeling of guilt, as if she were a burglar in her own house. In the hall she saw a silhouette of a head and shoulders at the door. She knelt down and with shaking hands she pushed the envelope back into the suitcase and pulled the zip round. From upstairs she heard a door opening and her mum's voice. She stood upright, like a sentry, beside the suitcase, as though she were guarding it, keeping it safe.

She knew the silhouette. It was Mrs. Livingstone. Her hair flicking out at the back of her neck, her head held high as though she was constantly looking for something that was on a top shelf.

Footsteps sounded on the stairs.

"Just a minute!"

She heard her mum's voice. A moment later, she was there on the stair looking sideways at her, doing her dressing gown up, her hair sticking up at the back as though she'd been lying down. How different she looked from the photographs.

"What's the matter?" she said, stifling a yawn. "I thought you were at the picnic."

The knocking on the door got louder, sounding impatient, angry even.

"Carol? Are you in there? Carol?"

Her mum shuffled toward the door. From upstairs she could hear someone moving about, the bathroom door opening and shutting. She stepped back into the living room, out of the hall, out of sight, away from the suitcase with the wheels that held the terrible pictures.

She heard the front door open.

"Is Jennifer here? She just ran off . . ."

Mrs. Livingstone's voice was cracking. She sounded tearful.

"One minute she was there on the grass with the others and we went for a short walk. When we got back she was gone!"

"Don't upset yourself . . . She's here . . ."

Jennifer heard her mum's voice and footsteps as the two women walked down the hallway to the kitchen. She stood on the other side of the living-room door listening, only hearing snatches.

"I thought she'd got lost . . . Michelle said there was an argument . . . Those Bussell brothers . . . We looked for her . . . I didn't know what had happened."

Her mum's voice was louder.

"Don't be silly. She probably got fed up . . . She's a bit

like that. Look at the day I had to go up to the school because she'd run off . . . She's scatty. She doesn't think . . . I'll have a good talk with her."

The kitchen door closed and the voices were too muffled to hear. The sound of water running and cups chinking meant that her mum was making a cup of tea for Mrs. Livingstone. Then she heard footsteps on the stairs, quick and precise, so light it might have been a child running down. She opened the door and saw Mr. Cottis bending over to put something in his suitcase. Over his shoulder was his bag. It suddenly swung forward and fell down his arm so that he seemed to lurch forward and stumble, trying to pick it up and turn the suitcase round at the same time.

"Silly me," he whispered.

She just stared at him. His bald head looked funny, like a baby's. He didn't have his glasses for once, so she looked at his eyes, watery, like colored glass.

Then he was gone, the front door closing without a sound, as if he knew how to get in and out of somewhere without being heard. Like a burglar. As if he had come into the house and stolen something from them.

Later, when Mrs. Livingstone had gone, her mum came into the living room.

"Doesn't the woman go on?" her mum said, flopping down on the settee beside her.

She didn't know what to say. Was she in trouble for running off from the reservoir?

"I'm supposed to tell you off, love. You mustn't run off by yourself and all that stuff. Trouble with these people around here is that they mollycoddle their kids. You can take care of yourself, can't you?"

"I thought you were coming to Lucy's picnic."

"I was. I got held up. When I got back I had a headache. You know what I'm like!"

Jennifer didn't answer. It was just another lie. She picked up the TV remote and clicked it on.

She got a phone call from Michelle. She was surprised. Michelle usually came over if she had something to say.

"I'm not allowed out," she said. "My mum's in a mood about the picnic."

"Sorry," she said woodenly.

"It's not your fault. It's those brothers. Stevie's really dirty and Joe's a dimwit! Even Lucy agrees with me."

Jennifer's eyebrows rose. She imagined Lucy sitting next to Michelle. She would agree with anything to get on Michelle's good side.

"I've thought of a way we can get back at them."

"Yeah?" she said, not really interested.

"Lucy knows where their den is. You know the one they've made up at the reservoir?"

"Yeah, so?" she said.

"Because it's half term, my mum's taking the both of them to see their mum in hospital tomorrow morning. So when they're gone we can go up there."

Jennifer waited to see what else Michelle had to say. "What do you think?"

"We're not allowed to go up there on our own."

The words came out before she realized what she was saying. Michelle wasn't allowed up at the reservoir, but *she* could go whenever she wanted. Her mum wouldn't lose any sleep over it.

"No one will know. My mum'll be out for hours. We can go up there and wreck their den. They'll never know it was us."

"Lucy said this?"

"Well, not exactly. She's going to show us the den. She doesn't know we're going to wreck it!"

"Mmm . . ."

Jennifer sighed. It didn't sound like much of a plan. She didn't like the Bussell brothers, but, honestly, she wasn't about to play war games with them. It was too silly for words.

"I've got to go. Mum's coming upstairs. Me and Lucy'll come and call for you as soon as she goes in the morning."

Her mum came into her bedroom as she was getting into bed. She was hugging a plastic shopping bag to her chest.

Jennifer stopped what she was doing and waited. Her mum hardly ever came into her room.

"Jenny, love, I've got a surprise for you."

She sat down on the edge of the bed and Jennifer sat up, her back against the headboard. Her mum looked hesitant and gave a couple of quick smiles as though she were trying to work out what to say.

"Mr. Cottis thinks it would be a good idea to take some mother-and-daughter photographs. For our family album. He thinks you look like me."

Jennifer frowned. She didn't like the mention of Mr. Cottis. She didn't like to think about him talking about her. In any case, no one had ever said she looked like her mum.

"He wants to take some photographs of us . . . you . . . the two of us together . . ."

"Why?" she asked.

Her mum answered, her words rapid, some running into each other. *A family portrait . . . Some pics of you . . . in school uniform . . . for a magazine feature he's working on . . . Won't have to do anything . . . Stand there . . . smile when he says . . . play around a bit . . . It won't take long . . .*

She wasn't really listening, though. She had a sick feeling in her stomach, remembering the photos in the suitcase. Her mum, the model, smiling and laughing, wearing nothing but a school tie round her neck. He'd taken the pictures in her room and brought pretend things with

202

him: books, rulers, a globe. He had been playing make-believe with her mum. The idea of grown-ups playing a child's game made her feel clammy and uncomfortable, and she pushed her duvet back so that her thin legs were there in front of her like straight lines down the bed.

Her mum was still talking. *He'll pay you some money . . . And he might ask you to dress up for a bit . . . Just play-acting . . . You don't have to do anything you don't want to . . . Thing is it'll have to be a secret . . . Too young for modeling . . . Our business, no one else's . . .*

She didn't like Mr. Cottis, his head was too shiny and his eyes were like steamed glass. He took pictures of other people and kept them himself in brown envelopes. It was a sort of theft. She didn't want him to steal her picture.

"I haven't got a school uniform," she lied, interrupting her mum.

"Yes. Mr. Cottis has brought one, here. You can wear it for the photos."

A white blouse and tie fell out of the shopping bag. A vest and dark blue knickers. A pleated skirt and long white socks. She held them all up, one by one. The tie had stripes across it. It was the same type that her mum had worn in the photos.

"I don't want to," she said abruptly.

Her mum looked surprised, as though it were the last thing she expected to hear.

"But I thought you'd like this. It could be your first

modeling job. You could grow up like me. A model. You could get your face on the front of a magazine!"

"I don't want to be a model," she said, pushing the clothes away with one hand so that they lay on the bed without touching her.

Her mum took a deep breath.

"Look, Jen, I need you to do this. Mr. Cottis is a very important man and if I don't . . . if you don't do this photo session, he might drop me. There're loads more models who would like to work with him. It'll just take an hour. No more. I'll be there all the time."

She stared at her mum, catching her eye, trying to hold the look, to keep her there on the bed, to tell her the truth of what she'd seen. But her mum glanced down and began to fuss with the school clothes.

"He's coming at twelve tomorrow. I want you to do this and I'll be there with you. Twelve o'clock. Otherwise I might not have a job, and you know what that means."

Her mum always spoke so softly, her words like velvet. Underneath though, the meaning was there, like small hard pebbles. She might lose her job; they would have no money; Jennifer might end up back at Gran's or, even worse, in care.

"Twelve o'clock. It'll be all right. You'll see. It'll be a laugh. Night, love."

When the door shut and her mum's footsteps faded, she got up and went across to her wardrobe. At the bottom was a shoebox and inside was Macy. She pulled the old doll out and took it back to her bed. Macy was grubby, her clothes tatty, some of her hair missing where Jennifer had combed it once too often. It didn't matter, though. She got into bed and laid Macy down beside her.

EIGHTEEN

MICHELLE started to annoy her as soon as they'd been walking for about five minutes. It was an uncomfortable day, chilly and hot at the same time. There was a sharp wind that seemed to be running all over the place, hitting them in the face, pushing them to one side, forcing them onward, along the lane toward the reservoir. There were clouds dashing across the sky, but every now and then the sun came out and for a moment it was blindingly hot.

"I'm boiling," Michelle complained. "Lucy, you can be my slave today, so you must carry my sweater."

She untied it from her waist and draped it around Lucy's shoulders. Lucy, looking sleepy even though it was past ten, pulled the sleeves into a loose knot at her throat. She smiled up at Jennifer, shielding off the glare of the sun by holding her hand up to her forehead. Then Michelle changed her mind.

"I'm cold, slave," she said, smirking at Jennifer. "Give me my sweater back."

Lucy took the sweater off.

"Here you are," she said.

"Here you are, what?" Michelle said.

"Mistress," Lucy said.

"Don't be stupid!" Jennifer said, a flash of annoyance coming out of nowhere. She should be used to Michelle's silly little ways.

"It's all right. We play this game all the time," Michelle said. "Don't we, Luce?"

Lucy nodded. Jennifer noticed that she was wearing her party dress again on top of grubby sneakers, her legs bare. Even though she had a sweater tied round her waist she looked cold, with goose bumps on her arms. It didn't seem to worry her, though. Michelle had dressed up. Freshly washed jeans and a T-shirt with the word BABE across it. Her sweater was newish as well, deep pink with a zip up the front.

Jennifer hardly noticed what clothes she'd put on while dressing. The shopping bag with the other clothes, the school uniform, sat in the corner of her room as far away from her bed as was possible. She'd shoved it there, out of her line of sight, even though her eyes had been drawn back to it from time to time. Even when the room was dark, when her mum had called out "Night, love," she looked across and saw its shape, crumpled and ugly.

When she woke up, her room was gray, the daylight forcing its way through her curtains. She got up and walked out into the hallway to look into her mum's room. Pushing the door open, she saw her lying half in and half out of the covers, one foot sticking up. Jennifer tiptoed across to the bed and pulled the duvet straight, causing her mum to move, her head shifting on the pillow. Then she was still. Turning to go out, Jennifer noticed the globe sitting on top of her mum's chest of drawers. She stood close and studied it for a moment. How had Mr. Cottis brought it to the house? It looked too big to fit in his suitcase or his bag. She put her hand up and touched the ball with her fingers, watching as it spun gently, the countries of the world floating by her. Why had he wanted it?

"Jen?"

Her mum's voice was husky from sleep.

"Do you want a cup of tea?" Jennifer said, walking back to the side of the bed.

Her mum shook her head, her hair rubbing against the pillow. Jennifer turned to go but her mum spoke again, her voice crackly with tiredness.

"Don't forget the photos this morning. Have a bath. So that you look your best!"

Jennifer didn't answer. She walked out of the room with feet of lead.

In the lane she let the others lead the way. She'd come along even though she hadn't really wanted to go to the reservoir, and wasn't interested about seeing the Bussell brothers' den. It was something to do, a journey to make, a place to go until she had to go back and face Mr. Cottis at twelve o'clock. Up ahead she could see the gate of the reservoir. Lucy was talking about her favorite subject. The wild cats. Michelle was full of it.

"Be careful you don't get too close to them," she said, in a loud voice.

Lucy mumbled something Jennifer couldn't quite hear.

"Because they hate people. They blame people for flooding the land and drowning them. Don't look straight at them because they might scratch your eyes out."

"Don't say that!" Jennifer said.

Michelle was irritating her. Pretending to know everything. Lording it over Lucy. Dressing up in new clothes when she couldn't be bothered to dress up for Lucy's party.

"Why not? It's true."

"It is true. That's why Stevie hunts them."

Lucy was wide-eyed, her expression deadly serious. Honestly. It was *cats* they were talking about, not tigers! Jennifer huffed and passed them, in through the gate of the reservoir, along the winding path, stepping out in front of the two girls, putting some distance between them.

She looked across the lake to the spot where they'd had the picnic the day before. She remembered Stevie Bussell, lying back on the blanket, his boots looking as though they were too big for him, touching his trousers with his hand in a disgusting way, his mean eyes looking at her, calling her mum names. Who would take his word for anything? Him and his dressing-up clothes, his den in the woods, his guns for shooting the wild cats. How could he call her mum a *prostitute*? Where had he got the idea from?

"JJ, don't go so fast," Michelle said, running up behind her.

Lucy came last, her face flushed, her eyes looking distant, as though she were thinking of something else, the cats, perhaps. For an instant Jennifer saw her brother's face there, just an expression, nothing more.

"Come on, slave, keep up!" Michelle said.

They walked along for a while, zigzagging the path, keeping to the edge of the lake, dipping in and out of thickets. They went in and out of small woods, their trees young, the bark silky and the branches thin like ladies' arms. Lucy turned round from time to time, and Michelle gave her another order, her voice friendly. It was only a game. Just pretend. Michelle wasn't really ordering Lucy around. It was just some fun. They passed a couple of people with dogs on their way round. It was a Monday morning but nobody looked at them strangely. Three girls walking round the reservoir. It was the school holidays, after all. In town the classrooms were still and the only thing moving in the playground was the breeze, picking up candy wrappers and throwing them down again.

There were some boats on the lake, cutting through the water, their sails billowing one minute and taut the next. When the sun came out, the water sparkled and the boats seemed to skate across the surface. When it clouded over they slowed down, bobbing up and down on the muddy ripples.

The path split. One section led around the lake and the other forked off up an incline away from the water. There was a sign a couple of meters along: WOODLAND PARK RECONSTRUCTION. PUBLIC ACCESS PROHIBITED.

"This way," Lucy said, ignoring the sign.

Jennifer paused for a moment. They weren't supposed to go. They would get in trouble if anyone saw them. She looked at her watch. It was almost eleven. They'd been out for an hour, walking round the lake for almost that long. If they carried on she wouldn't have time to get back for Mr. Cottis.

"Come on," Michelle said, linking her arm, pulling her onward.

And then it occurred to her. Why not stay out? Why not stay out all day? That way she wouldn't have to see Mr. Cottis or dress up in a silly uniform to have her photographs taken. She started to walk, her body feeling looser, lighter even. It was simple. Why hadn't she thought of it up to that moment? *She didn't have to go back and have her photo taken.*

They left the lake behind, went up the path, and into another wood. The trees there were bigger, older, more dense, as though they'd been there much longer than the lake. On either side of the path the branches leaned toward each other, touching above their heads, blocking out a lot of the sky. It made Jennifer feel secluded, as if she were in a different world. She felt a lightness in her step. Maybe, if she didn't go home until late, Mr. Cottis wouldn't want the photographs at all.

"It's in there," Lucy said, stopping, pointing to a gap in the trees that led downward toward the edge of the lake.

The three of them walked off the path and into the trees, stepping high to avoid the undergrowth, nettles, dry cracking twigs, and thorny bushes. The light was dull, and underfoot it became damp, their feet sinking into muddy patches.

"Oh no," Michelle said, holding up one of her white sneakers coated with mud.

"We're nearly there," Lucy said.

They emerged from the trees onto a small rocky ledge that dropped sharply into deep water.

"Where are we?" Jennifer asked.

Instead of reaching the shore as she'd expected, the lake was off to the side, distant, like a picture postcard, boats dotted here and there. In front of them, the water looked different, still and dense, almost black in color. It was the width of a river, the opposite bank close enough to hit with a stone.

"I don't remember this bit," Michelle said, still holding her foot up to look at her muddy sneaker.

"Stevie found it. Nobody comes here."

"Where's the den?" Jennifer said, looking around, half expecting a small wooden building or a cave.

"Here," Lucy said, climbing over some rocks and beckoning for them to follow. "Careful, the rocks are slippery and some of them are loose."

Behind a couple of big boulders was a pile of branches, their leaves withered, dry, and crackly. Lucy started to move them one by one, and Jennifer was struck with admiration. Had the Bussell brothers built an *underground* den?

"Here," Lucy said, becoming breathless, moving the branches behind her, passing them to Jennifer and Michelle.

When she got to the last couple, she sat back. Beneath the wood and leaves they could see a tin box, a large tin box.

"Where's the den?" Michelle said.

"This is it."

Lucy pulled the remaining branches off and put them behind her. The hole was about sixty centimeters deep. The tin box sat snugly in it, its corners scuffed. It must have been about thirty centimeters wide and sixty centimeters long. Jennifer couldn't quite see, but it looked deep, as though it might hold a fair bit.

"That's not a den!" Michelle said disdainfully.

"Wait till you see what they keep here," Lucy said, on

her knees by then, grabbing the handle on the side of the box with both hands and pulling hard to move it. Jennifer got to the other side and pushed, her legs slipping for a moment, and one of the loose rocks skidding away and dropping into the water.

"It's a box. It's not a den! A den is a place to sleep, to eat, not a stupid box."

Jennifer and Lucy struggled until the tin box was out of the ground. It sat crookedly between them, with a dent in the lid that Jennifer hadn't noticed at first. Lucy, breathless, flung it open. Inside it was packed: canteens for holding water, tins of baked beans and frankfurters, two sleeping bags rolled up on top of a skein of rope. There was an assortment of tools, screwdrivers, a hammer, a Stanley knife, even a baseball bat. Bit by bit they unpacked it, throwing things behind them, to the side. Michelle was sitting on a rock, rubbing at her filthy sneaker. When they came to the bottom, there was a small zip-up pouch.

"Where's the gun?" Jennifer said.

"They don't leave that here. It's too dangerous!"

"If it really exists," Michelle said sarcastically.

Jennifer sat back, disappointed. Even though she hadn't been keen to come, she had half expected to find something interesting.

"Stevie does have a gun!"

Jennifer picked up the pouch. She unzipped it and turned it upside down so that the contents spilled out onto the gravelly ground. There was some money, mostly coins, and a couple of cigarette lighters. Inside, something was stuck, so she put her fingers in and pulled out a couple of photographs. They were upside down when she first saw them and it took her a moment to register what was there. A face that she knew. Two shots of her mum, lying back on a sofa of some sort, naked except for a teddy bear that she was holding up to her cheek. Her mum. Naked. A child's toy rubbing against her skin. It didn't seem right. It didn't look nice. She held them in her hand for what seemed like a long time, her fingers trembling, her mind blank, like an empty room. Lucy, turning her head to see, made a small sound in her throat. It sounded like an *"Oh."*

"What's that?" Michelle said, in a bored voice.

"Where did your brother get this?" Jennifer said in a whisper.

"I don't know," Lucy answered, looking away, her voice barely making a sound.

She did know. Jennifer could see it in her face. *She knew!* She knew about her mum and the photos and the school uniform and the disgusting Mr. Cottis.

"Is this why your brother said that my mum was a prostitute?" she demanded, her voice louder.

Michelle stopped scraping at her muddy sneaker.

"I don't know why he said that," Lucy said, moving back a little, away from the tin box and the army stuff that was scattered across the rocks.

She was lying.

"Did you take these photos? Did you steal them from my house?"

"No, no."

"You did! You took them and gave them to your stupid brothers. That's why they said that my mum was a prostitute. She's not. She's a model. These are . . ."

Lucy shrugged her shoulders, the look of concern gone and replaced by some other expression. Disbelief, ridicule. For a second Jennifer saw that look again. Her brother's face, his lazy, mocking expression. It was there around Lucy's lips, the corners of her eyes. It flickered on and off for a second and then it was gone and there was just Lucy's little mouse face staring back at her.

"What pictures?" Michelle said, taking the photos from Jennifer's hand. "Oh my . . ."

"You took them from my house! You had no right!"

Lucy stood up, stumbling a little over the rough stones.

"I never took them. I didn't," she squeaked, taking a step backward, away from Jennifer.

"You must have! How else could your brother have got hold of it? How else?"

"Uncle Kenny gave it to him!"

"Uncle Kenny? Kenny? Who's Kenny?"

"Kenny Cottis. My uncle Kenny."

Jennifer stopped. She was breathing shallowly, as if she'd just run a great distance. Lucy's *Uncle Kenny*?

"That photographer's your uncle?" Michelle said, still looking at the pictures.

"He's not a photographer. He takes photos, but that's not his job."

"You haven't got an uncle. My mum said you had no relatives. That's why you have to stay at our house."

"He's not really my uncle. He's my mum's friend, but I always call him . . . uncle . . ."

Lucy had stepped backward, near to the edge of the rocks.

"Mr. Cottis is . . . your mum's friend?"

Jennifer couldn't believe it. It couldn't be true. Mr. Cottis was a proper photographer. He had equipment, cameras, and lights. He was her mum's agent. He was even going to take some photographs of her. That very day. At twelve o'clock. The dressing-up clothes were in the shopping bag. All she had to do was put them on and Mr. Cottis would take some photos of her.

"Some uncle!" Michelle said. "He's just a dirty old man. He likes taking pictures of people with no clothes on. That's disgusting."

Jennifer stepped toward Lucy. She looked straight into her face. Mr. Cottis had probably been at her house, showing off his photographs to Stevie and Joe. Maybe he'd also been boasting about the photographs he was going to take of her.

"I never took the photos, honest!" Lucy said, edging away.

There was that expression again. Her brother Stevie, leering, drooling, rubbing himself while he looked at her mum. It wasn't Lucy anymore, just her despicable brother. Jennifer raised both hands up to push him away, to get him out of her sight. She stepped forward, giving a rough, hard shove until Lucy stumbled back away from her and toppled off the rocky ledge into the water.

"Oh no!" Michelle shouted.

She stood on the edge of the rocks and stared as Lucy bobbed up out of the water. The little girl made a gasping sound then sank down again, disappearing underneath the surface. Jennifer's face was rigid, her skin like concrete, her mouth unable to move.

"What have you done?"

Michelle was gripping Jennifer's arm fiercely. She turned to look at her best friend. Her mouth was hanging open in some kind of shock, but her eyes were glittering with excitement.

NINETEEN

LUCY surfaced. Her arms rose out of the water, and she seemed to thrash around for a moment before going underneath again.

"Her clothes are too heavy," Michelle said. "They're dragging her down."

But she resurfaced and began to splash out in some kind of doggy paddle, her mouth open, spluttering, spitting water out, her eyes rounded in astonishment. Jennifer, frozen to the spot, watched for seconds while Lucy made choking, gasping sounds. The water around her was calm and soupy, hardly moving at all. Lucy thrust her arms out toward the shore, gulping down mouthfuls, words gargling in her throat. Jennifer felt a swooning sensation, as though she was about to faint. She turned to Michelle who was standing watching with her arms crossed. *Why didn't someone do something?*

She swung round and scanned the stuff strewn across rocks. Holding down a feeling of dizziness, she strode across and picked up the skein of rope that they had tossed out of the tin box moments before. She pulled and pulled at it until it uncurled and tumbled loosely over her hands.

"Take this," she said sharply.

Michelle looked at her and gave a half shrug. She took the end of the rope in a resigned way; as if it were no use. Jennifer stepped to the edge of the rock and shouted as loud as she could, her voice cracking.

"Lucy, grab hold of the rope. LUCY, get the rope, grab the rope."

She tossed it into the water, close to the struggling girl. Lucy saw it and threw out one of her arms, continuing to paddle frantically with the other. It was just beyond her reach. Jennifer hauled it back. She took the end of it in her hand and lifted it above her head, throwing it with every ounce of strength she had. It flew past Lucy and flopped in the water. The little girl hadn't seen it and was looking tired, her arms moving more slowly, the water oozing up to her chin, her eyes looking glassy and distant.

"BEHIND YOU!" Jennifer shouted. "The rope is BE-HIND you."

"Lucy! Look behind you!"

She heard Michelle's voice joining in, and together they screamed at Lucy until she seemed to perk up and turn her head, reaching out wildly for the rope, grabbing it with one hand, and then a couple of seconds later with the other. Jennifer felt light-headed with relief.

"She's got it," Michelle said.

They pulled the rope together, as if in a tug of war. There was only a small girl at the other end but she was a deadweight, her clothes saturated. Lucy, her hands clenching the rope, had a look of fright on her face, as if she'd just seen a ghost. As moments went by her head seemed to loll backward.

"She's too heavy," Michelle said.

"Walk backward," Jennifer shouted. "Backward, come on . . ."

Michelle took a step back, straining on the rope, and Jennifer did the same.

"Again!" Jennifer shouted. "AGAIN!"

Lucy came closer to the edge.

"I'm letting go!" Jennifer said, throwing the words across her shoulder toward Michelle.

In a second she was by the rocky edge, grabbing Lucy's arms. She plunged her own feet in the water so that she could lean forward to pull the soaking-wet girl up.

"Let go of the rope. Come and help me," she grunted.

The rope went slack, and then Michelle was kneeling at her side, bending down, helping to pull Lucy out. She came up slowly, as if the water were reluctant to let her go. With a final heave the three of them fell back onto the rocks; Lucy, cold and wet, lying half across Jennifer's legs. After a moment, Michelle jumped up and was wiping herself down.

"I'm soaked!" she said crossly. "She's soaked. My mum'll kill me for this!"

Lucy struggled to her feet, the water dripping from her new dress.

"I want to go home!" she said, amid hiccuping sobs.

"You can't!" Michelle said. "My mum'll go mad! You'll have to dry off first!"

"She can dry off at home," Jennifer said, and was about to add *She can dry off in my house,* but then remembered that Mr. Cottis would be there expecting to take photographs.

"It's all right for you. I'm supposed to look after her!" Michelle said, grabbing Lucy's arm and pulling her along.

"I don't need anyone to look after me . . ." Lucy said, her voice disappearing at the end.

"Don't pull her like that, she might have hurt herself in the water!"

"Mind your own business. If you hadn't lost your temper, she wouldn't have been in the water at all, and I wouldn't be in trouble," Michelle said, raising her voice.

"I'm telling your mum," Lucy said, shaking off Michelle's hand.

"No, you won't. Otherwise you can go back to your own house!"

Lucy looked up sharply, her pale skin the color of a wax candle.

"Don't say that to her!" Jennifer said. *Hadn't Lucy had enough?*

"Why not? What's it got to do with you, anyhow? You're the one who called her Mouse. You're the one who said her brothers were morons. Me and her were friends before you came!"

As soon as the words came out, Jennifer looked around at Lucy. She looked pathetic, soaking wet, her hair flattened into her head. Without a word, Lucy turned and walked away into the trees and out of sight.

"Lucy, wait!" Jennifer shouted.

"Don't come all goody-goody! You threw her in the water!" Michelle said, pointing her finger at Jennifer. "What kind of friend are you?"

"I didn't mean . . ."

"You're mental, you are. Look at that time you hit Sonia with the recorder. Now Lucy. Someone like you ought to be locked away."

"Don't say that!" Jennifer said, her fingers stiffening with annoyance.

"I'm telling your mum about this," Michelle said, straightening her back.

"Don't you say anything to my mum!" Jennifer said, taking a step toward her.

"That reminds me. Your mum. *You* said she was a model. You didn't say she showed her tits off to everyone!"

The words were like a smack, and Jennifer reeled back.

"Gross!"

She hadn't known. Jennifer hadn't known. Not really, not until the day before when she'd looked into Mr. Cottis's suitcase on wheels.

"And Stevie Bussell's right. There are loads of men who visit your house. I heard my mum telling my dad last night at dinner."

Michelle's mum and dad *at dinner.* The picture of it infuriated her.

"My mum's a model," Jennifer said, her throat tight like a fist.

"Yes? And my dad's Father Christmas!"

Michelle turned and began to walk away. Jennifer watched her go for a second before realizing what was happening. Her friend. Her best friend hated her.

"Wait!"

Jennifer moved to follow but caught her foot on a rock. She stumbled forward, putting her hands out to break the fall. One hand hit the ground full on, the other skidded across the baseball bat that had rolled there earlier. Her chin hit the ground with a thud.

Michelle stopped abruptly and turned back. With a sigh, she walked across and held out her hand. Her face was full of pity and Jennifer couldn't bear it. She turned on her side and pulled herself into a sitting position. For some reason she found herself holding the baseball bat.

"Please yourself!" she heard Michelle's voice from behind. "To think I used to feel sorry for Lucy—now I feel more sorry for you."

Using the baseball bat as a prop, Jennifer got to her feet. Her chin was throbbing and the skin on her hand was stinging. None of it mattered, though. Here she was, a girl without any friends, with a mum at home who wanted her to pose for pictures. A mum who took money and was probably counting up the pink fifty-pound notes at that very moment for the pictures Mr. Cottis would take of her. How would he want her? Lying on a settee with a teddy bear?

"It's not *your* fault." Michelle's mouth was dripping with sarcasm, and Jennifer clutched the baseball bat as though it was a crutch that she needed to lean on. "After all," Michelle continued, "we can't choose our parents."

With that she swiveled away from her and began to walk off. Michelle had the right parents. Jennifer went after her.

"Don't bother following me!" Michelle said, without turning round. "You and me aren't friends anymore!"

She would have no friends. Just her mum and her. Alone together. Her mum who loved her enough to offer her to Mr. Cottis. She felt a sudden sense of loss, as if everything important was walking away. She raised her hand to stop it, to reach out and pull it back. *Be my friend,* she wanted to say, she might have even said it as she raised the baseball bat and swung it at the back of Michelle's head.

Everything froze for a second and she swung it again.

Stop, she wanted to say. *Don't leave me.* And Michelle didn't. She dropped like a stone on the ground before her.

Silence filled the air and Jennifer stood uncertainly, blinking back the tears, looking round at the trees and the water and the rocks. She saw the cat then, creeping out of the bushes, standing for a moment over by the empty tin box. A wild cat. Its bones shining through its thin coat, like a skeleton in the sunlight, raising a single paw and licking it with relish.

It was a witness. It had seen everything.

part three

ALICE TULLY

TWENTY

THE trip to Brighton didn't take long. Once they'd packed the car up and got through the afternoon traffic it was less than an hour's drive. Frankie's home was in the outskirts of Brighton and it took a few minutes for them to find the right street. They pulled up across the road from Frankie's parents' house and sat for a moment, the engine idling. On the back seat was Alice's holdall. Beside it was a smaller bag, and some boots in case Frankie wanted them to go walking.

"It'll do you good to have a break," Rosie said, talking above the music station that was playing. "You're thinking about it all too much. I told you we'd work something out, that it would be all right!"

"I know," Alice said, her thumbnail pushed against her front teeth.

"It's a good compromise," Rosie said.

"Yeah, of course."

Neither of them moved, and Alice looked across the road at Frankie's home. It was a big Victorian house with bay windows. On the front of the roof she could see the skylights. The loft where Frankie's room was. It was something she had been excited about. Now it hardly mattered.

"Do you want to go in?" Rosie said.

"Not really," Alice said.

"Why not? You've been looking forward to this!"

Rosie opened the driver's door and got out, brushing down her wrinkled dress and fixing her beads. Then she walked around the car and opened the passenger door and stood like a chauffeur waiting for Alice to get out.

"I haven't got to pull you out, have I?" she said, cheerfully.

Alice felt a moment's annoyance. Rosie was making a scene. People would see her standing there in the orange flowery dress that she said she had rescued from a thrift shop a week or so before. Neighbors might be looking out of their windows wondering who this big lady was, her skirts dripping on the pavement, her beads swaying from side to side as she walked. There might even be members of Frankie's family wondering what the sudden noise was, Rosie's laugh and her gentle attempts to dislodge Alice from the car.

Alice got out.

"Shush," she said sharply, "I don't want the whole world to know I've arrived!"

There was a flicker of hurt on Rosie's face, but she covered it up in a flash, leaning past Alice to get her things out of the back. The car door clicked shut and the two of them walked across the street toward Frankie's house. Before they got there the front door opened and a girl with glasses stood in front of them. She was tall, almost as tall as Alice. Her face was young, though, scrubbed and freckled.

"Hi! I'm Sophie! Don't believe a thing Frank says about me. You must be Alice!"

Alice faltered. She wasn't sure whether to hold her hand out or not. How was she supposed to greet the ten-year-old sister of her boyfriend? She didn't know. Rosie made up for her disarray by giving Sophie a hug.

"Frankie's only said good things about you," Rosie said.

"Yeah, I wish," Sophie said, a slow blush creeping up her cheeks. "Come in! My mum and dad are in the garden. Frankie's upstairs. Wait a sec. That sounds like him now."

Footsteps sounded from above, gaining in speed as Frankie appeared at the top of the stairs. In a flash he was there in front of her, grabbing her with both arms.

"Hi, Rosie," he said, burying his face in Alice's neck.

"Give the girl a chance, Frank!"

Alice saw Frankie's dad over his shoulder. Behind him was a woman in jeans and a loose shirt. She walked to within a few feet of them and stood waiting until Frankie let Alice go.

"I take it you're Alice? I'm Jan," she said. "You've met

Peter, my husband." Smiling, she held her hand out for Alice to shake. "And you must be Rosie," she said, turning to the side.

Rosie gave Jan a hearty handshake.

"Come into the garden. Sophie will make the tea, won't you, darling?"

Sophie nodded her head enthusiastically and Alice and Rosie followed Frankie and his parents through the house and out of the French doors into a large back garden. Frankie flopped down on a blanket on the grass and Alice joined him. The others sat in cane chairs, in the shade of a giant white umbrella. Frankie's parents were talking to Rosie about the journey, the traffic jams, the problems of living in a popular seaside town. Alice could hardly concentrate on their words because Frankie had slipped his fingers up the back of her T-shirt and was stroking her skin and playing with her bra strap. Through tight lips she told him to stop it but he ignored her, joining in with his parents' conversation from time to time.

After a while Sophie appeared at the French doors, holding a tray in her hands. On it were cups and saucers and a two-tier plate stacked with cakes. It looked heavy and Alice wondered if anyone would move to help her. No one did, and Sophie took each step carefully, her arms and shoulders tensing until she reached the table.

"There!" she said, pleased with herself.

"How lovely!" Rosie said, putting her fingers out to touch the two-tier plate. "I've always wanted one of these."

"It used to be my mother's," Jan said. "You don't see them in the shops these days. Now, Sophie. What have we got?"

"Right," Sophie said, straightening her glasses, "fairy cakes, scones and cream, and chocolate chip muffins."

"Did you make these?" Rosie said, her face beaming.

Sophie nodded proudly, took her glasses off, and cleaned them with the end of her T-shirt. Alice turned to Frankie. His face was breaking into a smile.

"What can I say? Sister of the year! She only does it to make me look bad!"

While the others were still sitting in the garden, Jan showed Alice upstairs to a pretty little bedroom next to Sophie's and told her how pleased she was that Frankie had found such a nice girlfriend. On the pillow there was a gift-wrapped package that Jan told her to open. Inside was an old-fashioned white cotton nightdress, with real lace around the sleeves and neck. Alice held it up against her, the hem touching her ankles.

"Frankie told us you were tiny so I bought the smallest size."

"Thanks so much," Alice said, embarrassed. She hadn't brought any gifts with her.

"It's nothing. We just want you to make yourself at home while you're here. And don't mind Sophie. She's been dying to meet you, and she'll probably drive you mad! You know what ten-year-olds are like!"

Just then the door opened and Sophie was there.

"Mum! I'm nearly eleven," she said, looking shyly at Alice.

Rosie left soon after, carrying a bunch of flowers picked from the garden and a handwritten recipe for chocolate chip muffins. Sophie had scribbled it out, drawing a row of muffins across the bottom of the page. Rosie seemed relaxed, more like her old self than she had been in days. Frankie's family had welcomed them with open arms. It made Alice feel a little overwhelmed. Standing by the car, as Rosie started the engine, she had an urge to get in beside her, to drive away, back to Croydon. There was something unnerving about being greeted so enthusiastically.

"And don't worry about anything. I'm seeing Sara Wright in a couple of days to finalize the arrangements for the interview. It's going to be all right. I'll ring you and let you know what she says."

Alice nodded. Rosie called the newspaper reporter *Sara Wright* now, in a formal way, as if she were a stranger, not someone who had lived close and become a sort of friend.

"Bye," Alice said, as Rosie's car drove off up the street.

There were footsteps behind her, and then Frankie's arms around her, hugging her to him.

"Come up and see my loft," he whispered, kissing the back of her neck.

She waited until Rosie's car turned right and then disappeared before turning round and returning Frankie's embrace. She stood on tiptoes and gave him a long kiss on the lips. She was lucky to have him, she knew that.

The loft had only been built a year or so before and still had a new smell. Frankie showed it off with the flourish of a real estate agent.

"You can see the sea from this skylight! And down here is a tiny window seat. Look, it opens. When I'm home, I read there and sometimes have a smoke."

He had his own shower room and built-in wardrobes.

"Look at this!" he said excitedly, pointing to a miniature fridge. "The minibar!"

She had to smile. He was so full of it, so pleased with himself.

"It's like my own flat," he said, pulling her by the arm over to his double bed. "And much better than that dump in Croydon."

She found herself half sitting, half lying on the bed, Frankie flat on his back. She braced herself, expecting him to start kissing her, to roll over on top of her. Sex with Frankie. It was something she had wanted right from when she first met him. The first kiss outside the Coffee Pot when he'd waited hours for her to finish her shift. She'd held on to him with her mouth and felt a surge of energy racing through her, making her skin tingle and breasts harden. That had been months before. She'd made him wait a long time, and he'd become impatient. What he had never understood was that it wasn't him she'd been trying to hold back but herself. Did she deserve that kind of pleasure? She didn't think so.

Frankie pulled her toward him so that she was lying across his chest. She could feel his heart thumping, his ribs digging into her face. Now she was ready. More than ready, a heavy ache spread across her chest when she thought about the two of them together. It wasn't that she deserved it *now*. It was just that since Sara Wright had come into her life, there was an urgency about everything she did. As if she had to fit a lot of things into a small amount of time.

He was stroking her short hair, his fingers like the teeth of a comb. She moved her hand and put it under his T-shirt, rubbing at the hairs on his chest, her knee moving up to lie across his legs. He let out a groan, and she felt a powerful rush as if she were in charge. It was time.

"Wait," he said.

She raised her head, feeling dazed. Did he want to *stop*?

"Wait. Thing is," he gasped, sitting up, "thing is since

you said that you were a virgin, I've been feeling odd, funny. Like there's a lot of pressure . . ."

"What do you mean?"

"Like it's got to be right. It's got to be special."

"But it would be special. With you."

"That's the thing. If I hadn't known . . . Now I feel awkward. I'm worried. I've never been with a virgin before. I don't know what it would be like. I might hurt you. It's making me feel . . ."

"You mean it's put you off."

"Not put me off you. I just think we shouldn't rush it."

Alice sat up. She didn't know whether to feel relieved or insulted. The sound of footsteps could be heard running up the stairs. A tiny knock on the door made Frankie sigh.

"That's the other problem," he whispered. "Sophie thinks you've come to visit her, not me. While she's awake, we'll have no peace."

"It's great," Alice said. "I like her. I like all your family," she added truthfully.

The door opened and Sophie stepped into the room, carrying an armful of books and files.

"I wanted to show Alice my project on Elizabeth the First. You did say she was an expert at history."

Frankie lay back on the bed as his sister came in carrying a big three-ring binder and some books.

"Ah," he said, "Elizabeth the First, the virgin queen. How interesting!"

Alice nudged Frankie, her face breaking into a mischievous smile.

"What's so funny?" Sophie said. "I don't get it!"

"Nothing. Your brother's an idiot, that's all."

"I knew that!" Sophie said, lowering herself onto the floor, her books and folders scattering at the last minute.

The family had a special meal for Alice's first night. It was at eight o'clock on the patio outside the French doors. The big umbrella had been closed up and the dining table carried outside with candles dotted all over it.

"We usually eat in front of the telly," Frankie said.

"No we don't!" His mum slapped his arm.

"Takeout and pizzas," Peter said, joining in.

"We never have takeout!" Sophie said. "Do we, Mum?"

They had three courses and two different types of wine. Sophie was allowed a glass of each, and she grimaced as she drank the first sip. After they'd finished eating, Sophie insisted on making the coffee and the sound of beans being ground reached their ears.

"Where did we get that girl?" Jan asked.

"We stole her from a well-balanced family so that she could be our servant," Peter said.

Later, when the dishes had been cleared away and Jan and Peter had gone inside, taking a reluctant Sophie with them, Frankie and Alice were left alone on the patio.

Frankie pulled out a couple of the garden loungers and sat them side by side. The sound of classical music spilled out into the night, and they sat in the dark, looking out at the dense shapes of the garden and the lights of other houses in the distance. It was a perfect night. Alice stretched her arms up until her bones cracked. A few days before she had thought that such a night was out of reach for her. When Sara had come into the flat and said that she knew the truth, Alice had thought that everything she and Rosie had built over the past six months was over.

She'd been wrong.

There had been hasty conferences between Rosie, Jill Newton, and Sara. The three women sat round the table in Rosie's kitchen, trying to salvage a future of some sort for Alice Tully. Alice wandered around the flat in her pajamas, peering cautiously through the windows. There were phone calls between attorneys and newspaper editors, between senior probation workers and Patricia Coffey. There had been long faces and angry words. Rosie's kitchen, once a place of warmth, pungent with the aroma of herbs and spices, now smelled of compromises and deals.

They couldn't just ignore Sara and her newspaper. The scoop was too good for the editor to pass on. While the rest of the press thought Jennifer Jones was in Holland, they knew the truth, and they had the right, they thought, to splash it across their front page. The threat of an injunction did not seem to worry them. They had a sister paper in Scotland and would publish there.

Unless Alice Tully agreed to be interviewed.

They would withhold her name and whereabouts if she was prepared to tell her side of the story: the killing of Michelle Livingstone, her life in Monksgrove, her new life in society. It would be an intelligent piece of investigative journalism, and it would lead to a book that would be published in a year or so. The information in the book would be thorough, leaving no stone unturned. But none of it would break Alice's cover.

Rosie had been unconvinced. Wearing the same clothes two days running, she slumped across the table looking tired. Sara Wright, arriving punctually, wore crisp suits and carried a wafer-thin laptop. On the third visit she closed the laptop until it gave a soft click. She looked from Rosie to Jill and then round to Alice.

"The press are only interested in you because you are such a mystery. If you let me interview you, write up your story from your point of view, you'll cease to be a mystery and they will give up on you."

Rosie looked up. Jill Newton picked her glasses up off the table and put them on.

"The newspapers are racing with each other. Once they see that we've won, they won't be so keen for Alice's story. It'll be yesterday's news."

Sara tapped her nails on the laptop and looked at Rosie and Jill. Both women looked weary, Rosie fiddling with her earring.

"I'll do it," Alice said suddenly. "Just one interview. I'll answer your questions, but then you'll leave us alone. You won't come back for any more?"

Sara Wright nodded.

The one interview was to be a whole-day affair, on the Saturday after she got back from Frankie's. It was to take place in a hotel in the center of London, and there would just be Sara, Alice, and Rosie. The article would appear about a week later. Then it would be over.

"Hey, you two." A voice broke into Alice's thoughts. "Come in and play charades. Girls against boys!"

Sophie was standing at the French doors, one leg on the patio.

"My family!" Frankie said under his breath.

"Don't say that!" Alice said, standing up, using her hand to pull Frankie back on his feet. "I think they're lovely."

TWENTY-ONE

THE house was dark when Alice heard the patter of footsteps coming down the stairs from the loft. She'd been awake for a while, lying in the strange bed looking around the room. Even though she was exhausted and a little woozy from the wine, she couldn't seem to keep her eyes closed for more than a few seconds. She was troubled. Her conversation with the reporter was weighing heavily on her. It was years since she had talked about Berwick Waters.

The footsteps reached her door. It was Frankie, she knew.

He came cautiously into the room with a finger on his lips, as though she might suddenly call out. She pulled herself up, fixing her pillow so that it made a backrest. He sat down on the bed and kissed her hard, his fingers on her shoulders, pressing into her skin.

"I thought we weren't going to do this," she said, when he finally moved back.

"We're not! I've just come to say good night," he said,

running his fingers down the front of her new nightdress, his hand resting on her breast.

"Good night!" she said severely, moving his hand.

But he didn't go. He lay down beside her, his head on her chest.

"They all love you, I can tell," he said, his voice crackly, as if he were about to fall asleep.

"They've only just met me," Alice said, stroking his hair. "They don't know me."

"What's to know?" he said.

Alice's breath became shallow and she spoke before thinking.

"You don't really know me, either. I mean, about my life. When I was younger, a kid."

"You never talk about it," he said.

"What if . . ." She stopped, hardly daring to go on. "What if . . . I'd done something bad. When I was younger?"

He didn't speak, and she was aware of his arm moving under the covers, his fingers pulling at her nightdress. She gripped his hand and pulled it up to her face.

"Frankie," she whispered, "what if I'd done something awful? In my past? Would you still want me then?"

He raised his head and looked at her, his face in shadow but his eyes dark and penetrating.

"Of course I'd still want you. I love you, silly!"

He kissed her again, softer this time, and then sat up, rubbing his eyes with his fists.

"I'd better go and get some sleep. We've got sightseeing to do tomorrow!"

She waited until he'd gone before lowering her pillow. The bed felt empty, her own body hardly making a dent in it. She let her eyes shut and pulled the duvet over her face. All she could see was darkness, but it still didn't help her to sleep. How could she rest when she had to tell it all again? When it meant dragging up images and memories that she had buried long ago.

The wild cat didn't stay for long. Once it had looked at the small girl standing with the baseball bat and the other lying face down on the rocks it made a slow turn and gracefully leaped away.

Jennifer's body was rigid, her thin hair moved by a sudden breeze that came from nowhere. A bird shrieked from up on high and the sound pierced the air. Then it was all still and she looked at Michelle's back, her jeans and pink top, her sneakers, one of them dirty from where she had sunk into the mud. She looked at the ginger hair springing out from her head, in the middle a dark wet patch that seemed to be getting bigger before her eyes.

"Michelle," she whispered, the word hardly leaving her lips.

There was no answer. There couldn't be any answer.

She sank down, onto her knees, the very air wavering in front of her. *What had she done?* A thin cry came, but it wasn't from Michelle, it couldn't be. The sound came from somewhere deep down inside Jennifer, hardly loud enough to be heard. She glanced down. In her hand was the baseball bat. It shouldn't have been there, but it was. She raised it to look. Blood on the wood; a terrible red stain that had soaked into the fibers. Her hand began to shake and she turned and started to half walk and half run along the water's edge until she came to the lake itself. In front were giant grasses standing high, as tall as she was. She shoved the bat into them, stretching her arm as far as she possibly could, and then let go. There was no thump or splash and she hesitated for a moment before pulling herself back, drawing her breath in great gulps as though she'd just surfaced from underwater.

The sun came out, sending a dazzling light on the surface of the lake. She shielded her eyes and looked through the top of the grasses to the other side. There were people there, standing in a tight knot, some dogs scurrying around them. It was too far to make out anything about them, who they were, whether they were young or old.

She walked backward, away from the water and into the wood. Something scooted by her foot and she jumped back, gripping onto a branch while she looked down to see what it was. Nothing. A water rat, maybe. Whatever. It was gone and she was alone. After a moment, pulling herself together, she crept back through the trees and bushes until she came to the spot where the three of them had emerged earlier, when they had first walked out to the place where the Bussell brothers had their den.

She hardly dared to look.

Michelle was facedown on a rock, her hair as springy and curly as ever. In the middle of it was a great brown stain, wet and sticky. It looked like molasses.

"No, no, no . . . ," she said, her head bobbing up and down, her hands in fists, her teeth welded together.

She began to walk distractedly back and forward and saw the hole where the tin box had been. Beside it was a mound of branches. She looked back to Michelle and then back to the hole. She was breathing lightly, her chest hardly moving. She walked toward Michelle's still body, her feet hardly touching the ground.

She had to do *something*.

She bent down and pulled at one of Michelle's shoulders, turning her over so that she was lying on her back. Her pale face was there among the untidy ginger hair, and Jennifer backed off, looking at it with awe. Inside her chest everything was still, as if her own heart had stopped beating. She stood for a long time, putting the flat of her hand against her ribs. There was no feeling there, no life inside her, and yet she was still standing.

She had to *do* something.

She stepped closer and bent down. Averting her eyes

from her friend's face, she put her hands underneath her armpits and pulled her a few inches before resting. She did it again and again until she had her in front of the hole. It wasn't deep, two feet or so. She pulled her by the arms one last time until the girl's motionless form slipped into the earth.

She became busy, picking up the branches one by one and laying them gently across Michelle, taking care not to cover her completely. The sun had gone in and she felt chilly, hugging herself to keep warm. She noticed the stuff from the box then, the rope, the sleeping bags, the things that they had unpacked earlier. The whole place looked messy, untidy. It would draw attention to what was there, under the branches. She piled it all up and pushed it under a bush. The only thing that was left out in the open was the empty tin box. She pulled it to the edge of the water and inched it over the side, dipping it in so that it began to fill. When it got too heavy she let it go and in seconds it disappeared from sight.

Then she turned away, not daring to cast her eyes in the direction of her friend. She walked into the trees and strode off, tears coming, her chest heaving, her shoulders shaking with emotion. She walked down the path and round the edge of the lake. It took almost an hour but she met no one. When she left the reservoir her face was wet and her eyes felt raw and puffy.

What had she done?

Alice sat up. It was no good. She simply couldn't sleep. She switched the tiny bedside light on and looked around the room. She'd thought it pretty earlier in the day but now it seemed garish. There were too many flowers: on the wallpaper, the curtains, the duvet cover. The carpet was too thick, the chest of drawers too shiny. Looking down she saw the white nightdress that had been given to her as a present. A simple style, just some lace around the neck and sleeves. White, the color of purity. She pulled at it for a moment and then took it off over her head and threw it down at the side of the bed.

She lay naked, staring into the light for a long time. After a while she drifted into sleep.

Jennifer's breath was punching in and out of her chest as she ran down the lane, leaving the woods and the lake behind her. She found Lucy on a swing in Michelle's back garden. The little girl was moving back and forth in a dull way. Jennifer walked straight up to her and put her hand on her shoulder. Her dress was still damp and her teeth were chattering.

"There's no one in," Lucy said dejectedly.

Jennifer hopped over the fence and went carefully into her own house. Only then did she remember the photographs. Mr. Cottis and his camera and the bright lights. The hallway was empty, no bag or suitcase on wheels. She looked at the clock in the kitchen. It was almost three o'clock. The day had disappeared, and so had Mr. Cottis.

"Mum?" she shouted up the stairs, but there was no answer.

She pulled Lucy by the hand into her house and up to the bathroom. She ran a hot bath and made Lucy get in and wash herself including her hair. She felt like a mum fussing over the girl, sorting out some of her old clothes for her to wear. Then she used hot water to dab at her own grazed hand and chin.

"Where's Michelle?" Lucy suddenly said, getting out of the bath and wrapping herself in a big towel.

"We had a row. She walked off."

When Lucy was dressed, Jennifer took her downstairs into the kitchen and made some tea and toast. Lucy ate hers while Jennifer's sat untouched on the plate in front of her. Lucy talked about her mum and her brothers. It didn't seem to worry her that Jennifer was not paying attention.

"Thing is," Jennifer said, finally interrupting, "I think it's better if we don't tell anyone about what happened today. About you falling in the lake . . ."

Lucy stopped eating, her little mouse face looking straight at Jennifer. She hadn't fallen in the lake, she'd been pushed in, but Jennifer hadn't said that.

"Me and Michelle will get in trouble because we were supposed to be looking after you. Your mum might not let you play with us again."

Lucy nodded, her eyes shifting from side to side as though she were thinking it through.

"And . . . it might be better not to mention that we went up to the lake. You know Mrs. Livingstone doesn't allow Michelle to go. She might blame me. Or even blame you, and you don't want that."

Lucy shook her head.

"So we'll just say we went to the park. You fell over and dirtied your dress. Michelle walked off in a huff and I brought you back here to change. That's all we need to say."

They watched television, and for a while Jennifer seemed to relax. She kept her eyes on the screen as program after program started and finished. She concentrated on the sound, the words, and the music. She let it fill her head so that other thoughts were pushed aside, covered up.

When the doorbell rang it surprised her. Lucy, engrossed in the program, didn't look up but Jennifer stood and walked over to the window to see who was there.

When she saw Mrs. Livingstone standing at the door it was a shock. Her hair was loose, blowing around in the wind, ginger and curly. She rang the doorbell, bending over to call through the letter box. Jennifer stumbled her way toward the front door, opening it just a few centimeters.

"I'm back. I left Stevie and Joe up at the hospital. They're going to stay overnight and get a train back later tomorrow. Are Lucy and Michelle in there?"

Jennifer couldn't speak, her fingers holding fast to the door. Lucy came up behind her so she opened the door wider for her to go through.

"Michelle's not here." She forced the words out. "We had a row down at the park and she walked off."

"Oh no, that's a shame. You'll make it up. She'll be home soon, I'm sure. Come on, Lucy, let's go and get tea ready."

She turned and walked away and Lucy trotted behind her. "What happened to your dress?" Mrs. Livingstone was saying as she walked down the path. Jennifer closed the door tightly, standing against it, pinning it shut with her forehead and shoulders as if she thought Mrs. Livingstone might come running back toward it, demanding to know what the truth was. When a while had passed, she ran up the stairs and sat in her room, on her bed, with Macy on her lap, the cardboard box of her clothes beside her.

Her mum didn't come in until six. The front door banged shut and Jennifer sat tensely. Her mum's voice called from down in the hall, two, three times, the room doors opening and shutting. Footsteps sounded and then she poked her head into the bedroom, breathless from running up the stairs.

"Jen, there you are! Helen Livingstone wants to talk to you. She can't find Michelle anywhere."

Jennifer looked at her mum's smiling face and a thought took hold of her. She could *tell* her what had happened. It was a sort of *accident,* she could say. She hadn't meant to do it. Her mum would understand. She would explain to other people.

"I'm angry at you anyway," her mum said, glancing down at the bag with the school clothes. "Mr. Cottis waited for over an hour today. He was fed up, I can tell you! And now I find that you were off playing with Michelle!"

A feeling of hopelessness hit her. She couldn't tell her mum anything.

"I don't know where she is," she said, her eyes fastened on Macy.

"No one does, I've told you! Helen hasn't seen her since this morning. She's rung the police. She wants you to go round there."

The police. Jennifer felt a swooning sensation and let her head loll back against the headboard.

Alice felt a hand on her bare shoulder. She opened her eyes and saw bright sunlight in the room. Sophie was standing by her bed. She was wearing a pink dressing gown tied tightly across some pajamas.

"I brought you a cup of tea," she said, pointing to a china cup and saucer sitting on the bedside table.

She bent down and picked up the white nightdress from the floor. Alice took it from her, embarrassed.

"I was so hot in the night!" she said. "I must have taken it off."

"Mum bought me one of those," Sophie said, using one finger to push her glasses up her nose. "I didn't like it, either. Don't worry, I won't tell."

Sophie sat on the edge of Alice's bed and watched as she drank her tea.

TWENTY-TWO

TWO days later they went for a walk across the downs. They packed Frankie's knapsack with food and drink and sun lotion. His mum drove them to a little village outside Brighton so that they could start a circular route. She would be back at five, she said, to pick them up. Sophie waved mournfully from the passenger window as the car moved away. She had wanted to join them but Frankie had said no, firmly, several times.

It had been his suggestion to go. He had wanted to get out of the house, away from his mum and his sister fussing over Alice. Alice hadn't minded. She liked Sophie and Jan, but she was a little weary of always having to look happy and in a good mood. Once alone she and Frankie could both relax and drift into companionable silence. That was the idea.

But Frankie's mood dipped soon after they started. He was too hot, he said; the knapsack was too heavy, Alice was walking too quickly, he complained. She slowed down, looking at the map and finding the right paths to take. Whenever she turned around he seemed farther behind.

There were other walkers on the downs and the paths were clearly marked with yellow arrows. They struggled up steep inclines and went through shady woods. They even passed a bench or two. Eventually, after a couple of hours they came to the halfway point of the walk and Alice rested on a grassy mound. When Frankie finally reached her, she waited for him to sit down before she spoke.

"What's wrong?" she said.

He shrugged his shoulders, getting out a bottle of water and drinking from it.

"Do you want me to go home? Are you fed up with me being here?"

He looked startled by her comment and leaned over and pulled her toward him, burying his head in her chest.

"Of course not," he mumbled. "I love you."

"What's wrong then?" she insisted.

"It's just that I can't bear to think of you going to uni. I know I'm going to lose you!"

She lay back on the grass and looked at the sky. She felt the weight of his head on her breasts and his hand stroking her leg. She put her arm across his shoulder and felt the tension that was there. They'd had this discussion a couple of times since she'd arrived at Frankie's house. In October he would be returning to Croydon to do the last year of his degree. She would be starting at the University of Sussex, just outside Brighton. Although the distance was only seventy kilometers or so Frankie had been talking as though they would be studying in different countries. What he really wanted, she knew, was for her to transfer to his college, to start her degree there instead of Sussex so that they could be at the same place. He'd even suggested that they share a flat together. "Think of the money we'd save," he'd said. But it wasn't about money, she knew. Frankie wanted her close by. He wanted to know that she *belonged* to him.

Since she'd been at his parents' home, he'd been desperately possessive, sitting close to her, his hand or arm always touching her skin in some way. She didn't mind, she liked it. He seemed uneasy, though, as if he had some second sight that she was going to pack her bags and leave him for good. As if she would.

There'd been no sex. She had wanted to, brought condoms with her, felt her chest aching for him. He had shied away, though. After laughing at her nervousness in his shared house or in Rosie's flat, he was now tense, always listening for Sophie's footsteps on the stairs or his mum's movements. The previous night, when everyone was asleep, he had crept down to her room and laid on top of her bed. After a couple of moments of kissing and touching she had pulled the white cotton nightdress off again and sat naked in front of him. She wanted him. Was it *love*? It had to be. But he covered her up with the duvet and lay beside her, eventually falling into a doze from which he woke with a start, not knowing where he was.

In a way she was grateful for his preoccupations. It

kept her from thinking about her meeting with the reporter in a few days' time.

"There's still time to change course. It's the easiest thing. You just ring up the college and ask about the history BA. You've already got your A-level results, so you'd be ahead of all the kids who have just finished school."

"I've already got a place. At Sussex," she said firmly. "And anyway, you're finishing your course in a year. Then I'd be on my own."

"But I'd stay round there, get a job, we could still be together. Then when you've finished your degree we could go traveling. The Far East, India. Anywhere. We could go anywhere."

"I like the course that Sussex offers. I don't know about your place."

"But you could find out," he said softly.

She felt herself wavering. Would it really matter so much, if she changed colleges? If it made him happy? Rosie wouldn't like it, she knew that. But could she be won over? If she knew how much Frankie cared for her? What would Jill Newton think? And Patricia Coffey? She would have to ask all of them. Otherwise she wouldn't have any confidence in her decision. A lot of it might depend on the newspaper article. Whether they could *really* keep her identity a secret.

Frankie rolled away suddenly and sat up.

"Don't bother answering," he said, his back to her.

He had taken her silence as a negative sign. She sighed. She wished he could be a little less childish.

"Most probably you'd rather be away from me anyway," he continued, his face in a sulk. "You'd rather start fresh among new people. Maybe meet someone less pushy than me."

"That's not true . . ."

"Then why won't you change? Why won't you come to my college? Is that too much to ask?"

Alice looked at him for a few moments, his forehead bunched up in a petulant frown. It only took her a moment to decide. Yes, it was too much to ask. She had made her plans over a year before. She wanted to go to Sussex and do a degree in history. She'd already arranged it. She stood up, shaking the stiffness out of her legs. Even if she did change, there was no guarantee that it would make him happy.

"I'm walking on," she said coldly. "Are you coming?"

He stayed on the ground, staring into the distance. She tossed the map at him and walked on, without looking back.

Using her compass and the posts with arrows she walked on for more than an hour, each step propelled by growing frustration. Didn't she have enough to worry about? Why couldn't Frankie just be happy? She was here, in Brighton, with his family. It was a glorious day and they were alone; he had her all to himself. The previous evening she had been prepared to take him into her bed, something he had wanted for a long time. Why couldn't he be *satisfied*?

Up ahead she saw a big tree, its branches making a canopy of shade on the grass beneath. She headed for it. She was thirsty and hungry and realized then that Frankie had all the stuff. Would he follow her? She looked back along the path, but there was no sign of him. It was too much. How could he be so childish and spoil their day? She lay on the grass, her head resting on her arm, and closed her eyes. Why was it like that with people? You got close to them. You began to love them. Then they let you down.

After a while she allowed the memory of Michelle Livingstone to come into her head.

A light breeze riffled the leaves above her and she opened her eyes and looked at the branches and the ragged bits of sky in between. Michelle let her down, just like everyone else. She didn't deserve to die, though. Not like that.

Jennifer stood in Mrs. Livingstone's living room and told the policewoman that they'd been playing in the park and had an argument. "Michelle just walked off!" she said, holding her hands out in a gesture of hopelessness. After more questions by different people they left her alone. She sat with Lucy Bussell in the kitchen and heard her mum and Mrs. Livingstone talking. The police were doing house-by-house inquiries, she said, and the neighbors and local people were helping with a search of the town. "She may have got locked in somewhere," Mrs. Livingstone said, hopefully, "in someone's garage or shed."

"Or maybe she's with some other friend, someone you don't know about," her mum answered. Mr. Livingstone said similar things, his voice cheerful.

"What's happened to Michelle?" Lucy whispered.

"I don't know," Jennifer answered.

For a while, sitting in the big kitchen with the pots and pans hanging gaily from the ceiling, it began to seem as though she really didn't know. As if the events of the day were some kind of bad dream. The voices from the living room, the suggestions that Michelle had wandered off and got lost, or was playing with some new friend and had forgotten the time, seemed possible. Whenever there was a knock on the door, Jennifer looked expectantly around, as though Michelle and her ginger hair might bounce into the kitchen at any moment, laughing and wondering what all the fuss was about.

As it got dark the mood changed and her mum took her home and told her to go to bed. She didn't get undressed. She lay on the top of the bed, still wearing the same clothes she'd had on at the reservoir. There was noise from downstairs, neighbors calling round to see what had happened. At one point there was a man's voice and she

crept out of her room to see who it was. She heard Mr. Cottis talking and her mum hissing at him, telling him about the missing girl. He left immediately, without another word. Jennifer imagined him slipping out of the door and into the night, his glasses hardly having time to adjust to the darkness.

She went back to bed. Lying under her duvet, she closed her eyes and seemed to dip in and out of sleep, a heavy blackness then wild dreams. Opening her eyes she was immediately aware of her room, of unusual noises outside, car doors banging, voices talking. Then she would slide back into a dream. Once, she was sure she could see the feral cat sitting in front of her, on the end of her bed, licking its paw. A feeling of dread settled on her, and she wanted to put her hand out to ward off the animal, but before she could do anything she seemed to sink back into pitch-black sleep again. Waking much later, her room was no longer dark, only shadowy, a cold light glowing at the window. She got up, stiff and uncomfortable from lying in her clothes. She went out onto the landing and heard her mum snoring gently, her room door wide open.

Out of the living-room window she could see that the police car was still there. Otherwise it was quiet, and there was no one else around. It was six o'clock. The day lay before her, flat and empty. All she could do was wait.

She watched breakfast television and saw the reporter explaining that a ten-year-old girl had gone missing in

Berwick. She was pointing to a lamppost that had a poster stuck to it. HAVE YOU SEEN THIS GIRL? it said, flapping in the early morning breeze. The reporter's face was serious, although she was wearing bright lipstick and orange earrings that looked like boiled sweets. The scene changed and there was a shot of the reservoir, and talk of divers searching the lake in case the little girl had fallen in. Jennifer held her breath, looking hard at the screen, at the flat, black water of the lake. Once it had been fields and houses; now it covered everything, even some dead cats.

At midday everything changed. The sound of knocking on the front door alerted her. There was a bell that could have been used, but the knocking just got louder. It was insistent, urgent.

"All right, all right!" her mum said, shuffling along the hall.

There were sharp questions, demanding words, footsteps that were determined to walk up the hallway and find her. The muscles in her back tightened until her chest had sunk and her shoulders were rounded balls. The living-room door swung open and they were standing behind her. She could see the shape of them reflected in the television screen.

"Jennifer Jones. You must come with us. This minute."

Lucy Bussell had told them the truth. In a way she was relieved.

———

Alice sat up cross-legged, looking around her. Ahead the path led upward and she judged that she only had a few kilometers to go before getting back to the village. Then she would wait for Frankie's mum. Looking back she could see the fields and meadows that she'd walked across. In the distance was a small figure. She relaxed, sure it was Frankie. They could make up. All he needed was a little reassurance. She felt calm watching him. He was walking alongside a field of corn and looked small, like a child, beside the giant stalks. It would be ten or more minutes before he reached her. She stood and waved anyway and the figure paused for a moment and waved back. Then she slumped down, her back against the trunk of the tree, and waited.

Lucy had told them everything. They were angry with her and demanded to know what had happened after Lucy had left the reservoir. Jennifer wanted to tell them. She wanted to open her mouth and let the words come out, but something was stopping her. Their faces were all around, firing questions at her. *Why had she lied? What had happened? Did she know where Michelle was?* All she could do was nod. Yes, she did.

Mrs. Livingstone's face lit up. She gripped on to her husband. *No, no,* Jennifer wanted to say. *She's still dead. It's just that I know where she is.*

They got into the police car, she and Lucy and a policeman and woman. Behind them were Michelle's mum and dad, getting into their car. On the pavement her mum was moving back and forth, a confused expression on her face. She wasn't coming. Jennifer peered out of the back window of the car as it went slowly up the lane, and she saw her mum getting smaller and further away. Sitting beside her, Lucy was talking all the time, explaining about what they'd done and the accident that had happened when she had fallen into the water. Her voice was steady as she told the policewoman that Jennifer had saved her from drowning. "What do you say, Jennifer? Is this what happened?" The policewoman's voice made her turn round, away from the sight of her mum disappearing in the distance.

Jennifer couldn't speak. Her tongue seemed numb, incapable of making a sound.

Moments later they swept into the official car park of the reservoir, followed by Mr. and Mrs. Livingstone. A park ranger in a waterproof jacket and green trousers was waiting for them. He nodded to the policeman and pointed to a Land Rover. There was a holdup, though. The policewoman said that Mr. and Mrs. Livingstone had to stay with her in the car park. There was an argument, with Mrs. Livingstone raising her voice and getting upset. Jennifer stared at her, letting the words of the argument go over her head. Mrs. Livingstone's skin looked dry and yellow, her mouth hanging open, her lips sucked of color. The only living thing about her was her eyes—dark and

wild, they turned from speaker to speaker, and then finally they rested on Jennifer.

Another police car came into the car park, and the officers pulled Michelle's parents back, saying things about ambulances and doctors.

Jennifer, Lucy, one of the policemen, and the ranger got into the Land Rover. It drove slowly along the lane, going over the uneven path and dipping in and out of holes. It skirted the lake in no time. They got out at the point where the lane split and forked off up into the wood. The park ranger was mumbling about a *prohibited footpath* and *no public right of way*.

Lucy led the way and they walked in a line. Jennifer looked round to see that the ranger was carrying a small case with the words FIRST AID on it. That's when it dawned on her. They were all making the same mistake that she and Michelle had made. When Lucy had told them that her brothers had a den they'd thought of a cabin or a tent or a cave. Something proper; shelter, a place where a person could survive. They'd misunderstood. They didn't know it was only a hole. She stopped for a moment, her legs giving way underneath her. They thought they were going to find Michelle *alive*.

"Come on now, Jennifer!"

The police officer's voice was sharp, like the crack of a whip. She walked on, behind Lucy, in front of the adults; a strange procession winding up the incline. At the gap in the trees she slowed up, her feet heavy and her legs thinning away to nothing. Lucy said, "It's along here," and they all went in through the trees, walking carefully through the darkened undergrowth, twigs and dried grass cracking under their feet. Stepping out into the light, they all stood by the side of the water, looking disorientated.

"Where are we?" the policeman said.

"It's an outlet. In case the water level gets too high, they let some of it drain away," the ranger said.

Jennifer wasn't really listening. She was staring at the branches that covered the hole, more untidy now than she remembered leaving them.

"Where's this den, Lucy?" the policeman said.

Lucy pointed and they all looked mystified. Jennifer almost wanted to smile. *We were exactly the same!* she wanted to say. *We were disappointed, too.*

"Where, Lucy?"

"Over there, where all those branches are."

The policeman strode over. He glanced down onto the branches and Jennifer held her breath.

"It's just a hole," he said, looking puzzled.

He hadn't seen her. She was underneath the branches. He had to look more closely.

"It's where my brothers keep their stuff. You've seen it, haven't you, Jen? Sleeping bags, food . . ."

Lucy nervously listed the things they'd unpacked the day before until the policeman interrupted her.

"But where's Michelle?" he said.

"Underneath the branches," Jennifer said, her voice squeaking.

She'd been quiet for hours, it seemed, and now she was the one sounding like a mouse. They stared at her with surprise. The policeman looked down again. He shook his head in a mystified manner and used his foot to dislodge a couple of the branches. He mumbled something to the park ranger. He wasn't taking it seriously. He didn't believe her. She walked across and bent over, pulling at the branches.

"She's in here," she said. "SHE'S HERE!"

But there was just a hole. The earth was damp and smelled of the lake. Pulling the branches away, one by one, she stared with horror. There was no one there. Michelle had gone.

Frankie was smiling when he finally got to the shady tree. His hands were joined in a kind of mock prayer. Then one of them turned into a fist and he started to bang his own head with it.

"I am an idiot," he said. "I'm sorry, I'm sorry."

He put his arms round her and lifted her off her feet.

"Do you forgive me?" he whispered.

She smiled. Of course she forgave him.

"I need a drink," she said. "Otherwise I'll die of thirst."

He laughed, dropping the knapsack to the ground. He pulled out the bottles of water and the blanket they'd brought with them for their picnic. Alice sat on it and drained the bottle, feeling the cold water cooling her throat. Then he was beside her, kissing her, gently at first, then with fervor, making her head spin as she lay back on the blanket with him leaning across her, his whole body pinning her down. She closed her eyes and felt the breeze on her face, the sound of the leaves rustling gently above. When he moved on top of her, she put her arms around his neck and held him tightly. After a few moments he arched back and looked at her questioningly. She nodded and he sat back, fiddling in his pockets, undoing his trousers, while she eased up, pulling her jeans and panties over her thighs and off.

When he lay on top again, she felt the warmth of his skin on her stomach and legs. She sensed his hesitation as he reached for her, then a rush of energy with his mouth on her face, her neck, and her shoulders, his hands pulling at the few clothes she had left on. Then it was over and he was slumped on her, his breath coming in great gasps as if he'd just climbed a mountain.

"I love you," he said.

She closed her eyes. Was it fair? That she should be so happy?

———

They were around a hole in the ground. The policeman, the ranger, Lucy, and Jennifer. The hole was empty even though Jennifer was scrabbling in it, crying hysterically, shouting out incoherent nonsense about wild cats.

Something caught the policeman's eye. A flash of pink from further up in the bushes. He didn't say anything at first, just moved his head to get a better view of whatever it was.

"Oh no," he said, moving away.

Jennifer stopped and looked up. Lucy was already following the policeman.

"Oh no, my god!"

Jennifer heard his voice and the radio crackle into life. She walked toward where the policeman was and saw, on the ground, the garish pink of Michelle's sweater.

"Don't let the children see this!" the policeman said.

The park ranger, his mouth hanging open, turned to the two girls and tried to shoo them away. His heart wasn't in it, though, and Jennifer broke through and stood beside the policeman, looking down at her dead friend.

TWENTY-THREE

THEY took Sophie to the beach to make up for the fact that she hadn't gone on the walk. She spent ages getting ready, showing Alice a variety of outfits while Frankie sat on the bottom stair, flicking through the newspaper. When she finally came out of her bedroom, Alice noticed a hint of eyeshadow. They got the bus to the seafront, and Frankie sat on one seat and she and Alice on another.

"What's that terrible smell?" Frankie said suddenly, sniffing around like a dog.

Sophie and Alice looked puzzled.

"Oh, it's just Sophie's perfume!" he said, grinning.

"You!" Sophie said, pushing her glasses up her nose.

She linked Alice's arm as they walked along the front. The sun was low in the sky, too bright to look at, and Alice held her hand up to shield her eyes. In front, Frankie was walking casually, his arms swinging confidently, a swagger in his step. She thought of him earlier on, lying beside her on the grass, his body still, his hands resting on her skin, all his urgency gone. A ripple of desire went

through her, and she forced herself to smile at Sophie and pay attention to her chatter.

"Her real name's Charlotte, but she told me to call her Charlie, but her mum doesn't like it. She hates her name. She says she's going to change it when she grows up."

Alice raised her eyebrows.

"She's mad, she is. She's always cheeking the teachers and last week one teacher found some"—she stopped for a moment and then said—"*cigarettes* in her bag."

"She's a bad influence." Frankie threw the comment backward. "I think Mum should stop you from seeing her."

"You wish!" Sophie said, a look of disdain on her face. "She's my best friend."

"Take no notice," Alice said, rubbing Sophie's arm. "He doesn't mean it. You should see some of the friends he hangs round with at college!"

"Don't tell on me!" Frankie said, in mock anger.

"Sometimes," Sophie whispered, when Frankie had walked a little away from them, "I wish I had a big sister instead of a brother!"

After being persuaded to go on some of the rides with Sophie, Frankie suggested fish-and-chips. Sophie only wanted chips.

"I'm a vegetarian," she said to Alice.

"Since when?" Frankie said.

"Since recently. Charlie and me have given up meat. It's cruel and totally unnecessary. Humans don't need to eat meat."

"What about those shoes? Aren't they leather?"

Sophie looked at her sneakers, picking one foot up and then the other.

"Leave poor Sophie alone," Alice said, poking Frankie in the ribs. "If she wants to give up meat it's up to her!"

"Next week it'll be something different." Frankie sighed. "Depending on what Charlotte wants to do!"

"It's not *Charlotte*! It's *Charlie*!"

They ate their food sitting on the beach wall. The chips were hot and salty and the fish crumbled in Alice's fingers. Even though it was almost seven, there were still families on the sand, digging, making sandcastles, playing football. One couple was sitting on a small towel, their arms round each other, kissing, oblivious to anyone else. The rides seemed far away, although the air was full of distant shrieks and echoes of music. Behind it all, the sun was slipping down into the sea.

A bleep sounded. Alice put her food down and pulled her mobile out of her bag.

"It's a text," she said, pressing the right buttons to show the message on the screen. It was from Jill Newton.

When U R alone ring me asap. Jill

She frowned at the screen. She wanted to return the call immediately but couldn't. A feeling of alarm made her sit up straight. From beside her she could hear Sophie whispering, "Who's it from?" And Frankie, playing along, his answer in a hushed voice, "Maybe it's her other boyfriend."

She composed herself. It's nothing, she thought. Some last-minute detail about the interview with the reporter. If it was anything really important Rosie would have rung. She put the mobile carelessly back in her bag as if it weren't important, just some tedious communication that she had received. She turned, picked up her chips, and popped one in her mouth.

"Just Rosie," she mumbled. "Checking that you're looking after me."

Frankie rolled his eyes, but Sophie looked serious.

"She's nice! I liked her," she said, giving her brother a sideways swipe.

They got the bus back soon after, Alice sitting beside Frankie this time and Sophie in the seat in front, her body turned to them. They played a game. Each had to say a girl's name that began with the last letter of the previous name.

Anne, Emily, Yvonne, Ethel, Lorraine, Elizabeth, Harriet, Tina, Amanda, Amy, Yvette, Ellen, Nell, Lily . . .

When they got off the bus, Sophie was stuck.

"*Y* is so hard!" she said, grumbling.

"Give up?" Frankie said.

She shook her head.

Alice walked on, reaching the front door before them. When Frankie caught up, he put his arm round her.

"You okay?" he said.

"Fine. Do you think your mum would mind if I had a soak in the bath? I've got a bit of a headache. Probably too much time in the sun!"

"Course," he said, a knowing expression on his face.

"There are only two names. Yvonne and Yvette! It's not fair!" Sophie said.

"Give up?" Frankie said.

Alice dashed up the stairs, leaving them behind. In her room she picked up her towel and toiletries and went into the bathroom, locking the door behind her. She clicked on the small radio that sat on the shelf above the sink. Classical music started to play. She put the plug in the bath and turned the hot tap on, slowly, so that the water was no more than a trickle. Then she sat on the floor and rang Jill Newton. The call was picked up immediately.

"Alice," Jill said.

"Is Rosie all right?" Alice said.

"Yes, yes, she's fine. There's nothing wrong with her, but . . ."

Alice sat very still. Behind her the water was barely dribbling into the bath.

"Alice, I'm so sorry but I've got bad news."

The music was soft, just the notes of a piano tinkling above the running water.

"There's been a leak at Sara Wright's office. She's terribly upset. It seems that someone she trusted had access to some of her papers and decided to sell them to one of the tabloids. They've been sacked, of course, but . . . The thing is, they're going to publish tomorrow!"

"It's going to be in the papers?" Alice said, pushing her thumbnail into her teeth.

"We've been trying all afternoon to get an injunction, but the judge was unsympathetic. The fact that we were prepared to deal with one newspaper means that we have somehow waived our right to privacy. At least that's what the judge said. We are appealing to another judge and we might still stop it, but I must tell you, Alice, there's a very real chance that your story and your photograph will be in the newspapers tomorrow morning."

She looked at her watch. It was almost nine o'clock. In nine hours everyone would know who she was. Everyone.

"I want you to pack your stuff because Rosie's on her way to pick you up. She should be there by about ten, ten-thirty. The best place for you is at home. I'll be there tomorrow morning and we can see just how bad the newspaper article is. Then we can decide what strategy to take."

She rang off and Alice was left thinking about the word *strategy*. As if it were a battle of some kind and they had to work out their next move. She let her mobile slip onto the floor and then, crossing her arms, she hugged herself tightly as though she were in a kind of straitjacket. The moment had come. They had thought they could get away with it, but they were wrong. Now people would know about her and what she had done. Her throat was hard and dry and she had to suck air into her mouth so that she could breathe. Behind her she could hear the water still running. Somehow she had to get herself up off the floor and get her things packed so that she would be ready when Rosie came.

Instead of rushing out, though, she took her clothes off and stepped into the bath. The water was scalding hot, but she sank down into it anyway. She washed herself from head to foot, busily, with purpose, as if it were the most important thing in the world. When she finished she closed her eyes and lay flat down, submerging her head, rinsing her hair. Sitting up, she inhaled the steam and heard the piano still playing on the tiny radio. A knock on the door sounded and she tensed. If only she could stay there, in that room, alone.

"Yes?" she said, surprised at the strength of her own voice.

"Alice, I didn't give up!"

Sophie's voice came through the door, loud and gleeful.

"I thought of one. Yolanda. That's a girl's name, isn't it? Frankie says it's not, but it is, isn't it? When you come out you'll tell him that I've won?"

"Sure," she said.

That wasn't all she had to tell him.

TWENTY-FOUR

FRANKIE gave a soft knock on her room door before pushing it open slightly.

"You all right?" he said.

She had almost finished packing. He saw her holdall immediately and came into the room with a frown on his face.

"What's going on?"

"I've got to go. Something's happened—" she started.

"Why? What's wrong? Is something wrong?"

"Yes . . . No . . . Nothing's wrong with us . . . I just . . ."

"Is it about this afternoon? Are you sorry that we . . . ?"

"It's not about us."

He was standing by her bed. He looked a bit sleepy, his hair tousled, as if he'd been having a nap and just remembered that she was there. He was stretching his arms up and yawning. She felt a need to hug him, to encircle him with her arms, to push her head into his chest. He was too big for her, though. He had always been too big for her.

"You'd better sit down," she said, taking a step backward, away from him, pulling her holdall off the bed and onto the floor.

Frankie plonked himself on the duvet. He seemed resigned in some way, as if he expected to hear something bad. Alice sat beside him and put her hand on his shoulder. He had no idea how terrible it was going to be.

"The other night? When I asked you if your feelings toward me would change? If you knew that I'd done something bad?"

She was deliberately keeping her voice light.

"Alice, if you're going to dump me just do it," Frankie said, his words flat.

"Listen to me. I am not going to dump you. I love you!"

It was the first time she had said it. Those three little words. His head was bowed, though, and he didn't seem to notice. He was so sure that what she had to tell him had something to do with *him*.

"My name is not Alice Tully," she said, as forcefully as she could.

He looked up, puzzled.

"How do you mean?"

"Alice Tully is not the name I was born with. I've only been calling myself by that name for seven, eight months. All the time that I've been living with Rosie."

He didn't speak. He leaned back on his hands, a look

of interest on his face. He was sure now that she wasn't going to dump him. If only he knew how much worse it was going to be.

"There's no easy way to tell you this. My real name is Jennifer Jones, and seven months ago I was released from a secure unit. I . . . I . . . My name was changed to give me a chance to start fresh. To begin a new life."

He was just looking at her. The name hadn't rung any alarm bells for him. She decided to keep going.

"Frankie, six years ago, I was involved in . . . I caused . . ."

"Jennifer Jones?" he said, as if there were cogs turning inside his head.

"Six years ago I killed my best friend. Then I went to prison."

There was silence. Not a sound. Alice held her breath and looked straight at him, her eyes searching his face, her hand moving swiftly to take his.

"I . . . I did do it. I can't make any excuses. I killed her . . ."

Her voice broke and she found herself choking back the need to cry.

"I was only ten. We were messing around, by a lake, with another girl, and I hit her with a bat. I can't really explain except to say that it was a moment of madness."

"You're Jennifer Jones?" Frankie said, a look of awe on his face.

"Yes."

"You can't be," he said, giving a false laugh. "I remember reading about it in the paper. She's only just been released. There was a load of publicity about it. She's living abroad somewhere."

"It's me. I was released six months early. Only a few people knew. The press stuff about the official release? That was all a bluff, to put the media off my trail. You see, I'm big news."

She was crying. She had his hand sandwiched in between hers and she was holding it tightly.

"You killed your friend?" he whispered.

"I did. I can't explain exactly why. All I know is that it did happen. I wasn't myself. I didn't know what I was doing."

Alice stopped. That wasn't right. To deny responsibility. She had spent too much time talking to counselors to fall back on excuses.

"That's not true. I did know. I did know what I was doing. I can't explain. It was I who killed her, and yet at the same time it was a different person altogether."

"But . . ."

Frankie started to speak but seemed to notice then that Alice had his hand. He pulled it back. He stood up and walked across the floor, his fingers pushing his hair up at the front.

"I read about this. Weeks ago. I think I even knew about it at the time. Jennifer Jones. It was in the woods or somewhere."

"A reservoir. Berwick Waters. It's near Norwich." Alice's voice was firmer. It was easy to give the facts. "She was ten and I was ten. There was another girl, but she wasn't involved."

"It was all over the newspapers."

"Yes. It was a scandal. A terrible thing. One child killing another."

She was talking about it as though it had happened to someone else.

"And it was *you?*" he said.

She nodded as he lapsed into silence. What was going through his head? Part of her wished she knew, but part of her was glad she didn't.

"This kid, this girl, she wasn't killed outright. That was it. She was buried alive."

Alice felt a swooning sensation. She pushed her feet into the ground, but it felt soft and spongy. The room seemed unsteady. Out of the corner of her eye she could see Frankie standing upright, one hand leaning on the wall. He looked bigger than she'd ever seen him. She felt tiny, as if she might fall off the bed and disappear between the floorboards.

"No, that's not true . . . I didn't know that she was still

alive. I was only ten. I thought she was dead. I never would have left her if I thought she was still alive. I would have got an ambulance . . ."

She couldn't say any more because something shocking occurred to her. *Would she? Would she have got an ambulance?* If Michelle Livingstone's eyes had flickered open as she covered her with branches would she have done anything to save her? Frankie's voice seemed to be droning on. He was saying stuff about *honesty* and that this was *something he would have to think about* and that he would *need time and space.* She didn't care, though. All she could see in her head was a girl lying underneath the foliage, her ribcage moving up and down. It was a moment of madness, she had always said that. And yet what if she'd known that Michelle was *alive?* Would she have lifted a finger to save her?

The front doorbell sounded. It forced itself into her head. It rang again, with purpose, as if someone were in a hurry. She could hear it, loud and clear, as if she were standing next to it.

"That'll be Rosie," she said hoarsely.

"I can't believe you kept all this from me," Frankie said. "You lied to me."

"That was part of the agreement I had with my probation officer. No one knew."

"Rosie knew?"

"Except for Rosie. She had to know, obviously. She

had to know what she was taking on, who she had living in her house . . ."

"What about me?"

There was noise from downstairs, the sound of Jan talking loudly to someone in the hall.

"Didn't I have a right to know who you were? Who I was getting involved with?"

"We didn't think . . . At the time I had no idea that I would meet . . . someone like you."

Jan was calling Alice's name from downstairs.

"I've got to go . . . Wait here . . ."

She said it softly. Then she turned from him and walked out of the room and downstairs.

Rosie was standing at the bottom of the stairs, her car keys hanging from her hand, her face anxious. Jan was beside her, looking uncertain. Sophie appeared at the living-room door, the sound of the television coming from inside.

"Is everything okay?" Jan said.

"A family situation. I've got to take Alice home," Rosie said tactfully, her keys moving and sounding like the tinkling of bells.

"Oh, I'm sorry," Jan said.

"Is Alice going?" Sophie said, her voice dropping.

"Yes, she is, love," Rosie said.

"I'll only be a minute," Alice said.

She gave Rosie a kiss on the cheek, just a peck, and then turned to go back upstairs. Sophie followed behind her. She went into her room and found Frankie sitting on the bed, his head in his hands.

"Frankie, I . . ."

She sat beside him, her arms around his neck.

"I was only ten. Only a child. I'm a different person now."

He was rigid, though, his shoulders and arms solid, as if he were closed against her. He was strong and she was weak. That had always been the way. She stood up, her throat closed in a knot. She picked up her holdall and heard the door creak and Sophie come in.

"Tell Alice not to go," Sophie said, linking her arms through Alice's.

Frankie looked up at his sister, and then his eyes, heavy and dark, moved to Alice's face.

"Get away," he said.

Alice flinched, thinking that he meant her, that he wanted her to get away from him. It was worse, though, much worse than that.

"Sophie, get away from her. Let go of her," he said, lifting himself off the bed and pulling his sister's arm so that she let Alice go.

He stood, holding his sister, his big arms around her. Sophie looked annoyed, as if she were about to argue with him. He moved back, as far away from Alice as he could. That's when she understood. He was protecting his sister

from her. He was keeping her *safe* from the child-killer in his house.

Grabbing hold of her bag she turned and left, Sophie's protestations in the back of her head. She walked down each stair uncertainly, as though she weren't sure where the next one would be. Rosie was chatting to Jan, a half smile on her lips. The moment she saw Alice she opened the front door, her keys up and ready.

"Thank you for having me," Alice said woodenly, when she got to the door.

"That's all right!" Jan said, leaning across and giving her a perfumed kiss on the cheek. "We'll see you again, soon, I shouldn't wonder."

But Alice knew that she would never see them again. Any of them.

TWENTY-FIVE

SHE woke early in her own bedroom. Her eyes popped open but the rest of her body was weighted down with sleep. She turned her head and looked at the bedside clock. It showed the time: 5:32. It wouldn't be long till the newspapers started to drop through people's front doors. The manager from the Coffee Pot; Pip and Jules; Rosie's mum, Kathy; Rosie's work colleagues and her friends; Frankie's housemates; Frankie's parents; the neighbors; her own mother and her new husband. The list went on.

Yesterday she was Alice Tully. Who was she now? She turned over, away from the clock, and looked around the room. She'd been there for almost eight months. She'd decorated it, rearranged the furniture, bought herself a chair and a small stereo system. She'd added some cushions and a mirror and a special lamp with fringed crystals hanging from it. Rosie had wanted to pay for them, but it was important for Alice to buy her own things, to make her own stamp on the room.

It had seemed like home.

Now it looked odd, as if nothing quite fit. She'd been away for four nights in Frankie's tiny spare room, so at first her own room had seemed far too big, the ceiling too high, the floorboards too uneven and creaky. As soon as she'd taken her shoes off, she'd felt the draft seeping up, making her feet feel icy and causing goose bumps to rise on her shins.

She'd got into bed immediately, covering herself with her duvet.

"It's stuffy in here," Rosie had said. "I'll open this window slightly."

"No," she'd insisted, "I want it closed. And the door, close it tightly when you go out."

Rosie had given her a hug and kiss and then left, shutting the room door behind her, her footsteps along the hallway, heavy, as if she were burdened with something.

Alice looked at the lamp. It was too flashy, she could see that now. It didn't go with the stripped-wood dresser and the Victorian curtains. She had carried it carefully home from the shop and set it up on the kitchen table to show Rosie. Her first reaction had been to say, "What's that?" When she explained, Rosie had clapped her hand over her chest and said that it was *absolutely beautiful.* It didn't fit, though. Rosie was only being kind. A rush of affection filled her chest like a fire warming her from inside. Rosie. The one good thing in her life. Somehow she drifted back to sleep.

A knocking on her door awoke her. Rosie came in with a mug of tea in her hand. Strangely, she was formally dressed, wearing her court suit. Alice sat up, bleary-eyed even though looking at the clock, she could see that she'd had a couple of extra hours' sleep. She stretched her arms up.

"Have the papers come?" she said, knowing that they must have arrived.

Rosie nodded and Alice took a gulp from the mug of tea. There were some sounds from outside, voices, louder than she would expect at that time in the morning. Rosie pulled the curtain back a few centimeters and looked.

"Damn," she said.

Alice got up, her feet hardly touching the floorboards until she stood next to Rosie. Out through the gap in the curtain she could see a car parked across the street and two people sitting in it with the door hanging open. Standing talking to them were two men, one with a camera.

"I thought you said they weren't allowed to print my address?" Alice whispered.

"They haven't. Those reporters are probably from the paper that's printed the story. They're hoping for another picture of you. Before anyone else."

Just then another car drove up and parked further up the street. Jill Newton got out of it and walked along the pavement toward the house. Rosie mumbled something about opening the door and dashed off, leaving Alice

standing on her own. The reporters ignored Jill, but the moment she turned into the pathway they sprang toward her, calling out, the camera flashing. Alice heard the front door opening and shutting as Rosie let Jill in. Then the reporters walked back off to their car, and Alice could see curtains opening at other windows, one of the neighbors across the way coming out to see what the commotion was.

How long before everyone knew?

Jill Newton seemed calm. She gave Alice a hug and tutted when Rosie pointed out the newspapers. She was neatly dressed as usual, light-colored trousers and jacket. When they sat round the kitchen table, she refused a drink and held her hands together. Only then did Alice notice the peeling varnish on her nails. Looking closer at her, she could see a weariness around her eyes, and her glasses looked speckled, as though they needed a polish.

"I have a safe house for you to go to, Alice, just while this is going on. When the stories in the newspapers have burned out we need to reassess the situation, see just how much damage has been done," she said, her fingers drumming lightly on the tabletop. "I was going to take you there later this morning, but I'm afraid there's been a development and we'll have to leave soon, within the next thirty minutes or so."

"What's happened?" Rosie said, laying a protective hand on Alice's arm.

"I've got information that your mother is on her way here."

"My mum?" Alice said. "Why?"

A strange sensation took hold of Alice. Her *mum* was coming. *To see her? To look after her?*

"I hardly know how to tell you this, but she's made a deal with this newspaper," Jill said, pushing it away with a sneer. "Let's face it. It's not the first time she's done this."

Alice gave a tight nod of her head. Rosie pulled a chair up beside her and sat only centimeters away.

"What the newspapers have got here is hardly worth reading. They have your name, where you work, the area, and so on, but what does it amount to? Not much. They want excitement. They want drama. They're paying your mother to come down and try to meet with you. Maybe they're hoping for a public reconciliation. Either that or some embarrassing scene. Anything that'll help them sell more newspapers."

"How do you know all this?" Alice said in a tiny voice.

"I have a contact who works in the press. She does me favors, I pass her stuff. It's a good arrangement. I always tell her the truth, so I told her to ignore the Holland rumors. She phoned me this morning. I trust her."

"Why such a rush?" Rosie said. "Alice's mum lives up north, surely?"

"They brought her down yesterday. She's due here in about an hour. That's why I want Alice out."

"I'll pack a few things."

Rosie lifted herself off the chair and walked into the bedroom.

"I'm so sorry, Alice. That it's turned out like this," Jill said.

Alice couldn't answer. She shook her head with disbelief. Her mum. Coming here. Paid for by a newspaper. At long last she would get her photo on the front page. It was what she'd always wanted. The very thought of it made Alice feel sick.

"I'll get dressed," she said, and left Jill on her own.

It wasn't the first time Carol Jones had made a deal with the newspapers.

In the beginning, when Jennifer was sent to Monksgrove, her mother had managed to visit her regularly. Every month for over a year she stood in the queue of visitors and waited her turn before being allowed through to the lounge where the visits took place. Little groupings of chairs dotted the big room. Half a dozen for a big family, and even then there might be a sleeping baby in a carrier. Jennifer and her mum usually sat by the window, one chair at an angle to the other. It always started with an awkward kiss on the cheek and then some chatting. The same questions each time. What was her room like? Her friends? Her schoolwork? Then it was Jennifer's turn. Where was she living? Was she working? How was Gran?

Mostly her mum came dressed up, her blond hair carefully styled and her mouth perfectly lipsticked. Jennifer always liked to see her like that because it meant things were going well. A couple of times she looked unkempt, her hair greasy, wearing jeans and old tops that Jennifer vaguely remembered. She talked about her modeling career then, about how she was going to get back on some agency's books and earn enough to buy them a small place. That way Jennifer could come and live with her when she was released.

The counselors said that Jennifer was tense for days after these visits. She liked to be on her own and avoided the other children. Her eating became erratic and sometimes she would hurt herself. Patricia Coffey asked her once if she would like a break from her mother's visits. A chance to reflect, to work out her feelings toward her mum. She'd shook her head vehemently. Of course not. How could she not want to see her mum?

For a while Carol stopped coming. Three, four months, over the summer period. She wrote a short letter saying that she was working abroad and would be back in September. She came, tanned and beautiful, a tiny T-shirt showing her rose tattoo; her flat stomach was the color of honey, a gold ring through her belly button. The other kids and parents looked with envy.

The next month she looked grim. She'd been ill, she said, a chest infection. Her hair looked orange, and for the first time Jennifer noticed dark roots and shadows under her eyes. She was out of work, she said, living with a friend. All talk of modeling had stopped. After that she missed three, four months. There were a couple of post-cards, telephone calls, last-minute excuses. She returned the following April without explanation. Jennifer had been at Monksgrove for almost two years.

Her mum looked like her old self. She had a leather coat on that was belted at the waist. Her hair looked lemony and her eyes were the brightest blue. They were allowed to walk out in the grounds, through the long grass, past islands of daffodils. They sat on a bench and Carol told Jennifer about her new job as a receptionist at a fitness club. After a while of chatting, she took a small camera out of her handbag.

"I don't have a photo of you," she said. "And you're changing. You've got taller and your face is fuller."

Jennifer smiled with pleasure as her mother took some pictures. She sat back on the bench, looking casual, the daffodils in the background. Then she leaned forward, her shoulders hunched, grinning wildly for the camera. She was pleased. *Her mum wanted a picture of her.*

Unlike before, at the time of the trial. The only picture they had of Jennifer was the one taken by the police. A face, staring at a camera. Bangs and long hair. Staring eyes that looked surprised to be there. The newspapers had called it *The face of a killer.*

There were no other pictures of her. In a house full of photographs of her mother, there wasn't a single one of the ten-year-old Jennifer. Baby shots, a couple of early school photographs, but nothing else. Everyone who she spoke to wanted to know why: the social workers, the counselors, the teachers. She couldn't explain. Mr. Cottis had been about to take some pictures of her, but Jennifer never told anyone about that.

When her mum left, she gave Jennifer a hug and kiss and said she'd see her soon. A few days later Jennifer's picture was in a national newspaper. The same long hair and bangs, only this time her face was smiling brightly. A KILLER'S SMILE the headline said, and inside there was an exclusive interview with Carol Jones: MY LIFE WITHOUT JENNIFER.

Patricia Coffey had shown her the article. She'd sat quietly at the other end of the settee while Jennifer read through the paper. Behind her were the stuffed animals, one or two new ones that she hadn't seen before, a panda and a puppy dog.

Carol Jones, attractive mother of the notorious Berwick Waters killer, tells of life without her daughter. Thirty-year-old Miss Jones, former model, sat in the living room of her new flat and wept for her daughter. "She's not a bad girl," she said.

The article went on to describe Jennifer's life at Monksgrove as told by her mother: a lovely house in the middle of breathtaking scenery, a private room with her own television, sports facilities, an education block, small classes, music tuition, good food.

The editorial in the newspaper gave its opinion:

Is this justice? This girl killed her friend in cold blood. The state is paying for her to live in a place that sounds like a five-star hotel. What about Mr. and Mrs. Livingstone? How will they feel when they find out that their daughter's killer is living like this at the taxpayer's expense?

Jennifer put the paper down after she'd read every line about herself. She was surprised to see Patricia Coffey still sitting at the other end of the settee, her hands clasped, looking nervous. Jennifer didn't speak. She was too full of hurt and fury. If she opened her mouth it might pour out like vomit.

Her mother, the model. The visits stopped. Jennifer didn't want them anymore.

Alice was dressed. She picked up her holdall, which Rosie had repacked for her. Rosie was hovering, brushing dust off the sleeves of her suit. She had pulled her hair back severely and for once had no jewelry on at all. It looked as though she were in mourning.

Jill spoke crisply:

"I am going to go out to the reporters and tell them I've got a statement for them. I'll walk down to my car and distract them for a few moments. You must slip out then and go to the end of the road. My husband's in a black sedan there and he's waiting for you. Don't do anything dramatic like covering your face, you'll only draw attention to yourself. Put some dark glasses on. That'll be enough. If you're quick, they won't be able to catch you."

"How long do I have to stay away?" Alice said, clutching her holdall.

"I don't know. We'll have to discuss it later. I'll come and see you tonight when I've spoken to a few people."

Rosie was at her side, quietly fiddling with her earlobe. Alice saw something in her face that she couldn't quite grasp, an expression she'd never seen before. It was the suit, probably, the lack of any makeup, the stress of it all.

"Let's go."

Jill said it with an encouraging smile. They walked down the stairs one behind the other. Jill went out first, leaving the front door ajar. The reporters followed her up the street to where her car was, and she started to talk to them about Alice. Rosie and Alice walked quietly out and turned in the opposite direction. Nobody, none of the reporters, noticed them. In moments they were at the corner and saw the black Ford waiting, its engine idling. They got in. Jill's husband said hello as he looked around, reversing back so that they could pull out and get away.

Alice, breathless, sat behind him and peered nervously out of the window, expecting to see the reporters turning the corner and running at the car. There was nothing, though. She focused on the indicator light that was blinking on and off. They were waiting to move out, but a car was coming. It slowed as it approached them, intending to turn into Rosie's road. They would have to wait for it to pass before moving out themselves.

When it drew level Alice looked in, her eyes drawn to the backseat where a woman was smoking a cigarette, her arm casually resting on the open window, flicking the ash onto the road. The woman's face turned toward her.

It was her mother.

The hair was shorter and stiffer, the face a little fuller. Carol Jones put the cigarette between her dark red lips and sucked on it. *When had she started to smoke?* Alice couldn't know. She laid her head on the glass, a pain across her chest, her ribs tightening like a vise. She pulled her dark glasses off and caught her mother's eye. It was brief, just a flicker of acknowledgment; one backseat passenger to another. Then her mother turned away, oblivious, and continued talking to the person next to her.

The car turned into Rosie's street, and then Jill's husband pulled out and the black Ford sped away unnoticed by anyone. In the backseat were two women. Only one would return later that day.

TWENTY-SIX

THE safe house was in Hampshire. It was the home of another probation officer and Alice was only to spend the night there. The woman, an old friend of Jill's, was named Margaret, and she greeted them holding a sleeping baby over one shoulder. Jill's husband left them there, and Margaret told them to come in in a hushed voice. Alice felt awkward walking into a messy living room, a baby carrier on the coffee table and bits of baby paraphernalia scattered everywhere. Rosie immediately began to talk to Margaret about the baby, its habits, its feeding, and its weight. Alice sat on a chair, tongue-tied, still clutching her holdall. She felt like she had landed in another world.

Margaret laid the baby in its carrier.

"This is Emmie," she said.

Then she made some tea and they sat down around a small kitchen table and talked about Alice's degree course; what subject she was going to study, where she was going, whether she was going to stay in halls or rent a flat. It was all nice chitchat and it made time pass. When it was over and Margaret was washing and drying the mugs, Alice started to cry. The ordinariness of the room suddenly distressed her: the teapot, the messy kitchen table, the baby's washed bottle upside down on the draining board. These were the important things of everyday life and yet Alice had no right to them. The upset came suddenly with no warning. Her jaw began to tremble, and in a single blink she felt her eyes blur and then the tears ran in hot beads down her face. Rosie didn't notice immediately. It was Margaret who stopped drying a mug and looked at her with concern.

"Oh, Alice," Rosie said, getting up and standing beside her.

Alice stood up and pushed her head into Rosie's chest. It felt odd, not so warm or soft as usual. It was the suit. The one she wore to go to court. The material was hard and dark and seemed, to Alice, like some sort of armor. After a few moments Rosie led her into the living room and she found a space to sit on the sofa. Margaret followed them in, carrying Emmie over her arm.

"Alice, I don't know you, but Jill tells me you're a really good person and you'll get through this," she said.

Pat Coffey, Jill, Rosie, now Margaret. They all thought she was a good person. Maybe she was.

"You could watch television, but I might as well warn you that it's bound to be on the news."

Alice nodded. She might as well see the worst. She

300

picked up the remote and switched to a news channel. After fifteen minutes or so there was an item on her. The newscaster giving brief details of the Berwick Waters story. In the corner of the screen was the photo of ten-year-old Jennifer Jones. The scene changed then to the street outside Rosie's house. There, amid a group of reporters, was her mother. There was no cigarette at her lips, just a bunched-up white tissue that she was holding like a wilted flower. Someone had just asked her how she felt about not seeing her daughter for so long. Her mum took a deep breath, as if it were taking every ounce of strength she had to say a word.

Alice turned it off. She didn't want to hear the answer.

Margaret lifted Emmie out of the carrier.

"Would you hold her for me while I get her lunch stuff?"

Alice sat back as Margaret placed the tiny baby on her lap. She seemed to weigh almost nothing and was struggling, moving her legs and arms, her eyes half shut and her mouth turning toward Alice's breast. Rosie was sitting beside her, whispering endearments. The sound of the telephone stopped her and she looked round.

"Rosie, it's Jill," Margaret shouted.

"I'll be back," Rosie said.

Margaret appeared with a bottle. She took Emmie from Alice's lap and sat on the other chair with her. The baby sucked hungrily at the teat and Alice watched as her hands seemed to pause in midair, her tiny fingers open, her body still and heavy with contentment.

While the baby was feeding, Alice tried to listen to what Rosie was saying out in the hallway. Pushing her thumbnail against her teeth, she wondered what Jill had planned for her. The tone of Rosie's voice was even, there were no exclamations or protestations. That was a good sign. There were long silences, though, as if Jill had lots to say, masses of information to get across. Occasionally Rosie's voice sounded businesslike: "Absolutely! As soon as I get off the phone! Right away!" It made Alice think of Rosie in court with one of her social-work cases. Wearing her special suit and sounding efficient and in charge. It made Alice smile. How different Rosie was at home. How simple it was to get round her; how easy it was for Kathy to boss her.

The call ended and Rosie came back into the living room. Alice looked closely at her face, trying to read what was there. Rosie's mouth was turned up in a half smile, her eyebrows raised slightly, expectantly. Alice tried to catch her eye but she couldn't. It gave her a bad feeling.

Margaret got up, cradling the baby.

"This always happens! She falls asleep before she's finished the bottle. I'll take her upstairs for a nap. Give you two a bit of space."

The room felt empty when Margaret and the baby

had gone. She was there and Rosie was there but there was something big missing. The baby's things looked awkward, at angles; a rattle had rolled under the seat opposite and looked forlorn, as if it would never be found.

"Alice."

Rosie's voice broke into her thoughts.

"What did she say?" Alice said, knowing full well that it was going to be bad.

"Nobody got any pictures of you this morning. Jill is really pleased about that. It makes her job much easier."

Alice had become Jill's *job*. Maybe she always had been. Not for Rosie, though. She and Rosie had something more, something Jill with her painted nails and her smart glasses couldn't have.

"Jill is organizing a new placement. It will mean a change of location. A new name. Everything else is just the same, though. You'll still go to uni. In time, if there are no leaks, the newspapers will forget you and you can live a normal life."

"I won't be going to Sussex?" she said, a fleeting picture of Frankie passing through her head.

"No. Some other uni. They all do history degrees."

"We'll have to move," Alice said under her breath, her hand clutching on to Rosie's arm.

Rosie was very still, her eyes on the carpet.

"You have to do this on your own, Alice," she said.

There was a moment's silence. Alice's chest seemed to swell up like a balloon. She pushed her bottom into the seat in case she rose up and floated away.

"But *you'll* be coming with me?"

Rosie shook her head, her lips closed together in a tight line.

"Why not?"

Rosie didn't answer.

"But you could!" Alice gushed. "You're a social worker, you could work anywhere. We could both change our names. You could buy a new house. You're always saying that the flat is too small. We could look for one together. It would be fun . . ."

Rosie was shaking her head.

"Why not?" Alice asked, the words floating up from somewhere deep down in her chest.

"Alice, I'd do anything to help you. You're such a sweet lovely girl and you've had such an awful time, but . . ."

"Why?"

"I can't leave my home, my job, my friends. I can't leave my mum!"

Her mum. Rosie loved her mum. Alice thought of Kathy with her smart clothes and her stiff lacquered hair. She was so different from what Alice had expected. She'd thought Rosie's mum would be an older version of her: plump, gray hair, good cook, always searching round thrift shops for clothes. But Kathy had burst through the flat door with her red hair and matching coordinates. She was always trying to persuade Rosie to go to Majorca when really Rosie wanted to go round the world. Why should Alice have thought they would be similar? Look at her own mum. She was nothing like her.

"We could go on a long holiday." Alice's words hiccuped out, her hands trembling.

Rosie shook her head. She seemed unable to speak.

"I'd go anywhere for you, Rosie. Why won't you come with me?"

"I can't. I have my life here," Rosie whispered, brushing down the dark hard material of her suit skirt.

Alice sat perfectly still, on the settee, among the baby clothes and jars of cream. She was looking at her reflection in the television screen. A small girl tucked into the side of a settee. At the other end a big woman with a life of her own. From above she could hear Margaret's footsteps, the boards creaking with fatigue.

"I've checked with Jill. We can still see each other. I can come and visit you, in your new uni. We can still be friends," Rosie said.

Alice didn't look around.

"Course we can," she said, even though she knew it wasn't true.

part four

KATE RICKMAN

TWENTY-SEVEN

KATE carried the last cardboard box of stuff into her room. She was winded from coming up two flights of stairs. She was out of shape, she knew that. She placed the box on the single bed in the corner and looked out through the window at the grounds of the campus. It was vast, green grass and trees stretching ahead, broken up only by student accommodation blocks. Three four-story brick buildings surrounded by parents' cars, their sons or daughters ferrying their stuff up to their rooms. Over to the left a road snaked past, leading to the teaching blocks a kilometer or so away. Kate remembered reading about the bus that ran up and down this road, taking the first-year students to their classes and back again.

In her second year she would move away from here, find a shared flat or house, possibly somewhere in Exeter itself.

Behind her she heard Rob and Sally talking. Rob was carrying her stereo system and Sally was carrying the crystal lamp that was too fragile to be packed in any of the boxes.

Rob squatted down and put the stereo on the floor. When he stood up he checked his sports watch. No doubt he had timed himself coming up the stairs, to see how fast he could do it. She looked at his tracksuit on top of bright white sneakers. He seemed to have a different one for every day of the week.

"I'll just put this here," Sally said, placing the lamp on the desk.

Even though it was warm outside, Sally still had her coat on, done up to the neck. She'd worn it in the car for the whole trip from Bristol to Exeter. "I feel the cold," she said at least ten times a day. It was a change for Kate. She was usually the one who didn't like the cold.

Sally began to unwind the Bubble Wrap that had been around the lamp ever since it had been taken from Croydon a few weeks before.

"Do you mind leaving that, Sally?" Kate said. "I'll do it later when I've sorted all my stuff out."

"Course," Sally said, moving away from the lamp.

Sally was always careful not to intrude, not to interfere.

"These places have improved since we were here," Rob said, giving Sally a nudge.

"They must have knocked those old blocks down. It was more like a blooming dormitory in those days!"

Sally hooked her hair behind her ears. She was always saying stuff like that: *blooming* and *blimey*. As if she didn't know any stronger words. Rob was the same. In the three weeks Kate had been living at their bungalow, she'd not heard either of them utter a single swearword. She'd heard a lot of other stuff, though. All day long they'd talked to her, about the news, the television, her course, the magazines she was reading. There didn't seem to be a minute in the day that they would allow to tick by without conversation. It wasn't their fault. They were nice people. They'd probably been told to keep her busy. *Look after Kate,* Jill Newton had probably said. *She's been depressed lately and needs perking up!*

Kate caught her reflection in the mirror over the wash basin. She pushed her fingers through her short blond hair. These days she was always touching and fiddling with it. Since she'd had it bleached, it *felt* different, coarser somehow, as if it weren't really her hair at all. And the glasses. They made a real difference. Plain black frames and lightly tinted glass. She'd looked like a serious student from the moment she put them on.

"Would you like to take a drive around the campus?" Rob said, his eyes crinkling up.

"No thanks."

Rob nodded his head lightly, as if he were searching for something to say. Sally gave a light cough. There was a moment of awkwardness.

"Thing is," Kate said, "I'd probably be better spending a bit of time on my own. You know what it's like, unpacking, finding places for everything."

They both nodded their heads, and there was a feeling of relief in the air. Rob started to jiggle his legs as if he were limbering up for a long run. Sally leaned across to give Kate a quick peck. Kate took Rob's hand and gave it a hearty shake.

"Thanks for everything. You've been real lifesavers."

"You've got our number. If you feel you need a place to escape to . . . ," Sally said.

"Absolutely. Any weekend that you'd like a break you'd be welcome."

"I know," Kate said. "I won't forget how kind you've been."

She meant it. Walking downstairs with them and watching Rob open the door for Sally to get into the car, she felt a huge debt of gratitude that she'd never be able to repay. The car juddered a bit as Sally waved out the window. Then it drove off and disappeared.

Sally and Rob's bungalow had been her refuge. Their lives, their routines, their everyday concerns; these had been places where she could hide while things in her world were out of control. The newspapers had bounced stories off one another: JENNIFER JONES FLEES FROM HER MOTHER; JJ SLIPS OUT OF THE MEDIA SPOTLIGHT; JENNIFER JONES GOES INTO HIDING AGAIN! There were talk shows where the issues were pored over: "Should JJ be left alone? Can people really change?" She'd switched on daytime telly once to see her mother talking about the problems faced by the relatives of violent children. "I had a lot to put up with," Carol Jones said.

Kate had rocked back and forth on the chair in the corner of Rob and Sally's living room and watched it all. She felt like a survivor from a road crash, sitting on the side of the motorway looking at the wreckage below. They'd known exactly who she was, but they never mentioned it. Not a word. They called her Kate without hesitation and only talked about the future.

It was to be Exeter University, not Sussex. She would stay on campus until the Christmas break, and by then Jill would have some news for her of another placement. It had been organized discreetly and only Jill and the director of studies at the uni knew the truth. He was an old friend of Jill's. How thankful Kate was. Jill seemed to know everyone.

Back in her room she began to unpack. It didn't take long. Her clothes and books fit the spaces and the wires from her electrical stuff reached the necessary plugs. She got her bedding out. It was all new things, sheets, pillows, a duvet, all bought from a shop in the last week. Lastly she unwrapped the lamp and saw, with dismay, that it definitely didn't fit in her tiny student room. No matter. She left it there, on the edge of her desk, its crystals tinkling for a while and then subsiding into silence.

Almost as soon as she'd finished there was a knock. Before she could get to the door it opened.

"Hi, I'm Lindsay, next door but one. You're doing history, aren't you?"

A girl of her own age walked casually into her room. She was tall with long dark hair. Her bangs were hanging in spikes and one of them kept catching her eyelid when she blinked. She was drinking from a big plastic bottle of water.

"This is a dump, right? My friend is at Durham. She got two As and two Bs. You should see their halls. She says they've got *en suite* and televisions in every room. Standard. Me? I only got a B and three Cs, but then one of my teachers had a nervous breakdown. How about you? What were your grades?"

Kate smiled. Here was something she could be proud of. "Three Bs and a C."

"Not bad," Lindsay said, plonking down on Kate's bed. "Hey, new stuff," she said, fingering the duvet cover, stiff with telltale lines where it had been in the packet. "Your parents shelled out for it?"

Kate nodded. Why not? She didn't have to explain a thing.

"Along this corridor? There are mostly humanities students: English, psychology . . ."

Lindsay chatted on, looking round Kate's room all the while. Her eye finally settled on the desk.

"Hey! A laptop? Brilliant!"

Putting the bottle of water carelessly on the edge of the bedside table, she got up and went across to the desk, flipping open the computer without a moment's thought. Kate decided, in that instant, that she didn't much like her.

"Great. My mum was going to get me one of these. But her bloke said they were too expensive. Still, maybe I can borrow yours."

Kate smiled benignly. No one was going to borrow her laptop. Rosie had bought it for her.

"Some of us are going to the uni bar later. Come along, if you like."

"Yes, I might," Kate said.

After Lindsay left she locked the door. She turned to the laptop and gently closed the lid. She moved it to one side, lining it up with the edge of the desk. There were some papers underneath. Her letters. She hesitated for a moment and then took her glasses off and set them on top, like a paperweight.

It was good to be completely alone. Her time at the bungalow had left her craving privacy. Sitting down on the bed and leaning back against the stiff pillowcase, she noticed her new mobile on the bedside table. The latest handset, a fresh number; most other teenagers would have been delighted. She picked it up, feeling its weight in her hand, its exterior smooth, slippery almost. Inside, it held the numbers she needed for her new life: Rob and Sally and Jill Newton. The old numbers belonged to the other mobile, the one she had to give back to Jill on the day she drove her to Bristol.

"This has all sorts of new features," Jill had said. "You can use it for e-mails and calls, and it's got a huge memory so you can save stuff. It's even got games on it."

She'd sat in the passenger seat of the car and played with it. It only took moments to find all its functions, which button to press, how to scroll, how to text. Jill talked on while she focused on the tiny metal object that fitted beautifully into her palm, its silver casing giving off a luxurious gleam.

It was her link to the outside world, but it lay silent in her bag. She hadn't bothered to turn it on. No one would ring. She was a new person, with no history. How could she be part of anyone's list of phone numbers? She only took it out when she was bored and wanted to play games. One day she turned it on and saw the message icon on the screen. Surprised, she dialed her voice mail and heard Rosie's voice. *Rosie's* voice. Both Rob and Sally had caught her excitement as she paced up and down the living room, listening to the message over and over.

That had been a week ago.

Kate pressed a couple of buttons and then put the mobile to her ear. She had saved Rosie's message and the sound of her voice still made her quiver.

This is a message for Kate Rickman . . .

Rosie sounded calm. Trust her to use her new name so easily, so naturally. She, herself, wasn't used to it yet and had failed to respond to several people who had spoken to her. That was why Sally and Rob had made a point of repeating it over and over again. *Kate* this and *Kate* that. It sounded funny to her, false, like a character in a film. *Alice* had been strange at first but then, after a few months, she had *become* Alice. She had left Jennifer behind in the past, a figure in a photograph, frozen in time, never to grow old. Now she had to leave Alice behind as well.

It's Rosie here. Jill gave me your number and I just thought I'd call and wish you luck when you start uni next week . . . Everything's okay here, all the fuss seems to have died down, you'll be pleased to hear . . .

There was a few moments' quiet and Kate pictured Rosie fiddling with her earring, not knowing quite what to say.

Hope you're getting on all right with the laptop. Everyone swears by them but, you know me, I'd rather use pen and paper . . .

Kate gripped the phone. Even though she'd heard the message a dozen times, she still felt that Rosie was there, on the other end of the line, waiting to hear her voice.

I got your letter and I'll keep it among my important papers. You know . . . Kate . . . I won't forget you. You brightened up my life for a long time . . . Don't lose that. When your life starts to calm down you'll have everything you deserve.

There were a couple of coughs and the sound of snuffles. Kate swallowed back, her teeth clenched together. What did *Kate* deserve? A life of some sort, she supposed. Like Alice Tully had? A home, a job, friends, a boyfriend. Those things had seemed real and solid. Instead they had been as fragile as tissue paper. One puff of air and they had floated away. Then she had nothing.

Thing is . . . you mustn't contact me in case . . . you know . . . in case anyone is trying to find you. But I'll write to you, when you're settled in uni. And who knows, one day I'll maybe pay you a visit.

The line went dead. No doubt Rosie had pressed the END button before she meant to. How typical of her. She let the mobile drop onto the bed beside her and closed her eyes for a few moments. There were sounds from all over the building. Plodding footsteps on the stairs, irritated voices moving along the corridors, the sound of furniture shifting and doors opening and closing. A shriek of recognition from a girl and the low rumble of male voices from outside the window. A horn tooting in the distance and closer, from underneath, the thudding sound of someone's stereo.

She sat up and ran her fingers through her stiff, unfamiliar hair. Her glasses were resting on the letters and she picked them up and put them on. She didn't need them in order to read, but she might as well get used to using them. She plucked up the letters and held them for a moment. Then, sitting on the very edge of the bed, her back bent over, her elbows rigid, she unfolded the two pieces of paper.

Two letters from Frankie. The first dated a couple of weeks after her trip to Brighton; the second a week or so later. When Jill Newton handed them to her, she'd told her to read them and get rid of them. Why hadn't she? She honestly had no idea.

Dear Alice, they both said.

Kate stopped for a moment and whispered the words, *Alice, Alice;* the sound susurrating around the tiny room. It was a name that would always be with her, an echo from her past.

The letters went on, both similar in content, Frankie's spidery writing growing larger in some places, the lines slanting down to the right.

> *I just want you to ring me. I've been a total idiot and I just need to talk to you. We can talk about what happened in the past. Maybe we can get over it. Just ring me. I need to hear your voice.*
>
> *I love you. I reacted badly, that was all. I understand. People can change. I want you to know that my feelings haven't changed, not deep down. I was just an idiot. Don't give up on me. Just ring me. So that we can talk . . .*

Kate folded the two pieces of paper up again and took her new glasses off. Poor Frankie. He thought he could make everything all right for Alice Tully.

But there was no such person as Alice Tully anymore.

Reader Chat

1. Alice is careful not to blame others for her actions. Do you believe parents are responsible for the behavior of their children?

2. How is Rosie different from the other adults Alice has known? How does the way Rosie treats Alice compare to the way Carol treated her?

3. What do you think of Frankie's reaction when he learns the truth about Alice? How might you react if a girlfriend or boyfriend admitted something similar to you? Do you think it was right for Alice to wait so long to tell someone so close to her the truth about her past?

4. In her moments of violence, JJ feels detached from the acts she is committing. What kinds of feelings trigger her rages?

5. What does Macy represent to Jennifer? How does Michelle's opinion affect the way that Jennifer feels about her doll? Have you ever let a friend's opinion influence your own?

6. Why did journalists want to find JJ and reveal her whereabouts to the public? Do you think it was fair for Sarah Wright to research her story the way she did? How would you feel if you found out that someone living in your community was guilty of committing a violent crime?

7. This story emphasizes the power of the media. How was the media's portrayal of JJ and her mother different from the way they really were? Do you think it is ever possible to get the real story from television or newspapers? Can you think of any contemporary figures who you feel are singled out for bad press?

8. How is Sophie different from JJ when she was Sophie's age? Do you think Frankie was right to want to shield his sister from Alice?

9. Jennifer never tells anyone that her mother had arranged for her to pose for pictures for Mr. Cottis on that fateful day. What other things does she do throughout the story to protect her mother's reputation? Why do you think she does this?

10. It is Alice's belief that she hadn't actually been abused as a child. "She hadn't been hit, punched, locked away. She hadn't had anyone screaming at her, ordering her

about, insulting her. She'd just been sidelined, forgotten about. She'd been left with friends and family, the social services, complete strangers; finally when there was no one else, she'd just been left on her own" (p. 107). Do you think that the way Alice was mistreated can have repercussions just as devastating as physical abuse?

11. Alice thinks that she doesn't deserve a future after taking someone's life, but Patricia Coffey tells her that she must go on: "Otherwise two lives have been wasted. You have to go on now and make a good life for yourself, to make up for what you've done" (p. 113). What kind of life do you think Alice must live in order to make up for what she has done? Do you think she will ever feel redeemed in her own mind?

12. Do you think Alice has any chance for a normal life? Do you believe it is possible for a person who has been through what she has been through to really change?